HEAR MY HEART

BAYTOWN BOYS SERIES

MARYANN JORDAN

Hear My Heart (Baytown Boys) Copyright 2018

Cover Design by: Becky McGraw

Editor: Shannon Brandee Eversoll

Proofreader: Myckel Anne Phillips

ISBN (ebook): 978-1-947214-29-3

ISBN (print): 978-1-947214-30-9

❀ Created with Vellum

ACKNOWLEDGMENTS

First and foremost, I have to thank my husband, Michael. Always believing in me and wanting me to pursue my dreams, this book would not be possible without his support. To my daughters, MaryBeth and Nicole, I taught you to follow your dreams and now it is time for me to take my own advice.

My best friend, Tammie, who for over twenty years has been with me through thick and thin. You've filled the role of confidant, supporter, and sister.

My other best friend, Myckel Anne, who keeps me on track, keeps me grounded, and most of all – keeps my secrets. Thank you for not only being my proofreader and my Marketing PA, but friend. I do not know what I would do without you in my life.

My beta readers kept me sane, cheered me on, found all my silly errors, and often helped me understand my characters through their eyes. A huge thank you to Denise, Sandi, Barbara, Jennifer, Danielle, Tracey, Lynn,

Stracey, and Jamila for being my beta girls who love alphas!

Shannon Brandee Eversoll as my editor and Myckel Anne Phillips as my proofreader gave their time and talents to making all my books as well written as it can be.

My street team, Jordan Jewels, you all are amazing! You volunteer your time to promote my books and I cannot thank you enough! I hope you will stay with me, because I have lots more stories inside, just waiting to be written!

My PA Barbara keeps me going when I feel over-whelmed and I am so grateful for not only her assistance, but her friendship.

Chas...thank you for all you do!

Most importantly, thank you readers. You allow me into your home for a few hours as you disappear into my characters and you support me as I follow my indie author dreams.

AUTHOR INFORMATION

USA TODAY BESTSELLING AND AWARD WINNING AUTHOR

I am an avid reader of romance novels, often joking that I cut my teeth on the historical romances. I have been reading and reviewing for years. In 2013, I finally gave into the characters in my head, screaming for their story to be told. From these musings, my first novel, Emma's Home, The Fairfield Series was born.

I was a high school counselor having worked in education for thirty years. I live in Virginia, having also lived in four states and two foreign countries. I have been married to a wonderfully patient man for thirty-seven years. When writing, my dog or one of my four cats can generally be found in the same room if not on my lap.

Please take the time to leave a review of this book.

Feel free to contact me, especially if you enjoyed my book. I love to hear from readers!

Facebook

Email
Website

I have lived in numerous states as well as overseas, but for the last twenty years have called Virginia my home. All my stories take place in this wonderful commonwealth, but I choose to use fictional city names with some geographical accuracies.

These fictionally named cities allow me to use my creativity and not feel constricted by attempting to accurately portray the areas.

It is my hope that my readers will allow me this creative license and understand my fictional world.

I also do quite a bit of research on my books and try to write on subjects with accuracy. There will always be points where creative license will be used to create scenes or plots.

Four years ago, my husband and I discovered the Eastern Shore of Virginia and fell in love with the area. The mostly rural strip of land forming the peninsula originating from Maryland has managed to stay non-commercialized. The quiet, private area full of quaint towns captured our hearts, and we rushed to buy a little place there.

It has become our retreat when we need to leave the hustle and bustle of our lives. I gather ideas, create characters, and spend time writing when not walking on the beach collecting sea glass.

Music blared over the noise of the crowded room as Aiden MacFarlane stood behind the bar serving drinks, talking with the locals, and chatting up the women who were vacationing in the area. Though Baytown was just a little coastal town on the Eastern Shore, it always managed to pull in those looking for a beach retreat.

Co-owner of Finn's Pub, along with his older brother, Brogan, and younger sister, Katelyn, he was used to the crowd. A longtime business in Baytown, originally owned by their grandfather, Finn, it had been deeded to them when he decided to retire. Finn's Pub was one of the few restaurants in the little town that stayed open all year and the locals made it their regular weekend stop because of it. Baytown vacationers looking for a drink, a good meal, and local color, filled the tables as well.

Winking at the woman in front of him, Aiden watched as his older brother carded a couple of young girls that looked to be in college. He laughed as they pouted and tried to flirt their way to getting a couple of drinks. They stood no chance of that with Brogan. As expected, not a second later Brogan shot them down with a glare that would make most people cringe.

"Don't mind him, girls. Just make sure to come back in a couple of years when you can try one of my specialties. I'll still be here and better than ever!" He grinned, his blue eyes flashing as he flexed his arms.

They smiled at him and, casting a glare back toward Brogan, moved away from the bar.

"Man, why you gotta flirt like that?" Brogan growled.

"Why you gotta scare away fuckin' potential customers?" he shot back.

"Why you gotta cuss in front of the customers?"

"'Cause they don't fuckin' care. Why you gotta get on my case all the time?"

"Both of you shut up and serve the drinks!"

They swung their heads around in unison and watched as Katelyn walked behind the bar. Her arched eyebrow and glare had both of them quiet, but grins played about their lips.

Brogan bent to kiss her cheek and asked, "How's my nephew?"

Her scowl fell off her face as her lips curved into a proud smile. "Wonderful, as always," she replied. "Mom and dad are babysitting Little Finn right now."

Aiden offered a chin lift to Garreth, her husband, as he moved in to wrap his arms around her.

Katelyn's long dark hair and lush curves were in

contrast to the slender blonde who slid behind the bar and immediately moved to Brogan.

"Who's keeping law and order in Baytown tonight if you're here?" he quipped, grinning at Brogan's wife, Ginny, one of the police officers in town.

"All's quiet and tonight's my night off," she replied, her sharp eyes glancing around the bar, landing on the young women at the other end.

"Before you say anything, Brogan's already carded them and read them the riot act," he said.

"Good," she retorted, shooting him a grin before lifting her gaze to Brogan.

He stood for a moment and stared at the two couples, both whom he loved more than life, but the usual feeling of *glad to still be free* did not come. Instead, he recognized that another feeling had been sliding through him lately...one of longing. For what, he had no idea, but it was replacing his carefree attitude more and more.

Sucking in a deep breath, he cast his gaze toward the back of the bar where a gathering of their friends sat, most in couples. Most of the men had been raised together on the bay, earning the nickname the Baytown Boys as children, and it had stayed with them into adulthood. Each had all joined the military after high school and had returned to live in Baytown as adults. Many were now married and some had children.

Looking back to Brogan and Ginny, he smiled. Even they were expecting now. Life was changing for the Baytown Boys, and the melancholy thought hit him in

3

the gut. *Is it passing me by?* A shout from the side jerked him out of his morose reverie.

"Aiden? You comin' tonight?"

Harvey, one of their young line cooks, was throwing a beach bash and he nodded. "I'll be there," he called out.

Turning back to the side, he caught four pairs of eyes on him. Lifting his eyebrow, he tossed the rag in his hand to the bar. "What?"

"Aren't you getting a little old for *those* kind of parties?" Katelyn asked, her blue eyes flashing at him.

Brogan threw in his two cents. "No food, just alcohol—"

"And probably college girls who are looking for a hookup," Ginny finished, her lips pursed into a thin line.

"Sounds like my kind of party," he quipped, ignoring the niggling voice inside that agreed with them. In truth, he enjoyed the Baytown Boys' parties more, filled with good food and good company, but Harvey's gave him a chance to find some *casual* action. At least, that was what he told himself.

"You need to find someone you can settle down with," Katelyn said.

"And leave all of this," he swept his hand down his tall, muscular body, giving off his panty-melting grin, "for just one woman? Not ready for that." He looked at the clock and said, "I'll head out in an hour. Time for me to get my prowl on." He laughed as the others rolled their eyes but, though he would not admit it, his smile did not reach his heart.

Sitting in the corner of Finn's Pub, Amelia Smith watched the antics of the people behind the bar. New in town, she had to admit she was envious of their easy camaraderie, but the one man's cocky bragging had her pinching her lips. Looking down, she tried to focus on the delicious fish tacos in her takeaway bag while she waited for her bill, but the bartender was hard to ignore. He was certainly handsome, but she had little room in her life for any man, least of all a stuck-on-himself, overgrown playboy. Still, unable to stop herself, she watched from under her lashes as he headed out, not a care in the world. Lost in her thoughts, she startled when the server brought her credit card back. Signing the receipt, she made her way out into the evening, hurrying to get home.

Even though the sun had just set, the beach party was in full swing by the time Aiden drove up to the small house and parked outside. With the Pub short a server, he had been unable to get there earlier.

Walking toward the beach, he spied Harvey and waved. Harvey, his arm around two women, gave a chin lift and he grinned in return. As he glanced around, he recognized the blow-out of a party was truly as Brogan had predicted—more alcohol than food. And girls. Lots of girls. Most of them he did not recognize from town, so they must be vacationers. And they looked young... spring break young. He sighed.

He accepted a beer from a kid standing next to the

washtub cooler and wondered if the keeper of the alcohol was old enough to drink. Chastising himself for thinking like a bartender with a business instead of a partygoer looking for a good time, he walked over to the bonfire.

Several girls lounged on a blanket spread over the sand, beer bottles propped next to their long, tanned legs. Their bikini tops barely covered their tits and he averted his eyes. Somehow it seemed like perving instead of appreciating. Sighing again, he smiled as one of them grinned up at him.

"Hi, handsome," she purred, and her friends giggled.

Purr? Did she just purr? He eyed their drinks and said, "You ladies enjoying the party?"

More giggling ensued and the blonde said, "Yes. At least here we can drink. We tried going to that dinky bar in town but some old guy carded us."

His eyebrows lifted to his hairline as he tried to think what she meant. The only bar downtown was Finn's, and the only *old guy* was his brother, who was only one year older than him.

Before he had a chance to respond, she leaped to her feet and clapped her hands. "I love this song!" she screamed and threw her hands into the air. "Dance with me."

As the other girls crowded around, all dancing in a group, their bodies rubbing up against each other's, she asked, "Don't you just love this song?"

"Can't say I've ever heard it before," he replied, and

more giggling met his ears. Frustration coursed through his veins and he begged off dancing. Moving back to the table that was supposed to have food, he spied a few bags of chips and one tub of salsa.

Turning to leave, he felt fingers grab his arm and looked to see the blonde had moved to him. She bit her lip and looked down slightly so that as she gazed up at him, her face was poised perfectly. Coy. Flirtatious. *Fake. Irritating.*

"You need something?" he asked, recognizing his voice was flat but unable to manage the practiced charm he used so often to entice women into his bed for a few hours. That was all he was willing to give them, but he found no shortage of willing women who wanted just what he had to offer.

"Sure, gorgeous," she grinned. "I thought maybe you and I could find a quiet place to get to know each other better." She leaned in, pressing her breasts against his arm. "The guy throwing the party said you like 'em hot. I promise that's me. We can even ask my friends to join if you wanna."

Irritation flew through him at the thought that Harvey would have said that. It had been a long time since he had gone with anyone this young. He stared into her wide eyes and saw surety. *And, I used to be a sure thing, too.*

Unable to summon the politeness necessary, he shook his head as he disentangled himself from her hand. "Sorry, not interested."

She blinked as though unable to process what had just occurred. "You...you're turning me down?"

"Just not in the mood."

Her fists landed on her hips and she arched her back. "You're nothing to get excited about anyway, you know. You're just some old guy." With that, she flounced back to her friends and he heard the burst of giggling again.

Sighing for the millionth time since he arrived, he tossed a wave toward Harvey and climbed back into his truck. As he drove home, he wondered when it had happened. The young man on the prowl who now came home early because the party was filled with people barely out of their teens. *And no longer my scene.*

2

As one bloodshot eye opened, the glare of the light coming through the window caused a sharp pain in Aiden's skull and he squeezed his eyes shut. The sun was rising over the horizon, shooting rays of pink, yellow, and pale blue across the sky, but he had no interest in that. Rolling over in bed, he smacked his lips, grimacing at the taste in his mouth. It felt like cotton balls had been stuffed in his cheeks. *Make that whiskey-soaked cotton balls.* He did not often drink as much as he had last night, especially alone, but...well, there were always a few exceptions.

As his brain slowly began to awaken, he lay sprawled across the bed, wondering for a few seconds where he was. Without lifting his head, he opened both eyes and determined he was, indeed, in his bedroom. Navy curtains. Boring brick walls with no adornment. Slatted wood headboard. Matching chest of drawers. *Yep, my room.*

Managing to sit up, he gingerly rubbed his forehead in a feeble, and ineffective, attempt to still the headache. Forcing his mind back to the previous evening, he remembered the beach party and coming home alone.

Scrubbing his hand over his face, he rolled out of bed and headed to the bathroom naked. After using the toilet, he stood at the sink, his hands on the counter, and stared at his reflection. Hair standing on end, as though he had run his hands through it numerous times. A scruff along his normally shaven jaw. He was not old, but right now felt every hour of his thirty years. Holding his own gaze, he sucked in a huge breath before letting it out slowly. *What are you doing man? What the hell are you doing?*

Hearing a knock on the door of his apartment, he walked into his room and pulled on the jeans he found left on the floor. "I'm coming, I'm coming," he called out, immediately wincing at the pain slicing through his brain.

He stumbled to the front door and, with a quick jerk on the knob, threw it open and stared at the face he knew as well as his own. "Come on in, bro."

Taking one look at him, Brogan entered and detoured straight to the kitchen, setting a bag on the counter.

Following him, he caught a whiff of comfort breakfast food emanating from the bag. "Hot damn, Brogan. You just got voted my favorite brother."

"I'm your only brother, dipshit," Brogan replied, opening the bag and pulling out a huge sausage, egg, and cheese biscuit smothered in sausage gravy. "Ginny wouldn't let me eat this artery-clogging breakfast, but she figured you'd need it this morning. Best hangover food there is."

He moved toward his kitchen counter, his mouth watering, and scooped up the food. Before taking a bite of the delectable breakfast, he leaned over and turned on the coffee maker. Brogan's words suddenly penetrated his alcohol–fuzzy mind and he jerked his gaze to him. "Wait a minute. How the hell does Ginny know I need hangover food this morning?"

Brogan chuckled, and said, "She knew you went to the beach party with Harvey."

Heat flooded his face and he ducked his head. "And Ginny figured I'd drink too much?"

"Nah, but she did figure you'd appreciate some breakfast."

Finally sliding his fork through the gravy-soaked breakfast biscuits, he shoved a huge bite into his mouth. The flavors exploded on his tongue, immediately making the morning seem better. Chewing the tasty morsel, he closed his eyes as he swallowed.

"Here," he heard Brogan say and opened his eyes to see a coffee cup shoved toward him on the counter.

"Thanks," he mumbled and took a sip, ignoring the sting of the burn.

"So, what happened last night? No one to hook up with?"

Brogan's question settled deep in his chest and he winced. "Honestly? I haven't hooked up since last month when that real estate group came to look over some property here on the shore and ended up spending the evening at the pub." Seeing his brother's eyebrows lift, he nodded. "It's true."

"Losing your touch or growing up?"

"Damn, man, you know how to cut to the chase first thing in the morning."

"It ain't first thing in the morning, sleeping beauty. It's after nine o'clock."

His eyes widened at that tidbit and he shoved another bite of breakfast into his mouth, using the chewing as an excuse to keep him from answering. Seeing Brogan settling his hip against the counter, he sighed. Emitting a rueful chuckle, he admitted, "The girls at the party last night were pretty—and young. Way too young."

Finishing his meal, he rinsed off the plate and with a jerk of his head, moved with his coffee cup into the miniscule living room. Sitting on the sofa, he watched as Brogan refilled his cup and joined him.

"You know how we've got high school girls on our team?" referring to the American Legion youth baseball teams that he and his friends coached. Brogan nodded his understanding.

"I swear, the girls at the beach party looked about the same age as them. Way too young for me to even be thinking about and believe me when I say that I wasn't even interested." Warming to the subject, he said, "And it's not just there. Even at the pub, the girls who come in, we always have to check their IDs." Shaking his head, he claimed, "Not interested. Not even a little. Used to be, I'd have no problem tapping that if they were legal and amenable to a few hours of company. But now? Hell no."

Brogan nodded his understanding. "Yeah. I came to that conclusion several years ago. Glad that you have too."

Leaning back against the sofa cushions, he drank more coffee, the caffeine easing through his system. "Hell, I didn't even know the music they were talking about. A couple of them were only twenty—not even old enough to drink—and I realized I was ten years older than they were." Sighing heavily again, he added, "So, I came home alone and drank my whiskey all by myself."

They were quiet for a moment, each left to their own thoughts as they finished their coffee. After a final sip, Brogan stood and rinsed out his cup at the sink. Turning, he stood with his hands on the counter, his weight leaning forward as he pierced him with his stare. "So, what got you drinking last night?"

He looked up quickly and his mouth tightened into a thin line.

"Nightmares? Or memories?" Brogan asked.

He remained quiet but had no doubt his brother knew more than he was saying. Both of them had joined the Marines after high school, Brogan the year before him. Like the rest of the Baytown Boys, they had felt the calling of the military and enlisted as fresh-faced young men, ready to see the world and break away from their tiny town on the Eastern Shore of Virginia. But, the world was more than they had imagined, and most of them had come home with nightmares that crept in when they were their most vulnerable.

"Yeah, figured as much," Brogan said, his chin dropping as he stared at his boots.

Scrubbing a hand over his face, he said, "Hell, I can't do any more nights like last night. Too old to drink like that, for sure." He needed to take a page out of Brogan's book. His brother had come back from his tour in Afghanistan and almost never touched alcohol, even though they co-owned Finn's Pub.

Chuckling, Brogan said, "Good." Looking at the clock on the microwave, he straightened his muscular, tatted body and said, "Gotta go. Ginny's home so I wanna hang with my wife."

"How's she doing? Morning sickness and all that?"

"Not a problem at all," Brogan shook his head. "She says she's one of the lucky ones and I'm not supposed to tell Katelyn that."

He chuckled. "Yeah, Katelyn was a nightmare."

Brogan blew out a breath at that understatement. "See you at Finn's this afternoon."

With a chin lift, he watched his brother move to the door. His hand on the knob, Brogan turned and looked over his shoulder, "You know, the Eastern Shore Mental Health Group has helped a lot of us. Just remember it's there if you need it."

He did not give an answer, but knew Brogan did not expect one. Watching him leave, he felt a pang of envy. It was a new emotion and one that he had trouble understanding. Brogan had returned from his time in the Marines even more taciturn than he had been as a teenager, but falling for the pretty, town police officer, Ginny, had given his brother a new outlook on life.

He loved his sister-in-law and was so happy for both of them, but had never felt the desire to settle down. Even in high school, he never dated just one girl. Known as the jokester of the family, he always said there was too much awesomeness for just one woman, a comment that never failed to elicit an eye roll from his mom and sister and a laugh from his friends.

Walking back into the kitchen, he washed out his cup and looked around at his apartment. Just a block off of Main Street where Finn's was located, it was in an old, renovated brick building. The outer walls were exposed brick and the inside walls were still the original, white painted drywall as when he had first moved in. The space was small, but open, with a kitchen in one corner and a small dining area next to it, which he had set up with a card table and four folding chairs for poker nights. The other side of the room was the living room, furnished with a sofa, chair, coffee table, and one end table. Obviously, a large, flat-screened TV sat on the opposite wall. After all, there were *some* things he spent money on. Other than that, he lived simply, saving his money for...something. He just had not figured out what yet.

Down a short hall were his one bedroom and bathroom, both modest, overlooking the yard of the back-door neighbors who had a little garden and a few trees.

Checking the time, he pushed off the counter and stalked to the bathroom to take a shower. He needed to wash off the rest of the whiskey smell and get ready for coaching the kids at the game. Standing underneath the warm spray of water, he wondered, *What more could I want?* Not having an answer, he nonetheless felt something was missing, and so the question rang and rang through his head.

3

The sun shone brightly down on the town's ball field and Aiden pulled his ball cap off to wipe his brow. Sliding it back on his sweat-soaked hair, he appreciated the shade it provided his eyes. Standing in the dugout, which was more like the sidelines behind the fence, he kept his eyes on the game and the young, uniformed kids nearby.

"Jeffrey, you're up next," he called out and nodded at the signals sent to him from Jason at third base.

Jason Boswell was not one of the original Baytown Boys but had come to live there at the request of Zac Hamilton, the town's Fire Chief. Jason and Zac had served in the Navy together. The Baytown Boys had experienced the comfort of a welcoming place to return after the military tours but knew many of their friends had not. So, they invited any who might need a friendly place to land, to move to Baytown and become part of the community and the active American Legion they had founded.

His gaze moved lazily around the rest of the ball field, seeing the other coaches, all good friends. Mitch Evans, the Police Chief, and Grant Wilder, one of the police officers in town, were coaching next to him. Gareth Harrison, Katelyn, and Ginny were standing near the teenage girl players. Hunter Simmons, another transplant from the Navy, was near first base, talking to the young boy on base as they eyed the pitcher. Callan Ward was still in the Coast Guard and was currently in the outfield.

Hearing the cheering from the stands, he glanced at all those who had come out. He was glad to see the crowd. A lot of townspeople came to support the kids playing. The AL sponsored the teams of boys and girls, of all ages, providing them with uniforms and coaching at no costs to the parents. With North Heron County listed as one of the poorest counties in Virginia, their donations of time and money were appreciated by everyone. Their efforts allowed children, whose parents might not be able to afford such a luxury as youth sports, a chance to participate.

He tossed a wave to the group of women sitting together, all wives of his friends. Tori, Jillian, Belle, and Jade were married to Mitch, Grant, Hunter, and Lance, respectively. Their eyes were hidden behind sunglasses, but he knew they had seen him when they waved in return.

Looking up at the blue sky with only a few white, fluffy clouds rolling by, he pulled in a deep breath of salty air. He had taken living near the bay for granted growing up but, after the mountains of Afghanistan, Baytown was a welcome reprieve and the breeze was blissful.

As the inning came to an end and the players switched places on the field, he noticed a small girl standing to the side, her eyes intently watching what was happening through the fence. He knew all of the children and youth who played on one of the AL teams but had not seen her before. The front of her dark brown hair was pulled up with a pink bow, letting the rest fall down by the side of her face and back. Her pink dress seemed incongruous to the sporting event, where most of the kids who were not playing were running around in shorts and t-shirts.

She cocked her head to the side in an interesting mannerism and he wondered who she belonged to. Before he had a chance to approach her, a woman came running up, kneeling directly in front of the little girl. "Emily, don't wander off. I could not find you."

"Want to see," came the simple reply, a sweet smile on her face.

"Then you ask Mommy and I'll take you closer to the other kids. But you can't just walk off by yourself."

He stared at the woman. He was sure she was a newcomer to town because he would have remembered her. Her long, mahogany hair, so like her daughter's, hung down her back in a low ponytail and he grinned at the pink scarf that held it in place. She wore a pink sundress that hugged her perfect figure without being ostentatious, thin straps crisscrossing her back and the front was modest, but flattering. Scanning her top to bottom, her tanned arms and legs, just enough on display, only served to make the entire package drool-worthy.

"Hi," he greeted, walking closer. "You must be new to town."

The woman stood, her gaze hidden behind sunglasses, but instead of the wide smile he expected in return, she reached down to take her daughter's hand and faced him stiffly. He noticed the little girl was still staring out onto the field at the other children. The woman hesitated before replying, "Yes, we are."

"Well, let me welcome you," he drawled, throwing out his best white-toothed grin. "My name's Aiden. Aiden MacFarlane. I'm one of the businessmen here in town."

The woman continued to face him, but her expression was unreadable. The little girl's gaze drifted up to his face and she smiled a snaggle-toothed grin before ducking her head shyly and stepping partially behind her mother's body, looking out to the field once again.

He looked at her a beat longer then focused on the woman again and said, "Uh...your daughter seems to be interested in the game. Is this her first time to one of our events?"

"Yes."

Her one-word answer might have put him off, had she not dropped her gaze down to her daughter, her face immediately softening. Deciding to push, he said, "We would love to have her play."

The woman shook her head slightly and replied, "No, thank you. We're just watching."

"Sure, but she's more than welcome to come to our practices. We have all age groups and there are no costs to parents. That allows kids from all backgrounds to be able to participate—"

"Thank you, but no." The woman's already stiff demeanor turned frosty and she glanced down to her daughter, whose rapt attention was still on the ballfield.

A slow anger began to burn in his chest at her attitude and snippy replies. Her daughter was clearly interested, which meant the woman had something against the game. And for some reason that really bothered him. "You know, just because you have a hang-up about the games doesn't mean your kid doesn't want to play." As soon as the words were out of his mouth he wondered why he bothered. Her reasons for not wanting her child to play were none of his concern.

Whipping her head back to him, she said quietly, "It's not that. She's not like *those* kids. Her needs are different."

Rearing back, he stared in stunned silence for a few seconds, not remembering the last time he had met someone so blatantly superior. Gaining his voice back, he leaned forward, his words aimed at the mother and not the child. "Whoa, judgmental much? I'll tell you, these kids are great and if you're too stuck up to appreciate that then I'm glad you won't be involved."

Filled with rage, he turned to walk away but, unable to stop his mouth, he twisted his head and tossed out,

"Too bad your little girl has to deal with parents that think they're better than everyone else."

Her face paled and she opened her mouth to speak, but suddenly snapped it closed. Squeezing her daughter's hand, gaining her attention, she said, "Come on, Emily. It's time to go." Together, they walked away, the little girl looking over her shoulder at the game the whole time.

Readjusting his ball cap, he moved back to the fence to cheer from the side. Agitated more than he probably should be at the encounter, he glanced over his shoulder and watched as the two of them walked away, heading toward the parking lot. He was surprised at the woman's unfriendly countenance and felt sorry for the little girl who so obviously wanted to be part of the other children. The mom may have been drop-dead gorgeous, but her high-maintenance, holier than thou attitude held no appeal to him whatsoever.

Turning back, Jason nodded toward the receding pair as he came over. "Mom's pretty. You get her number?"

Irritated at the assumption, he replied, "No, didn't even try. Thought maybe the little girl would like to play but uppity mom just stuck her nose in the air and walked off."

"Seriously?" Jason asked. "She looked familiar. I guess I've just seen her around."

Once the game was over, the kids all sent home, and the equipment put away, he and the others went over to the pub. An afternoon of good friends and good food was all he needed to forget about the ladies in pink.

"Mama, who was that man?"

Finished folding the blanket in her hands, Lia put it in the laundry basket and looked down at Emily, sitting on the couch, and smiled. "What man?"

"The one with the kids. The one who talked to you."

"Oh. He was just a coach."

"I liked the game they were playing."

Her heart panged at the longing in Emily's voice. "I know. It's called baseball. We can watch some on TV if you like."

Emily scrunched her nose and shook her head. "It's not the same."

"I know, baby." Her heart ached as she watched the myriad of emotions cross her daughter's face. The same feelings were swirling inside of her, too, but she had to be the grown up.

Emily sat quietly for a moment before looking back up at her. "Maybe I can play sometime."

Smiling softly, she reached her hand down and cupped her cheek. "We'll see. I'll try to find out what Baytown might have that would be a better game for you to play."

"I liked the other kids."

"I promise, once you meet more kids in your class, you'll have new friends."

Emily nodded, resigned, and her heart ached. "You go play and I'll fix dinner."

Grinning widely, Emily bounced up and ran down the hall, leaving her staring at her back. As she turned to the kitchen of their little house, she thought back to the coach. Aiden. More like asshole, she thought. Slamming the pan she had gotten out to make dinner down onto the counter, she winced. Slowly, she sucked in a deep breath and let it out. *After all, it's not the pan I'm pissed at!*

She continued to fix their meal, but her mind could not help but wander to the infuriatingly handsome coach. Tall enough for her to have to lean back to look into his blue eyes. A t-shirt that barely contained his broad shoulders and arm muscles. Hair that was too long, but looked soft enough to—

Giving her head a shake, she forced those thoughts from her mind. Handsome or not, his personality was not winning any awards. *I've been down that road before and it's one journey I don't plan on taking again.*

The next day's crowd at the pub was thinner so Aiden was able to work in the back stocking the bar for several hours. When he came out, he cast his gaze over the tables to make sure the servers were attending to the customers. At the end of the bar stood a lone woman, her back to him and a takeout bag sitting on the counter next to her. Not waiting on the server, he walked over.

"Can I help you?" he asked. His breath caught in his throat as she turned and lifted her gaze up to his. It was the woman from the ballpark, only today he could see her eyes. Dark, warm chocolate stared back at him from a face that was startling in its almost-perfection. Porcelain complexion, full rosy lips, thick lashes. His eyes were drawn to the slight scar that ran through her left eyebrow, but it somehow made her face even more interesting.

As he stared unabashedly, his mouth not connecting to his brain, he noted her gaze jumped to just behind him and he turned in time to see Cheryl, the server, come over.

"I'm sorry," Cheryl exclaimed. "I was delayed in the kitchen. Here's your card and receipt."

As the woman took the receipt and quickly signed it, he noted she was not wearing a wedding ring. Remembering he had made a comment about her daughter's parents, guilt speared through him. That had been an asshole remark, in spite of his anger. *Still, she probably busted her ex-husband's balls, as well.* Standing, she started to move past him but his feet remained rooted to the floor.

"Excuse me," she offered, turning sideways to slide by, her eyes not meeting his.

"Sorry," he said, unable to think of anything witty to say. Finally, he tossed out, "Listen, I'm sorry about—"

"Save it," she said through tight lips. Stopping with her hand on the door, ready to push it open, she twisted her head and held his gaze, unsmiling. "I come for the food, nothing else. Certainly not the antics of an over-grown Peter Pan."

His hands landed on his hips, his apology fading to a glare. "What the—"

"Oh, you know, all that," she waved her hand up and down in front of him, "for just one woman?" Her eyebrows lifted as she pushed opened the door and walked out into the sunshine.

He stood stark still for a moment, her words—or, rather, his words—slamming into him. He wanted to be pissed at her uppity attitude but knew he had made an ass of himself at the bar the other night and she had obviously overheard him.

Turning, he shoved the barstool, pushing it out of the way roughly as he headed toward the back. Seeing the receipt still on the table, he scooped it up. Amelia Smith. *Okay, Miss Amelia. We'll just avoid each other from now on.*

4

"What's up?"

Aiden walked into the office of Finn's, seeing Katelyn and Brogan already sitting in the cramped room. He glanced around, appreciating how Katelyn was able to keep the office from becoming overrun with piles of papers, receipts, orders, taxes, employee forms, and everything else they needed to run the business. She no longer worked on the floor, having become a partner in her husband's business, Harrison Investigations, but there was no denying she kept Finn's running behind the scenes.

When Gareth, a private investigator, first came to town and opened his business, he needed a receptionist who could understand the operations. Katelyn had jumped at the chance and had become so fascinated with investigating, and Gareth, she had studied for and received her PI license shortly after beginning work there. Now, her work for the pub was mostly taking care of the paperwork, for which he and Brogan were grateful.

"It's that time again," she quipped, waving some papers in front of her.

"What time?"

"Taxes," Brogan cut in. "Jesus, Aiden, don't you keep up with any of this shit?"

Glaring at his brother, he said, "Of course I do, but didn't we just do these?"

"Yes, but we pay quarterly and it's time again," Katelyn said, her blue eyes scanning the papers on the desk in front of her. "And, it looks like there's a necessary change as well as a slight problem last time."

His eyes widened as he glanced between her and Brogan, whose normally taciturn expression now included a tic in his jaw.

"What?" he asked, his heart sinking at the thought of an accounting error that might sink the business.

"First of all, Thomas Redding is retiring," she announced, referring to the accountant in town who handled most businesses.

Blinking, he jerked in his seat, ignoring the creak of the old wood. "Retiring?" The one-word question came out as more of a squeak, as he tried to remember a time when Mr. Redding's accounting business was not taking up a small office off Main Street. Even as a kid, he ran past the office on his way to visiting his grandfather at Finn's.

Katelyn chuckled and shook her head in mirth. "He's eighty years old. He's been in business for fifty-five years!"

Rearing back, his chair now groaned as though ready to break and Brogan shot him a look.

"Jesus, Aiden, sit still. The furniture's gonna fuckin' fall apart if you keep moving like that!"

Ignoring him, he continued to shake his head. "I had no idea he was that old. We should give him a retirement party here at Finn's—"

"Already on it," Katelyn agreed, "but what we need to focus on is our taxes right now."

Remembering she mentioned a problem, he turned his attention back to the task at hand. "What's up?"

"Well, the good news is that he has sold his business to a new accountant. I've met with her, just this morning, and I like her. She's quiet. Serious. Very professional. She's also the one who let me know there was a problem last time." Sighing, she continued, "It appears Thomas made a slight error and we underpaid by about five thousand dollars, which is not horrible, but that means we need to make it up this time so we don't get hit with penalties."

"Fuckin' hell," he said, blowing out his breath while leaning forward, his forearms planted on his knees.

"Any good news?" Brogan asked.

"Well, Lia, the new accountant, said that she's going over our past accounts and might have found a way that we were also overcharged in a few areas, so that might counter-balance the deficit."

"Good," both he and Brogan replied at the same time.

"She needed more of these forms and receipts," Katelyn explained, picking them up and placing them into the open file on the desk. Gathering up the folder, she held it out to him.

"What am I supposed to do with that?" he asked, brows snapping down together.

"Take it to the accountant, of course."

"Why me?"

"Because it's your turn to deal with the taxes. We agreed that it was a burden we would share equally—"

"Isn't it Brogan's turn?" he continued to argue.

"No, Brogan did it the time before last. I dealt with Thomas last time, therefore, you win the prize this time."

"But you've already talked to this new lady. You know what the hell y'all talked about."

Katelyn's face softened and she said, "Aiden, you'll be fine. You don't have to do anything but deliver the file and answer some general questions about the business. If she has questions beyond that, she can call me."

"Fine," he bit out, his jaw tight and hands clasped in front of him. Standing quickly, he asked, "Anything else?"

Brogan answered, "No man, we're good."

He snatched the file from Katelyn's hand and mumbled, "Sorry," as he headed out, missing the shared look that passed between his siblings.

Standing outside Thomas' office, the title Redding, CPA, LLC painted on the window in gold letters, Aiden paced. He stared at the words, realizing that the new accountant had not added her name yet. Trying to remember if Katelyn mentioned her last name, all he could come up with was her first name. Lia.

He glanced down at the folder in his hands, noting the edge was becoming moist from his sweaty palms. Quickly wiping first one hand, then the next, on the thighs of his jeans, he sucked in a fortifying breath. Blowing it out slowly, he pushed open the door and stepped inside.

The outer office was the same as the last time he had been there. Dark, hardwood floors, buffed to a shine. A heavy wooden desk sat in the corner, elderly Mrs. Markham sitting behind an open laptop, the only modern accoutrement in the room. She looked up and smiled widely.

"Mr. MacFarlane," she greeted, peering at him over the top of her glasses.

He smiled in return. She had called him Aiden until Finn had deeded the pub to him and his siblings. Once he became a business owner, she referred to him as Mr. MacFarlane. It always made him feel like she was talking to his father or grandfather, but he recognized that was her way of maintaining professionalism.

"I understand I'm here to meet with the new accountant," he said, hoping his voice did not show his anxiety.

"Absolutely. In fact, she's ready for you now. I'll show you to her office."

He inwardly chuckled, since he knew there were only four rooms in the back and, with one a conference room, one a bathroom, and one a staff room, that only left one as an office. Following dutifully, he entered the same room as he had when meeting with Thomas.

"Ms. Smith, Mr. MacFarlane is here."

Mrs. Markham stepped out of the way and closed the door behind him, leaving him staring at Amelia Smith. His eyes popped open as her brows lifted in unison. "You? You're the new accountant?"

She looked up, her mouth in a tight line and her mahogany hair pulled back in a bun, and focused her brown eyes on him. "Yes. I'm Lia Smith." Her eyes narrowed slightly and she added, "I thought I was meeting with Katelyn MacFarlane."

"Well, looks like you've got me," he snapped, sliding into the seat in front of her desk.

"Fine."

She smoothed her hair back, but he saw no discernable strands out of place to warrant the action. She reached her hand out for the file in his hand and if she noticed the sweat-damp edges she did not say anything, for which he was grateful. As she scanned the contents, he took the time to carefully peruse their new accountant.

She wore a white blouse with a lace collar, a single strand of pearls around her neck. Paired with a navy pencil skirt, she had a timeless, classic appearance. Classic, but cold. She gave off no warmth and he wondered, given how kindly she had looked at her daughter, if she could really be as cold as she seemed. Moving up, her skin was just as beautiful as he observed earlier. He mentally shook his head in derision. *What did I think was going to happen in the last couple of hours, that she would*

have sprouted witch's warts? And why do I even care?
Rolling his eyes at his wayward thoughts, he startled
when she began to speak.

"As I told Katelyn, I'm a forensic accountant, not a
tax specialist and expect to hire another accountant
soon to help with the tax work. But, I'm certainly able
to check over what Mr. Redding had worked on and
give you my opinion."

He made no comment, so she continued. "It appears
that Mr. Redding made a slight arithmetic error last
time, causing your business to underpay your quarterly
taxes by about five thousand dollars. That could easily
be made up this time, but when delving a bit deeper, I
also found an area that I think we can make that
amount up and even save you a bit more."

"Good," he nodded, glad that she could be professional in spite of their obvious dislike for each other.

She swung a stack of papers around on the desk
toward him and, with a yellow highlighter, began
marking several of the lines of numbers. "If you'll look
here, you will see what I am talking about. These figures
do not add up to what he has down here. And, with the
missing tax-exempt additions, you can see where I have
included those in our bottom-line figures."

"Uh huh," he said, forcing his voice to have more
conviction than he felt.

She lifted her gaze to him and said, "Please, just look
at the numbers and you'll be able to verify what I'm
saying."

"I trust you," he bit out.

Her eyes narrowed on his, but he ignored her.

"Yes, but I'd like for you to verify the—"

Standing suddenly, he said, "I've got to get back to work." Walking to the door, he hesitated and looked over his shoulder, "Thank you, for what you're doing. Really, we appreciate it. Just let us know what we need to pay, and we'll sign the forms." With that, he walked out of the office, tossing a wave toward Mrs. Markham, and then out into the sunshine. Sucking in a deep breath and letting it out slowly, he felt the tension ease off him.

Walking back into the pub, he offered a chin lift to Brogan behind the bar and headed back to the stock room. He was halfway through the reordering when Katelyn walked in behind him.

"Everything okay with the accountant?"

"Yep."

"Anything we need to know about?"

"Nope."

Huffing, she walked around so that she was staring into his face instead of at his back. "Aiden?"

Stopping, he put his hands on his hips and glared down at her. "Come on, Katelyn. Ms. Smith is obviously good at what she does, but she likes to make sure everyone is one the same page. Sending me in there to talk to her about the finances was kind of a shit move."

Sucking in her lips, her face fell. "Oh, Aiden, I'm sorry. I thought you would just deliver the files and answer any specific questions she might have. I didn't expect her to start showing you what she was working on."

He heaved a sigh, dragging his hand through his

hair. "Yeah, I know. I'm sorry, sis. I shouldn't have bitten your head off."

"Did it get uncomfortable?"

Nodding, he admitted, "She wanted me to take a look at some of the numbers with her, but...I just said we trusted her."

She reached out and clasped his arm, moving closer. "It's okay, you know."

Lifting his eyebrow, he said, "Oh, really? When's the last time you got numbers switched backward?"

"Aiden, there's nothing to be ashamed of with how you switch numbers in your head. You understand math concepts perfectly. It's just that visually you read them backward."

Snorting, he said, "Yes, and it drove my math teachers crazy."

Arching a perfect eyebrow, she retorted, "No, I think that was you being such a jokester in class!"

Chuckling, he nodded. "Yeah, you're probably right!" He lifted his shoulders in a shrug and threw his arm around her. "It's okay. Really. I just felt like a bug under a microscope when I was in her office. Ms. Smith reminds me of a really uptight teacher."

Katelyn hesitated for a moment and he tilted his head, saying, "Cat got your tongue? That's unusual."

She punched his shoulder and laughed. "I wondered what you'd think about Lia."

Recognizing the mischievious glint in her eye, he questioned, "Lia? Seriously? Listen, if you've got some cockamamie idea about hooking me up with her, you can get that outta your head right now."

"I just thought that—"

"Sis, you're smart, driven, and right now so crazy in love with Gareth and little Finn that you want the whole world to fart rainbows. But, don't worry about me. I'm good. And, believe me when I say, there is not one little spark where Ms. Smith is concerned."

The two of them walked out of the storeroom and, ignoring Katelyn's fallen face, he thrust the stock form into her hand. "Want to check this over?"

She elbowed him in the ribs and said, "Nope. There's one thing I never worry about and that is you ordering the wrong alcohol!"

As they entered the pub, he walked behind the bar, his mood lighter—as long as he kept his mind off the pretty accountant. What he had told Katelyn was almost true. He had no intention of getting anywhere near Ms. Smith because, even as gorgeous as she was, as a person, she was uptight and judgemental. But at the same time, unfortunately, remembering the way she looked as she stared at him, there was definitely a spark.

5

Still reeling from her slam-bam meeting with the infuriating Aiden, Lia looked up as Mrs. Markham knocked on the door frame.

"I hate to bother you, but the Mayor is here to speak with you." Stepping further into the room, Mrs. Markham whispered, "I'll warn you, he's a bit pompous and rather pushy. But, he's been mayor for a number of years here in Baytown." Leaning down closer, she added, "He usually summons people to see him in his fancy office in the Municipal Building. For him to come here, alone, is...out of character, to say the least."

Nodding as she digested her secretary's words, she stood and, smoothing her skirt, said, "Please show him in."

Rounding the corner, Corwin Banks entered her office, his smile wide and his hand out. Clasping hers, he vigorously pumped her arm up and down. He wore an expensive, tailored suit and his hair was meticulously styled. The image of a big fish in a little pond came to her mind.

"Amelia, I'm Corwin Banks, mayor of this fine town. Been meaning to get over here to see who was taking Thomas' place."

Managing to retrieve her hand without it being crushed, she waved him to a seat and settled back down. "It's nice to meet you, Mayor Banks. What can I do for you?"

He shifted his girth into the sturdy chair and held her gaze. "To the point. I like that. Well, uh, normally, I like to have people come to my office when the business is official, but...uh...I have a delicate situation. One that I'd like handled with discretion."

Intrigued, she leaned forward, her pen and legal pad ready for notes.

His gaze dropped to the writing utensils on her desk and he hesitated for a moment. Finally, he said, "I need to have a forensic accountant take a look at our books. The last audit found a...um...discrepancy."

Her interest piqued, she said, "I would need to be hired by the Town Council—"

"Is there any way we can circumvent that process?"

"Mayor Banks, surely you know the legal process must be followed for any possible theft to be handed over to the county attorney."

"Yes, yes, I'm fully aware of the legalities, but you must understand my position."

Laying down her pen, she stared at the blustery man in front of her. His ruddy cheeks grew redder and she noted a sheen of perspiration over his forehead.

His eyes darted around before finally landing back on her.

"Mayor Banks, I know that having a forensic accountant come in makes everyone nervous. After all, it would be my job to investigate and discover where the financial discrepancy has occurred and the person who caused the discrepancy. Essentially, pointing the finger at the person who stole money from the town." She watched his shoulders slump and his body deflate but waited to see what he would say.

"Yes," he finally agreed, his face pinched. "It's just that…well, you see…it's an election year and gosh darn, I had hoped this would not become public."

"Then, you have a choice, Mayor Banks. Disregard the audit and continue forward, possibly allowing a member of your staff to continue to steal from Baytown and face the press when it inevitably becomes public," she paused for emphasis. "Or hire me to investigate. It's purely your choice, but if you decide on me, I can give you my word that I am professionally discrete but will not shirk from asking questions and doing the proper digging."

Corwin nodded and stood, offering his hand. "I appreciate your time. I'll let you know what the Town Council decides."

She watched him leave and slumped back into her chair. Glancing at the clock on the wall, she was stunned it was only a few minutes after three o'clock. She was ready to go home already. Checking her calendar, she remembered she had an introductory Auxiliary meeting that evening and was leaving Emily with a sitter. Tempted to skip it, she grimaced, knowing she needed to do more to get out into the community.

Sighing heavily, she opened the Finn's Pub file on her desk and continued to work, trying to ignore the irritating thoughts of Aiden MacFarlane that kept creeping into her mind. The way his long, dark hair was swept back from his face as though his hands had continually brushed it back. His blue eyes, the intensity that pierced directly into her. He was tall, and muscular...and a complete jerk!

Dropping her head to the desk, she groaned. As much as she wanted to deny it, even considering his horrible attitude there was something about him that sparked an interest. And it had been a long time since anyone had done that.

Rapping the gavel upon the podium, Jillian called the Baytown American Legion Auxiliary's meeting to order. Lia looked around at the gathering, her attention brought back to the front as Jillian spoke.

"Rise for the Advancement of the Colors," Jillian announced.

The large group of women in the building rose to their feet as Ginny Spencer, the Sergeant-at-Arms, marched forward carrying the American flag.

A Methodist minister from the town said the prayer before Jillian led the group in the Allegiance to the Flag. After Ginny had taken her seat again, Jillian read the preamble to the Constitution of the American Legion and then called Nancy Evans to the podium for the reading of the last meeting's minutes. She was still trying to remember who everyone was and how they were related to each other. She had met the Police Chief, Mitch Evans, and knew that Nancy was his mother and Tori was his wife. She was fairly sure Nancy was also Jillian's aunt, but was uncertain the exact relationship.

After Nancy completed her task, Jillian called Corrine MacFarlane, Katelyn's mom, to read the treasurer's report. She leaned slightly to the side to get a better look at Corrine. She could see the familial resemblance between mother and daughter, but it was Aiden's face that came to mind. He had been so dismissive of her today in her office. Just one more example of his arrogance. *How can his sister and mother be so nice, and he be such a jerk?*

Katelyn, as Vice President, took the podium and her focus jerked back to what was being said. Katelyn called upon the committee chairs to report as well.

Tori, taking the stand, said, "The music festival in the park is coming up and we still need more baked goods to sell. The entire proceeds of the festival go to the American Legion and Auxiliary. Let me know if you can send some baked items in."

Several other committees reported as well, then Jillian announced, "At our next meeting, we will be inducting several new members to our chapter of the American Legion Auxiliary. Last time, we met a couple of them and, tonight, I'd like to acknowledge Amelia Smith. I hope that you will make her welcome as she and her daughter are new to Baytown. Lia, would you like to introduce yourself to the group? You can just stand and say a few words."

Glad that Jillian had informed her earlier that she would be doing this, she stood and smiled nervously toward the large gathering. "Hello. I'm Amelia Smith and I have an accounting business here in town, taking over for Mr. Redding. I'm pleased to be considered for membership in your organization. My...uh...husband was in the Marines, serving in Afghanistan. He..." Her mouth suddenly dry, she licked her lips, stunned that she had gone blank. The smiling faces of the women near her did not penetrate the cold that surrounded her heart.

"Your husband? You were talking about your husband," one of the elderly women sitting next to her prompted.

With a mental shake, she blurted, "I'm a widow." As soon as the words were out, she could see the sympathy in everyone's eyes. Her gaze jumped to Jillian, still standing at the podium.

"That's fine, Lia. Thank you," Jillian rushed, her face registering regret.

"No...no, it's fine. Uh...my husband was killed in action three years ago. Uh...anyway, thank you for allowing me to serve alongside you in the Auxiliary." Sitting quickly, she clasped her hands together, hoping to still the shaking.

With a final prayer and the retirement of colors, Jillian read the Auxiliary Charge. "Till we meet again let us remember that our obligation to our Country can be fulfilled only by the faithful performance of all duties of citizenship. Let service to the community, state and nation be ever a main objective of the American Legion Auxiliary and its members. Let us ever be watchful of our organization and ourselves, that nothing shall swerve us from the path of Justice, Freedom, Loyalty and Democracy." After that, she pronounced, "If there is no further business to come before this meeting, the meeting is adjourned."

She listened numbly to the end of the meeting and then plastered a smile on her face to greet the many members who came to meet her. Their names and faces began to run together, but she desperately tried to keep them straight in her mind, some telling her about sons and husbands, brothers and fathers all lost at war.

Just as the walls were beginning to close in around her, she was left with a small group of women she knew, having met them around town or at the school or work.

Katelyn wrapped her arm around her shoulders and said, "Come to Finn's with us."

She wiped her brow with a shaky hand, looking at the friendly faces of Jillian, Tori, Madelyn, and Belle. Jade, Emily's new school teacher, was also part of the gathering. Looking at the group of women she mentally titled *Katelyn's Crew* she felt torn between wanting to spend more time with them and feeling exhausted.

Making the excuse of needing to get back to relieve her babysitter, she accepted Katelyn's hug and, with a wave goodbye, walked outside to her car. She lived in North Heron County, just outside of town in a small neighborhood along one of the bay waterways.

Thankful for the short drive home, she nonetheless sat in the car for a moment, attempting to still the shaking of her hands. Thinking of her husband, Carl, always had that affect on her now. Forcing a calm façade onto her face before she went in to see Emily, she climbed from her vehicle.

Opening the front door, she walked into her small living room, spying Emily in her pajamas, piled up on the sofa, watching a movie with one of the teenagers in the neighborhood who was babysitting.

"Don't you all look comfortable," she called out, gaining Susie and Emily's attention.

Emily jumped up and ran to her, throwing her arms around her waist and giving her a hug. Bending to kiss the top of her head, she shot a look toward Susie. "Everything go okay?"

Susie, a pretty, blonde, high school junior, stood and smiled. "We were fine, weren't we, Emily?"

Emily did not respond immediately so Susie moved closer to her and repeated her words.

Emily's face brightened with a huge smile. "Yes, we had fun! We watched movies and ate popcorn and played games."

"Fabulous," she said, kissing her daughter's forehead. "Let me pay Susie and you head on to bed. I'll be there in a few minutes."

Emily hugged Susie before running up the stairs. Taking out her wallet, she turned to Susie, holding out the money. "Thank you so much," she said with sincerity. "It means a lot to have someone I can trust with her."

"She was a doll. We had no problems at all, Ms. Smith. Call me anytime." With that, Susie headed out, jogging across the street to her house.

Watching until Susie was safely in her front door, she closed and locked hers. Refusing to give into the thoughts threatening to drown her, she sucked in a deep breath and headed to the stairs.

She found Emily, teeth brushed, and already in bed with her doll tucked in next to her. "My, my, you are ready, aren't you?"

Emily grinned the snaggle-toothed smile that always melted her heart. Sitting on the side of the bed, she tucked her in. "Since tonight was Mommy's night out, I've got a surprise for this weekend." Seeing her daughter's wide eyes, she laughed. "There's a music festival in the park and we're going to go."

Emily scrunched her nose and cocked her head to the side. "What kind of music?"

"Hmm," she thought, her forehead crinkled. "I really don't know, but I do know that there will be food and games, as well as the music."

That brought a smile to Emily's face. "I might see some of my friends there."

Nodding, she pulled the covers up to her chin, making sure to tuck her doll in as well. "I'm glad you're making friends at school. And I'm sure your teacher, Ms. Greene, will be there also."

Another huge smile met her with that statement and she made a mental note to specifically thank Jade for being so helpful with Emily's transition to Baytown Elementary.

"Okay, baby girl, it's time for you to go to sleep." With a final kiss, she turned out the light and headed back downstairs. Walking directly to the kitchen, she pulled down a wine glass and opened the refrigerator. Pouring a glass of Riesling, she moved into the living room.

Standing at the fireplace mantle, she stared at the framed pictures. The photograph of her holding newborn Emily drew her in. Carl was not in that picture. Taking a large gulp of the wine, she worked to steady her breathing as memories flooded back.

Their wedding with his military squad in attendance, Carl resplendent in his uniform. Setting up house in a tiny apartment outside the military base. Her disappointment in his immediate tour taking him overseas. Working for an accounting firm while he was in Afghanistan, feeling like she was living only half a life. Reveling in his trip home, celebrating it by barely leaving the apartment, and then discovering she was pregnant. Skyping with him during her pregnancy until she was due. They even skyped as she was delivering.

Carl taking a stateside position after his overseas tour was over. The feeling of bliss at their perfect life, perfect marriage, perfect family.

The concern that turned to fear as they watched Emily appear disinterested in her surroundings and her struggle to speak. Then discovering she was completely deaf in her left ear and had partial hearing in her right.

The doctors. The diagnosis. Sensorineural hearing loss.

The speech therapists. The audiologists. The tears, the fears. The promise she made to her daughter that she would do everything in her power to help her. Watching helplessly as Carl began to distance himself from Emily...and then her. The arguments. His refusal to learn basic sign language in case she needed to communicate with her hands instead of her voice.

Then came the argument that occurred the night he came home and told her that he had put in for another overseas tour. More tears, more fears. But they fell on ears that could hear but did not care.

This tour was unlike the first. Few calls. Few letters. No skyping. Until the letter that came where he said that he did not know what would happen when he returned, but it was too painful for him to be around Emily...that her deafness was something he did not know how to handle.

Her tears dried up and her fears turned to anger. How dare he think that a father could pick and choose the difficulties their child might face. How dare he leave her to be the parent while he simply removed himself from her life.

But, before she had a chance to let Carl know just how much of a coward he was, the visit came. The Chaplain. The Commander.

Her husband...the war hero...the slain Marine. Leaving behind a sweet three-year-old daughter who already had enough obstacles to face.

She accepted the condolences. She buried her husband. She kept the folded flag, to give to Emily someday. She had a framed photograph of Carl in his uniform on Emily's bookshelf so that she would have that memento. And, deep inside, she also buried the shame of knowing if he had lived, he planned on leaving them both. She wished the anger could be buried as easily.

Taking another large gulp of wine, she finished the glass quickly. She kept the photograph on the mantle for Emily, but also to remind herself that things are not always what they seem. The steadiest man can fall short.

Blowing out a long, slow breath, she walked back into the kitchen and rinsed out her glass before heading upstairs. Once inside her bedroom, she slipped out of her clothes and pulled on her silk pajamas. A smile slid over her face as she ran her hands over the smooth material. It was one of her few indulgences, but she told herself that the softness made her sleep better.

With a shake of her head, she moved into the bathroom. After removing her makeup and brushing out her hair, she moisturized her face. Standing, she stared at the reflection looking back. Carl used to tell her she was the prettiest woman he ever met and how lucky he was that she accepted his marriage proposal. At the time, it warmed her heart but, now, she saw the words as shallow.

She had been an adornment. And so had Emily. But, when Emily had been less than perfect in his eyes, he had no idea how to cope. *So weak...such a weak man.* As she continued to stare into the mirror, she reached over to flip off the light, plunging the room and her reflection into darkness.

Climbing into bed, she lay, her mind sliding to her meeting with Aiden MacFarlane—again. There was no denying he was gorgeous. If she let herself, she could stare into his eyes for hours, getting lost in their intensity. He was the first man she found herself attracted to since Carl, but that was just surface level. The first time she saw him he showed himself to be a player and then, when they officially met, he judged her nearly instantly. Rolling over, she knew he was exactly what would never be right for her or Emily. *He would never be able to accept someone with special needs...someone who had to be placed above all individual needs.* As she continued her restless tossing and turning, she wondered if there was such a man.

6

The music festival was in full swing as Aiden scanned the area looking for his friends. He stood near the band, who was set up in the white gazebo on one end of the park. Baytown was developed on a grid, streets running straight east to west and north to south. The beach was on the east side of town with Main Street on the south side. The Baytown Park was located in the middle of the town, taking up several blocks in each direction, which made it the perfect venue for an event like this.

Blankets and lawn chairs littered the area and, spotting his group, he walked to the side of the park where his friends had settled. The music could still be heard and yet was not too loud, so conversations did not have to be screamed.

As he made his way over, he surveyed who was already there. Mitch and Tori, Jillian and Grant, Lance and Jade, Katelyn and Gareth, Brogan and Ginny, Zac and Madelyn, and Belle and Hunter all sat together on blankets spread in a circle. All couples, some with children, some expecting. It really put into perspective how the Baytown Boys had grown.

Coming up to them, he greeted everyone and kissed his mother's cheek before shaking his father and grandfather's hands. Mitch and Jillian's parents sat nearby, as well as Grant's parents. He waved to them, smiling at the familiarity of the scene. Having noted that almost everyone was paired, he was glad to see several of his single friends were there also. Callan had brought some of his Coast Guard buddies and Jason was hanging with one of his mechanics.

Colt Hudson, the Sheriff of North Heron County and Hannah Freeman, the Police Chief of Easton, came by to call out greetings, both stopping to chat with the gathering.

The music came to a stop and the crowd turned toward the gazebo, seeing Mayor Banks moving to the microphone. Dressed in a suit in spite of the heat, he grinned widely at the crowd and said, "Just giving the band a break so that I can welcome you to the Baytown Annual Music Festival." As applause broke out, he waved congenially, his jowls shaking as he bobbed his head.

"And I wanted to take this opportunity to remind everyone to come out for the next mayoral election. Of course, I'll be running again and hope to count on your vote to keep Baytown moving forward as one of the best coastal towns in the south."

The applause came again, but Aiden and his friends

just grinned. His mother sighed, "He's a blowhard, but I can't fault what he's done for the town."

Others nodded in agreement before turning their attention back to the gazebo where the tall, thin town manager, Silas Mills, moved up beside Corwin.

"I also want to say that our intrepid town manager, Silas Mills, will be continuing to serve and has my support as he brings new ideas to our fair city, such as this Music Festival."

"Ohh, posh," Jillian grumbled. "Silas has done nothing but complain every time we come up with a money-making project for the community. I can take Corwin, in small doses,but Silas is such a little—"

"No name calling," Tori said, hushing her friend as she looked at her little one playing nearby.

Jillian stopped, but said, "You know I'm right. He's always complaining about our husbands and the whole police department as well."

The others nodded, glad when Corwin and Silas left the stage and the band began to play again.

Standing close to Katelyn, Aiden accepted a soda and gratefully took one of the sandwiches she had brought from the pub. Enjoying the music, he startled when she called out, "Lia! Over here!"

Wincing, he turned to find Lia standing almost directly behind him. Unintentionally, his gaze took her in from head to toe…slowly. Her thick, dark hair was pulled back from her face with a clip, the heavy length flowing down her back. A white, lacy, sleeveless shirt was tucked into light blue capris, both showcasing her curves. Flat, decorated sandals were on her feet, showing off pink, painted toenails. Unlike the blatantly sexy women he used to zero in on, she exemplified understated sexy. Suddenly, he found his bite of sandwich stuck in his throat.

Coughing, he gasped for air as Brogan pounded him on the back. "Shi—uh...geez, Brogan. Way to make it worse." He glowered at his brother as he tried to catch his breath, then scanned to make sure none of the kids heard his almost-cuss word.

"Are you all right?"

The soft voice came from the side and he turned again, looking at Lia, her eyes holding obvious, and unexpected, concern.

Clearing his throat, he nodded tersely, replying, "Yeah. Thanks."

Feeling the need to separate from her, he offered a chin lift before walking over to Jason and Callan. As he walked away, he heard his mom ask Lia about Emily and could not help but eavesdrop on her answer.

"Emily has a new friend from school and she's having some ice cream with Judith's family over by the picnic tables."

"Judith is a sweet child," Jade said, her smile wide. "I'm glad she and Emily are friends."

"Yes. It's kind of hard for Emily to make new friends. She's shy and, well, sometimes other children can be a little...uh...difficult."

Hearing Lia speak so derogatorily of other children reminded him of his first meeting with her. Without hesitation, he turned and said, "Like the kids on the ball teams?"

Lia blinked, her head cocked to the side as if she misunderstood him and was surprised at his ire. *You know exactly what I'm talking about.* Her mouth opened but he jumped in again. "If you'd ease up a bit, I bet Emily could find all kinds of friends that she'd find acceptable, even if you didn't. How you can be so judgemental and put yourself before your kid is beyond me."

He heard his friends gasp at his remark as Lia reared back as though slapped. Opening her mouth to retort, her words appeared stuck and he smirked. Someone needed to put her in her place. Moving to go he heard a strangled sob and turned back in time to see her quickly turn and hurry away.

"Aiden, you arrogant prick," Katelyn began while the others sputtered their outrage.

Throwing his hands up in defense, he was about to tell them of the conversation he had had with her at the ball field when he heard a scream. His head immediately swung in the direction of the sound, it was so full of agony and panic.

A woman was standing with Lia, crying and waving her hands. Without thinking, he moved in their direction. "What's going on?"

Tears running down her face, Lia turned and looked at him, unseeing. "Emily. She's gone. I have to find her!"

Her eyes frantically searching the crowd, she started to move away from him but he gripped her upper arms, halting her. "It'll be okay. Tell me what happened and we'll find her."

"Judith…Judith's mom turned around and Emily was

gone. She told Judith she wanted to find me. She's looking for me. I need to find her."

She tried to pull away again but he held her steady. Her strident voice, full of anguish, cut through him. Looking around, he started to form a plan when Ginny approached and asked what Emily was wearing.

"Pink shorts...uh...pink tennis shoes. Uh...a...uh... white shirt."

Mitch assured, "We'll get the music stopped and have an announcement made over the loudspeakers."

"No, no," Lia cried, tears streaming down her face. "That won't work. She's deaf. She can't hear that clearly!"

Jade, obviously knowing about Emily's special needs, rushed to Lia, pulling her in for a hug. "We'll find her," she said, her eyes glancing around to the group that had jumped up, ready to search.

"How does she communicate?" Colt asked.

"Uh, she has a hearing aid in her right ear but is completely deaf in her left. She can hear if you speak on her right side and she also reads lips. Loud noises are muffled and if you approach her from the left, she won't hear you at all," she said, her chest heaving with sobs.

"Does she know not to talk to strangers?" Mitch asked.

"Yes," Lia replied.

"Good. That's good," Mitch assured her. "Is there something we can tell her so she knows she can trust us?"

"Uh..." Lia looked to Aiden and his heart stuttered at

the lost expression on her face. "You...you can tell her to hear Mommy's heartbeat."

"Okay. Don't worry, we'll find her."

Mitch, Colt, Hannah, Ginny, Grant, Lance, and Hunter all grabbed their police radios and immediately spread out in the crowd.

Aiden's feet rooted to the ground for a moment, and he stared at Lia's ravaged face. Pain stabbed his heart at the realization he had completely misjudged her and her motives. Forcing his mind to clear of his fuck-up, he turned and raced away, determined to find Emily.

As the group dispersed, Lia moved to follow them but Jade held her back.

"What are you doing? I have to find Emily."

"This is the last place she knew you were. If she's moving and you're moving, you make it harder to find one another. You need to stay put."

Looking around at the crowd of comforting faces standing close by, she nodded. That made sense. Everyone was gone except for Tori and Katelyn, both holding their children, and Jade, whose arms were still around her. That was a lot of people looking for Emily.

"They'll find her," Katelyn promised, her eyes darting between her baby and Lia's face.

"She's never wandered off before. She's always stayed right with me." Tears started to choke her throat as she thought of all the possibilities. "Oh, God, she wanted to find me and now she's lost."

No matter what words her friends said, her heart screamed for her child. Stumbling back, she turned, saying, "I can't just wait here and do nothing."

"No," Tori said, reaching out to grab her arm. "We've got tons of people looking for her. When they find her, they'll bring her here to you."

Torn between wanting to search and wanting to be here for Emily, she hesitated. Breaking down in sobs, she cried, "I want my baby...I need my baby."

Tori and Katelyn sobbed with her, clutching their children, as Jade's arms encircled her once more.

Aiden's mind raced along with his feet as he searched the crowded park. His gaze landed on one of their friends, also searching, but they shook their head as he made eye contact. Stopping, he forced his mind to clear. What did Lia say? *She can't hear loud noises clearly.* Looking toward the speakers near the gazebo, he headed in the opposite direction. Sure that she would go where she might be able to hear better, he raced toward the back, not too far from the ice cream truck.

Turning in a circle, he fought the desire to call out her name. *Fuck! This is like searching for a needle in a haystack.* The crowds were standing near the food trucks and he instinctively knew, as tiny as she was, she would want to get to where she could see better. Turning, he ran past the picnic tables and circled around the far corner of the park where more people were sitting.

A flash of pink caught his eye and he turned to see a

dark headed child, her hair pulled into a ponytail with a big pink bow, moving away from him toward the edge of the crowd. Remembering her bow from the day at the ball field, he raced toward her, darting between families on blankets.

Not wanting to scare her, he slowed his pace, making sure to approach her from the right. His heart pounded an erratic staccato as he quickly moved in front of her, squatting so that he would be at eye level.

She jerked in surprise, her wide eyes full of fear.

"Hey, Emily," he said, unsure if he should speak differently to her. But, then, he remembered she understood him at the ball field. Swallowing the lump in his throat, he smiled widely. "Do you remember me? From the ball game?"

She nodded, her eyes still wide. "Mama said you were a coach."

"That's right. I help the kids learn how to play the game. My name is Aiden. Um...I think your mom is looking for you now."

She nodded, her pink bow bouncing up and down. "I had ice cream with my friend but wanted to find Mama." Her chin wobbled and she continued, "But I don't know where she is."

"Can I take you to her? I promise I know where your mom is."

She took a step back, unsure. "Mama said don't go with strangers."

"You're mom is very smart. She told me to tell you to listen for her heartbeat, so you would know it was okay to go with me." She mulled that over and her face

59

relaxed. Sighing in relief, he said, "Let's go find your mom."

She nodded enthusiastically, her eyes now full of hope. He held out his arms and asked, "How about I carry you? We can get there quicker."

Without hesitation, her arms shot up toward his and she allowed him to scoop her up. "I got tired," she admitted. Laying her head on his shoulder, his heart skipped another beat, but this time not in fear. This time, his heart filled with happiness as his arms held her slight body tightly.

Looking ahead, his long legs made quick work of getting him to the other side of the park. As he approached the area, he caught Mitch's eye and his face broke out in a huge grin. He twisted his head just long enough to see Mitch on his radio, alerting the other law enforcement personnel that Emily had been found.

Seeing Lia, her tears evident even from a distance, surrounded by Jillian, Katelyn, Tori, and Jade, he hastened his steps. Just as he was about to call out, Lia looked up, her gaze landing on him and then dropping to the precious bundle in his arms.

"Emily!" she screamed, throwing her arms into the air and racing toward him. They slowed just enough to keep from slamming into each other and squishing Emily. He was ready to hand Emily off to her, but her arms surrounded him as well as her daughter. He could feel Lia's body sliding to the ground as her knees appeared to give out so, he knelt as well, the three of them slumping together. Feeling the sudden urge to comfort Lia, he managed to loosen one arm from Emily and throw it around her, pulling both of them into his embrace.

Lia's body bucked with a sob as she held tightly to her daughter. "Oh, baby, baby, I didn't know where you were."

Emily did not respond and he was not sure if she was unable to hear her mother or just wanted to be held. He was barely aware that they were surrounded by a huge crowd of his friends and family, only the pats on the back he felt reminding him that they were not alone. Something about holding them, protecting them in this moment...changed something in him.

He settled his ass to the ground, stretching out his legs, trying to make sure Lia and Emily were comfortable as Lia fought to control her tears. Not wanting to let either of them go, he was struck with how right they both felt in his arms.

7

After a few minutes, Lia gained control of herself and leaned back, her eyes on her daughter. "Emily," she said, making sure she was looking at her. "Never, never walk away from the adult you're with. You should have asked them to find me."

Emily nodded, tears still streaming down her face. "I'm sorry," she hiccupped.

Belle squatted next to the trio and asked, "Is she all right? Should I check her?"

She remembered that Belle was a nurse and, sucking in a deep breath, realized she needed to make sure Emily was fine. She loosened her arms and peered into her face. "Baby? Are you hurt?"

"No, Mama. I just went walking to find you."

Emily twisted around and looked back at Aiden and her lips curved into a smile. "You found my mama."

His eyes were warm on her and he grinned widely. "Yeah, Emily. We found your mama."

She watched as he lifted his warm gaze from her daughter to her and her breath caught in her throat. "Thank you," she whispered, her voice raspy with emotion. "If you hadn't—"

"No," he hushed gently, still holding her gaze. "She's fine. There were lots of people looking for her and she would have been found very quickly."

"But—" she began, her heart aching as fear returned.

He shook his head and said, "Lia...no. Don't go there. She's fine and in your arms. You can talk to her later about safety in a crowd, but don't go there in your mind. She's right here."

Gulping in a harsh breath of air, she nodded. "Thank you." Unable to look away, her eyes were mesmerized by his and the strength exuded by him. For the first time in a long time, a sense of safety swept over her.

"Mama, I'm squished."

Jerking back, she looked down at Emily, and said, "Well, young lady, getting squished is what happens when you get lost and Mama gets scared." A giggle slipped from Emily's mouth and to her it was pure heaven. Suddenly aware of Aiden's arms wrapped around her and her daughter, she blushed and struggled to move back.

He stood and offered his hand to assist her up as well. Holding Emily's hand, she turned to see the gathering all standing close. Remembering how they immediately jumped in to help, she rushed to thank them as well.

She was hugged by more people than she could remember ever being hugged by at one time. Eric

MacFarlane and his father, Finn, walked over and, after offering hugs, gave her a cold water bottle, which she drank thirstily from. For Emily, Finn handed her a tall, hand-squeezed lemonade in a frosty cup with a bright yellow straw.

Corrinne stepped forward and with tears in her eyes pulled her in for a hug, one lasting longer than the previous ones she had been receiving. Before she had a chance to ponder that, Corrine released her and stepped to Aiden, her arms circling her son for a long time.

That sight caused her chin to wobble once more, seeing this large, opinionated man being coddled by his mother and letting her do it in front of everyone. She battled back the tears and, with a grateful smile toward everyone, she accepted a seat on one of their blankets, pulling Emily in close by her side.

"Aiden?" Emily's voice cried out, drawing his immediate attention.

He walked over and squatted in front of her. "Whatcha..." Hesitating, he amended, "What do you need, pretty girl?"

Emily giggled and asked, "Sit by us?"

Lia's eyes widened, but she smiled and nodded. He might have been a jerk to her on more than one occasion, but he saved her daughter today and that meant something to her. He held her gaze for a moment and then smiled at Emily.

"Sure thing," he replied easily, but instead of sitting on the other side of Emily, he lifted her up and plopped down on the blanket next to Lia with Emily in his lap.

Lia looked down and realized his thigh was firmly pressed against hers. He did not seem to notice or, if he did, it did not bother him. At first, it did not bother her too much either, but the longer they sat side by side the more she felt a tingle of electricity passing between them. She shifted slightly but he only resettled Emily and shifted closer again, keeping his leg next to hers.

After a few back and forths of that, he turned his head and grinned at her. "Easy, Lia," he said, his voice soft. "You've been a wreck for the past half hour. Sit back, relax, and enjoy the music. Show Emily that you're fine and everything's okay."

She opened her mouth to retort, but snapped it shut, realizing he was right. Dropping her gaze to Emily, she saw her daughter was eating up the attention. Blowing out a long, slow breath, she nodded. Offering him a slight smile, she turned her focus back to the gathering and the music. Uncertain why he was being so nice to her all of a sudden, she wondered what he would think if he knew she was the master of pretending that everything was fine. After all, she had been doing just that for years.

Aiden was aware the moment Emily fell asleep on him, her little body slumping in his arms and her head laying on his shoulder. He looked over at Lia, whose face was now relaxed as she laughed at something someone had said.

Hearing a throat clearing, he cast his gaze to the

side, seeing his mom, dad, and Finn smiling at him. Unable to explain the sudden desire to hold Emily and Lia close, he reacted by tossing them a typical, goofy grin, but their continued smiles told him they were not buying his act. Rolling his eyes, he looked down and saw Emily's little mouth slack with sleep.

He turned his head to the other side and watched Lia as she listened to Jillian telling a story. Dark circles marred her perfect complexion and he knew she was exhausted. Her smile, while sincere, was strained. He felt her shoulder leaning against his, as though needing his body to help prop hers up.

That intimate touch, even though she probably did not realize what she was doing, felt right. He had never cared for a woman's clinging touch in public, not wanting to claim anyone or be claimed. But, sitting in the middle of a large group of his family and friends, having Lia and Emily pressed tightly to him had his heart pounding while at the same time, strangely, settling his mind.

Leaning slightly to gain her attention, he whispered, "Let's get you and Emily home."

She focused on his face for a few seconds before dropping her eyes to Emily, her features relaxing as her gaze roamed over her daughter's sleeping form. "Oh, I'm sorry. You must be tired of holding her—"

"Shhh," he said, drawing her eyes back to his. "She weighs nothing and, anyway, this isn't about me. You two have had an exciting and exhausting evening. We can leave now and I can get you home before the crowd breaks up when the concert ends."

Her mouth opened as her brows drew down. "We...you?"

"I want to see you home safely," he said. "Please."

She sucked in her lips for a moment, eyes roaming over his face, assessing him. He waited patiently and, after a few seconds, she nodded and pushed upward to stand. He followed, shifting Emily slightly in his arms to balance her on his chest without jiggling her head too much. Ignoring the grins flying at him from all his friends and family, he offered a chin lift to his parents and waited patiently with Lia as she offered heartfelt thanks to everyone once again. Then, with Emily still asleep in his arms and Lia by his side, he weaved through the lawn chairs and blankets to the sidewalk around the park.

"I drove," she said, pointing to a small SUV. "We live just outside of town."

"I got you," he replied and, with his hand on her lower back, guided her to the vehicle. "I'll follow you home."

She beeped her locks open and watched as he gently placed Emily in her booster seat. "Thank you for everything, Aiden. I've got it from here."

"Lia," he said, drawing her attention. "I know you can do it all yourself but, please, let me see you and Emily home." She looked skeptical, like she was trying to figure out why he was doing any of this. It was a question he was asking himself, to be honest. It just felt...right. When she nodded, he let out a breath he had not realized he was holding. "My truck is just down the street. Let me get behind you so I can follow, okay?"

She nodded again and he reached out, placing his hand on her arm, giving a comforting squeeze. "See you there." Jogging across the street to his truck, he felt sure of what he was doing...a feeling unfamiliar to him.

Lia glanced into the rearview mirror, first to check to see that Emily was still asleep and then to see if Aiden's headlights were still in her sight. They were. She sucked in a breath, wondering what she was doing. *He's being polite. He wants to make sure that his rescue of Emily does not go awry by my falling asleep at the wheel. He's...* She couldn't really come up with any other reasons for him to be doing what he was doing now, let alone why he had sat so close to her on the blanket or why his arms had stayed tight around Emily all night, as if fearful of losing her again. Since meeting him, her thoughts about him had swirled from incredulity at his arrogance, to irritation at his judgemental attitude, to thankful that he had found Emily and was really good to her. Too exhausted to consider the emotional whiplash, she turned into her driveway.

Stepping from her vehicle, she waved to him, indicating that she was good and he could go home content in the knowledge that she was safe. Instead of driving on though, she watched as he pulled into her driveway behind her and turned off his truck engine.

Before she knew what was happening, he got out and walked to Emily's door, bending to unfasten her from her booster seat. Gently lifting her, he moved to where she was standing, mouth open and frozen still.

"Go on," he encouraged. "Unlock the front door and I'll get her in."

Blinking out of her stunned silence, she turned and hustled up the steps, doing as he said. Stepping inside, he looked at her and cocked his head to the side.

Nodding, she headed up the stairs, hearing his footsteps coming behind her. The small house only had two bedrooms and she led him through the door on the right. She watched as he bent and placed Emily on her bed.

Turning, he said, "I'll let you get her ready."

Placing her hand on his arm, she lifted her gaze to his, her chest heaving with so many different emotions. "Thank you," was all she could think to say.

He smiled and walked out of the room, his booted steps moving down the stairs.

Alone at last, she blew out her breath and turned to her daughter. Slipping off Emily's sandals and shorts, she gently pulled her pajama bottoms up over her legs. Emily opened her eyes, blinking several times before seeming to realize where she was.

"Let's go to the bathroom, sweetie," she encouraged.

Emily nodded and padded into the bathroom and quickly finished her business. Taking the toothbrush she handed to her, she brushed her teeth and then moved straight back to her bed. Following her, she pulled her blouse off and placed her pajama top over her head, weaving her arms through the sleeves.

Tucking her in, she knelt by the bed, kissing her forehead.

"We'll talk in the morning, okay?"

Emily's eyes widened and she asked, "Am I in trouble?"

"No, baby. But we need to make sure you understand the rules when I'm not around, okay? What you did tonight was scary and could have ended up in a not-so-good way."

Emily nodded but then smiled. "I like Aiden. He found me."

Ignoring the mixed up feelings curling around her insides at hearing Aiden's name, she smiled in return. "All those good people went immediately to look for you, sweetheart. But, yes, Aiden found you."

Emily yawned and, deciding their talk was over for now, she pulled the covers up and kissed her once more.

Turning out the light, she closed the door and leaned back against it, exhausting emotions pouring over her. The *what-ifs* were slamming into her mind and she felt a sob in the back of her throat threatening to choke her.

The quiet house seemed to close in around her and she walked down the stairs, thinking the bottle of wine in her refrigerator was definitely calling to her.

At the bottom of the stairs, she stumbled at the sight of Aiden in her living room, standing at the mantle and staring at the photograph of her and newborn Emily.

"Oh. I thought you'd left," she said, her eyes moving over him. Now that she had seen Emily cradled in his arms, it was hard to not think of him as her hero. *God, I am tired,* she chastised herself.

71

Crossing her arms around her waist, in a protective stance, she considered whether or not she should offer him a drink. She had two different images of him now and she wasn't sure which one was the real Aiden. Maybe both were. Taking a deep breath, she asked, "I was just going to get a glass of wine. Would you like one? Or, um...a beer?" As soon as the words left her mouth, she wondered what she was doing, but before she had a chance to rescind the offer, his smile widened and he nodded.

"Thanks. A beer would be great," he replied.

Turning, before she lost her nerve, she moved through the eat-in kitchen, opened the refrigerator, and pulled out the wine and beer. Pouring a glass and popping off the top of the beer, she walked back into her small living room. He took the beer from her hands and took a swig. He seemed to be waiting on her, so she moved to the chair and nodded her head toward the sofa in silent invitation.

"I know you said it wasn't necessary, but I would be remiss if I didn't say, once more, how grateful I am that you found Emily."

He acknowledged her thanks, but deferred by saying, "I was just lucky. There were lots of people who were looking for her. Lots of people here in this town who care."

Gulping another large sip of wine, she nodded. "It's nice. Having lots of people who care. That's not something I'm very used to," she admitted. The wine was already easing through her frazzled nerves, not only relaxing her body but, obviously, relaxing her usually private emotions.

"Didn't you have a lot of friends where you used to live, before you moved to Baytown?"

She noticed that he had not drunk much of his beer, but she swallowed another large sip of wine. Offering a slight shrug, she admitted, "When we first lived near the base, I was surrounded with other military wives. After Emily was born, my life became increasingly more and more about her and her needs."

She caught him stealing a quick glance at her finger and shook her head. "Not married anymore. My husband was a Marine but…he was killed in action. It's just been me and Emily for, well, her whole life really."

He nodded, his gaze steady and said, "You're a really good mom, Lia, and it shows in everything you do for her. I was wrong earlier to think otherwise. I'm sorry for that."

They sat in comfortable silence for a few minutes, each to their own thoughts while they finished their drinks. Now, more relaxed than she had been in hours, she was about to suggest he leave so that she could go to bed, when he startled her with his next statement.

"I'm very sorry about your husband's death. I was also a Marine and feel a kinship with any others who served, and their families."

She had no idea why she spoke the words she said, but before she could stop herself, she bit out, "I know he was a hero. A hero to his fellow Marines and a hero to his country. But not to me. To me, he was not a hero. He was simply a man and not a very good one at that."

8

Stunned at Lia's words and honesty, Aiden watched the play of emotions cross her face. Anger quickly morphed into embarrassment and he hated that for her.

"Don't do that," he admonished. "You have a right to whatever feelings you have inside of you and never let anyone tell you that you don't." She blinked and her mouth opened, but no words came forth.

"Tell me about him," he prodded, desperately wanting to know more about her now that he understood all his preconceived notions were wrong. Somehow, he knew that her complicated feelings for her deceased husband held the key. Sure that she would not normally open up to someone who was essentially a stranger, he hoped she felt the tentative bond forming between them and would trust him to have a care.

Her shoulders slumped, as though in fatigue, and he was about to tell her it was okay, they would talk another time, when she set her now empty wine glass on the coffee table, leaned back in her seat, tucking her legs up under her, and offered, "There's not much to tell, and I can't imagine why you would be interested."

He leaned forward and, mimicking her actions, set his beer bottle on the coffee table as well. "Honestly? I look at you and see a beautiful, smart woman, who's a good mother. I made a horrible assumption when we first met and I regret that. I misunderstood the meaning behind your words about Emily, but that's no excuse. I made a snap judgment and, just like I don't like others judging me when they don't know me, I shouldn't have done that."

She did not reply but held his gaze in silence.

He continued, "Tonight, I saw a strong mother who went through agony at the thought that something had happened to her child. I saw strength in you and in the bond that you have with Emily." His forearms rested on his knees, open slightly, with his palms turned up. "I can't imagine any man who would not be doing every-thing he could to keep you and Emily in his life, so I admit, I'm curious."

They continued in silence for several minutes and he was willing to give her as much time to gather her thoughts as needed. Just when it looked like she was going to deny his request to talk, she heaved a great sigh and spoke.

"We met at a picnic some friends were holding and I thought it was love at first sight. He was tall, strong, handsome and he looked at me as though I were the only woman in the room. He was already a Marine and I suppose we knew we were on borrowed time. We had only dated for six months when he popped the question and I eagerly agreed to be his wife. We were young, in love, and very happy. We talked about having children and sure enough right before he was sent away for a one-year tour, I got pregnant with Emily. We were ecstatic, even though he was leaving and that meant I'd be going through it all alone. We skyped as much as we could, of course, but it was still just me. After Emily was born, I threw myself into being her mom. After my maternity leave was up, I went back to work part-time at the accounting firm I was with and my mom watched Emily the three days a week I was at work. Carl and I emailed and Skyped as often as possible. I know he was proud, because every time we were Skyping he would gather his squad members behind him and have me hold Emily up so they could all ooh and ahh over her."

He watched as her eyes slid to the side, her gaze unfocused as she stared out into the room. He could tell she was miles away and remained quiet, giving her time to sift through the memories he assumed she may have pushed away.

She looked down at her hands and he noted they were clenched in her lap. The desire to reach over and hold them moved through him, but he did not want to make her feel uneasy. His curiosity had turned into concern, and he could not remember the last time he had felt this way about a woman he had just met...or any woman, really. But there was something about her, a vulnerability lying under the strength, that called to him.

"By the time Emily was a year old, it was obvious

that something was not right. A loud noise on her left side would not cause her to startle or even turn her head. I was concerned about her hearing but knew that she was not completely deaf because if I spoke toward her right ear, she would look up at me and smile. She babbled the way babies should but her doctor did early testing and determined that she was deaf in her left ear and had partial hearing in her right. I was devastated, but also determined to do everything I could to assist Emily with her hearing and her speech."

"And your husband?"

Snorting, she shook her head. "At first, when I would try to talk to him about it when we were Skyping, he would cut me off and tell me that I did not know what I was talking about. But, over time, he no longer gathered people behind him and did not even want to talk to her. When his tour was over and he came home, I could tell he was starting to see what I'd been saying and I was relieved. I finally thought everything was going to be all right. The burden that I had carried by myself could now be shared with her father. He could go to the doctors' appointments with me. He would be able to talk to the specialists as well. It did not take long for me to realize that the more I tried to push him to be with Emily, the more he pulled away from both of us."

What an ass, he thought, but remained silent. Glancing down, he realized his fists were clenched in a similar manner to hers and he released them, stretching his fingers.

"I had gone to the Key Wives' meetings. Those were for Marine wives, so I knew it was very common for families to have a difficult transition when the military member came back to the home. I told myself he was simply having trouble adjusting. I told myself that as a Marine, he always wanted the best, and he struggled with Emily because he felt as though there should be something he could do to make it better. I kept telling myself that as soon as he became accustomed to how we needed to work with her and communicate with her, it would be better." She lifted her gaze to him and shook her head sadly. "But it simply wasn't happening. He finally told me that he had re-upped for another tour in Afghanistan because it was too difficult for him to deal with a wife that was spending so much of her time and energy on their child that had special needs."

Unable to help himself, he jumped to his feet and stalked toward the fireplace, resting his fist on top of the mantle. "Fuckin' hell," he ground out, barely remembering at the last second to keep his voice down because Emily was sleeping above. "What a fuckin' prick."

Hating that he lost control of his emotions, he quickly turned and his gaze landed on Lia, sure that he would see censure in her eyes. Instead, to his surprise, her lips were curved in a slight smile.

"I always thought the same thing," she confessed.

Pulling in a ragged breath of air, he let it out slowly. Moving back to the sofa, he sat down, this time much closer to her chair so that their knees touched. "I'm sorry, but just the thought of him leaving you and your sweet daughter makes no sense to me."

"Thank you for that. It was so hard because everyone else treated him as such a hero. A Marine's

Marine. Only I knew the truth—he was not running toward a battle, but running away from one. For the next year, he rarely wrote and did not Skype one single time. I finally received an email from him where he said that he thought it was best if we separated. He admitted that I was a good mother but felt that I was no longer a wife that could be one hundred percent supportive of him. When I asked him about Emily, his reply was that while he loved his daughter, he had no idea how to communicate with her, did not want to learn sign language, and that it was too distracting for him to take the time away from his job to focus on her."

As he watched Lia tell her story, the slight smile she had fell away. Each breath seemed to take more out of her and once again her shoulders slumped.

"You know he was fucked, don't you?"

Her lips twitched again and he was glad.

She nodded, and said, "Yes. I know he was fucked." Sighing, she continued, "I moved out of my apartment and back in with my parents. Emily was actually doing very well with learning language mixed in with some hand signals. It was not American Sign Language, but the combination worked for her as she continued to learn to speak. I was still working at the accounting firm and spending every spare moment with Emily. I assumed that when Carl came home, he would file for divorce. I wavered between thinking that I wanted to take him to the cleaners and not having anything to do with him." Shrugging, she added, "In the end, it didn't matter. He was killed in action, still married to me. I know, in my head, that he truly was the Marine hero that everyone made him out to be, but I also know, in my heart, he was a deserter to his family."

"And you suffered in silence." It was a statement, not a question. It was obvious that she had gone through the motions of becoming a war widow, which meant being forced to accept all the glories heaped upon her husband, while knowing he had abandoned her and Emily.

"My parents were the only ones who knew. So, I just kept moving forward. I had my accounting job and Emily was enrolled in preschool and doing well there. Not long ago I learned of Mr. Redding's retirement causing a job opening to be here in Baytown. I couldn't pass that up. I yearned for something new. A place where no one knew of Carl. A place where Emily and I could start over. And with my parents just thirty minutes away in Virginia Beach, I thought this was perfect."

He finally gave in to the urge and reached over to cover her hands with his. Her fingers were cold and he rubbed them gently, hoping to infuse some warmth. "I'm so sorry for misjudging you when we met," he said. "I have no idea why I did, I'm not usually like that."

She shrugged, and said, "You don't have to apologize anymore. To be fair, I did the same to you. I had seen your...um...flirtatious behavior and overheard comments made by Katelyn and Brogan, so when you approached me at the ballgame I wasn't the nicest. I decided the kind of person you were based on one thing, and that was not fair of me either."

He grinned and stood. With her hands still in his, he

gently pulled her to her feet. She stared up at him, tilting her head to the side. "I think we should start over." Dropping her hands, he lifted his right hand out and said, "Hello. My name is Aiden McFarlane. Pleased to meet you."

A giggle slipped from between her lips and she lifted her hand, placed it in his palm, and gave him a firm shake. "I'm Amelia Smith, but my friends call me Lia. I'm pleased to make your acquaintance also."

He did not let go of her hand, but instead, drew her closer to him. He watched her smile slip as her eyes lifted and searched his. "Now, we can start anew. No more misunderstandings, no more misjudgments." With that, he wrapped his arms around her, offering a hug.

She hesitated for only a few seconds before sliding her hands around his waist and resting her cheek against his chest. He felt her body relax and before he could think about it he kissed the top of her head. Her body, lined up with his and snugly wrapped in his embrace, felt right. Once more, he was struck with how differently he felt and acted around her. He had never offered just comfort and friendship to a woman that he was attracted to in the past, but in this moment, he gave no thought to taking it further, only wanting to offer what she needed right now.

After a few minutes they slowly separated and he held her gaze. "Thank you for sharing your story with me," he said. "And as much as I'd love to continue to sit and talk with you, you truly look exhausted and I know Emily will need you in the morning."

She nodded and escorted him to the front door.

Opening it wide, she looked up and he leaned forward, placing his hand gently on the curve of her waist and kissing her forehead. When he pulled back, he realized he might have been too touchy feely with her, but the soft smile on her face said it was alright.

Smiling in return, he headed out of her house and down to his truck. A strange sense of rightness filled him and he could not wait to see her again.

That night, lying in bed, Lia was filled with a sense of contentment. It had been such a relief to unburden her complicated feelings for Carl to someone who did not judge her harshly. She had been surprised at how understanding Aiden had been.

Rolling over in bed, she sighed. It had been a long time since she had had any friends and now, it appeared that Baytown offered a wealth of them. It had also been a long time since she had spent any time with a man in anything other than a professional relationship. And now, it appeared that Baytown was offering that as well, with Aiden.

9

Lia sat at her desk Monday morning, still exhausted from the weekend's anxiety. She and Emily had spent all day Sunday together, and while she had gone over the rules for when she and Emily became separated, she did not want to make that their entire day. So together they had watched Disney movies, baked cookies, and spent hours cuddled up on the sofa.

Even though it had been a good day, she was still tired from not sleeping well. Images of Emily wandering lost had filled her mind only to be replaced by the sight of Aiden striding toward her with Emily tucked safely in his arms.

Shaking off the thoughts, she got back to work. She managed to get halfway through the files for Finn's Pub, when Mrs. Markham called on the intercom.

"Ms. Smith? Mayor Banks has called to say that he would like to stop by at one o'clock this afternoon. You don't have another appointment so may I tell him that you will be available?"

Nodding, she agreed. "Yes, that will be fine."

Self-conscious about her appearance, she glanced down at her attire. Always one to dress professionally, she had on black pants and a simple, silk blouse today, not feeling the desire to wear anything fancier. With flats on her feet instead of her usual heels, she felt at a disadvantage knowing the Mayor was coming. *Oh well, this is Baytown and everyone keeps telling me that things are more laid back here. I guess this is my chance to see if that's true.*

Looking at the clock on her desk, she noted that it was almost noon. She had grabbed a yogurt on the way out this morning, but now wondered if she could make a trip to the pub for one of their sandwiches. Of course, the idea of seeing Aiden again did not make that an unattractive choice.

Before she had a chance to decide, Mrs. Markham's voice came across the intercom again.

"Ms. Smith? Aiden McFarlane is here with your lunch. Should I send him back or would you like him to leave it with me?"

Her heart leaped at hearing that he had come to see her and she was surprised at the giddiness in her voice when she replied, "Yes, please. Have him come back. Thank you."

It had been a long time since she had felt the spark of excitement at seeing a man but had no chance to prepare before Aiden stepped through her door. Just like the last time he was here, his hair was brushed back and his blue eyes were shining. This time, though, his smile brightened her day. His Finn's Pub t-shirt pulled tight across his chest and it was impossible to not notice his bulging arms. As her gaze drifted downward she smiled too, observing a large, plastic sack that she knew contained a delicious lunch held in his grip.

"Wow," she exclaimed, rising from her chair. "To what do I owe this surprise visit?"

"I just couldn't wait to see you again," he replied, stepping forward and placing the bag on her table.

She laughed, and said, "That's honest…and very sweet."

"If you really want to know," he said, "I've given a lot of insincere flattery over the years. But, with you, I find myself just wanting to be honest."

She smiled in reply but remained silent, leaning over to peer into the bag as he began pulling out the contents. Two wrapped sandwiches, a container filled with fresh cut French fries, two slices of cheesecake with raspberry sauce drizzled on top, and two cans of soda.

"Oh, my goodness. You really did bring a full lunch. And since I see two of everything, am I to assume that you're going to stay and eat with me?"

"I'd love to, if you don't mind."

She held his gaze for a moment, feeling at ease with his presence in her office and the sweet gesture of lunch. "Let's get out of this little office and use the conference room."

Together they scooped up all the lunch items and carried them into the other room, setting them around the conference table. Within a few minutes they were both enjoying the delicious food, as well as each other's company.

───

Aiden laughed as he told antics of he, Brogan, and Katelyn as little kids growing up in Baytown. As Lia encouraged, he threw in some stories about the Baytown boys, loving the way her face lit up when she smiled. It was hard to imagine that he had ever seen her as a stuck-up, uptight person when the reality was that she was warm, friendly, and had a great sense of humor.

Her beauty held his attention as well, her curves barely hidden under the blouse and pants she wore. She wore subtle makeup and her long hair was pulled back from her face, both exemplifying her clear skin. Surprised to see her in flats instead of heels, their height difference was more pronounced and he towered over her, making him feel like a protector. He recognized that was a caveman attitude, so he wisely kept that idea to himself.

He liked seeing her relaxed and enjoying herself. *When was the last time I sat with a woman that I was interested in, for the pure enjoyment of just being in their company?* The fact that he could not answer his own silent question made him ashamed.

"So, I've been talking. Now it's your turn."

Eyes wide, she exclaimed, "My turn? I think I did enough confessing on Saturday night to last a lifetime!"

He shook his head. "Nah, that was about the last

couple of years. Tell me something about the Lia from long ago."

She bit her bottom lip and rolled her eyes, definitely not knowing how seductive that little maneuver was to him. He inwardly groaned, but kept his eyes focused on her face hoping she would talk.

"I was born and raised in Virginia Beach," she began. "My dad was a civilian who worked for the Marine Aviation Training. I have one older sister who's married to her high school sweetheart and they have three children. My mom worked for many years in daycare, so she was a perfect choice to be able to take care of Emily when I went back to work."

He lifted an eyebrow. "Seriously? That's all you've got? I tell you about dropping a crab into the middle of Katelyn and Jillian's tea party when they were five years old and you tell me where your dad worked? I tell you that Brogan and I were running from one of the farmers after having nabbed some of his watermelons out of his field and I got my pants caught on the barbed wire fence, and you tell me you have a married older sister? Somehow, I don't think our stories are quite the same."

She giggled and said, "Are you calling me boring?"

He leaned back in his chair and stretched his long legs in front of him, crossing one booted foot over the other. "No ma'am, I'd never call you boring. But I do think you've got some stories you are hiding."

"Well, I once challenged my sister to a tree climbing contest. I was determined to win, even though my face got all scratched up in the process."

He looked at the tiny scar through her eyebrow and

she saw his unasked question. Laughing, she touched it self-consciously and said, "Yes, this is my reminder."

"So you were daring?"

"And kind of competitive," she admitted. "There was this one time that my sister and I were playing darts and she beat me. I was a sore loser and it made me angry, so I threw my remaining dart toward her feet. I never came close to hitting her, but she jumped back screaming anyway."

With a grin on his face he said, "So there's a temper behind that professional countenance. Should I be concerned?"

"Well, the last time I was in Finn's, I did notice a dartboard near the front."

"Is that an invitation for us to play?" he asked, loving the light now shining in her eyes. "And what happens if I win?"

She threw her head back and laughed heartily. "I suppose we'll just have to play and then you'll find out."

"It's a date," he said. Her smile remained at the turn of phrase, but in truth he wanted it to be more than that. Uncharacteristically nervous at the prospect of asking her out, he cleared his throat. "Speaking of dates, I'd really like to take you on one." His hands gripped the arms of the chair, fighting the urge to wipe his sweaty palms on his pants. Staring at her face, he held his breath as he awaited her answer.

"A date?" she asked, a crease settling in her brow as though uncertain what the word meant.

"Yeah, a date. You know, where I drive to your house and pick you up and take you somewhere nice to eat?"

"I...um... I don't know. I haven't been on a date for over seven years." She grimaced, and said, "That makes me sound like such a loser, doesn't it?"

He hated that she felt that. "Not at all. You were a devoted wife and are a devoted mother." She smiled, but didn't say anything, and it occurred to him that this might be her letting him down gently. It had been a long time since he had had to work so hard to get someone to go out with him. In fact, it had been a really long time since he had actually asked a woman out on a date that was not just a casual hookup. He opened his mouth to crack a joke, to relieve the tension of her turning him down, but she spoke first.

"I'd love to go on a date with you, Aiden," she said. "There's a teenage girl that lives across the street from me that babysits when I need her. I'd need to give her a couple of days notice to make sure that she could watch Emily."

His breath left his lungs in a whoosh and his smile widened. "Good, good. Uh...do you think you should give me your phone number so that we can settle on the details once you know when you can get a babysitter?"

She pulled out her phone and they quickly exchanged numbers. Feeling lighter than air, he stood and grabbed all the trash from their lunch, shoving it back into the plastic bag. She rose from her seat as well and walked over, leaning back to stare into his face, her smile matching his. Her eyes moved over his shoulder to the clock on the wall and she startled.

"Oh, my goodness, I've got to get back to work. I have an appointment in just a few minutes."

"No worries," he said. "I'll give you a call and we'll set up our date." Just like the other evening, he leaned over, placed his hand on the curve of her waist and kissed her forehead. Turning, he walked out of the conference room and back through the lobby.

Just as he reached the front door it opened and to his surprise he looked up to see the Mayor. With a nod of his head, he greeted, "Mayor Banks."

Corwin blinked, visibly surprised to see him there, but his eyes dropped down to the plastic bag in his hands and he came to his own conclusions. "I see your brother has got you making deliveries now."

Refusing to be irritated by Corwin's misplaced sense of humor, he quipped, "When you're the co-owner of a business, as I am, I can pretty much do whatever I like. Especially bringing lunch to a very nice lady." Glancing over his shoulder, he called out a goodbye to Mrs. Markham and headed out into the sunshine. Walking back to the pub, he could not help but wonder what brought the Mayor to Lia's doorstep.

Lia was still shocked by Aiden's invitation to dinner and barely had a chance to celebrate before Mrs. Markham walked Corwin into her office. Standing, she greeted the Mayor and invited him to sit.

"Mayor Banks, it's nice to see you again. Has the Town Council come to a decision as to what they would like me to do?"

HEAR MY HEART

For a quick moment, irritation flashed across his face before being replaced with a sigh of resignation.

"Yes, Amelia," he began. I brought the results of the audit to the Town Council and they are concerned. The vote was unanimous that they want the financial discrepancies to be found. I am reticent to bring this to the public but know that if someone from the inside is stealing from us we must know who."

She remembered his announcement at the music festival that he was running for re-election and could only imagine that an opponent would use the publicity of mismanagement of town money against him.

"In case the Town Council made that decision, I have already created a proposal based on forensic accounting procedures and what would need to be done. A time-line, which I must warn you will not be short, for me to be thorough and my fees are attached." She pulled out a file from her desk drawer and handed it to him. "I would suggest you call another meeting of the Town Council and have them look over my proposal. I will be available for any questions they might have."

With a curt nod, he stood and extended his hand. "I thank you in advance for your professionalism and also ask for your continued discretion. I will call an emergency meeting of the Town Council, but I can assure you that we will be accepting your offer. I will call you within two days to let you know of the decision."

With that, he walked briskly out of her office and she heard the front door open and close. She grinned, knowing that Mrs. Markham would be in her office momentarily and she was not disappointed. Seeing the

93

older woman walking in with an arched eyebrow, she could not help but giggle.

"Well," she said. "Unless I'm mistaken, it looks like I'll be doing work for the Town Council."

Shaking her head, Mrs. Markham replied, "You'll find that doing business in a small town is very different from the large accounting firm you're used to. I know you've already figured that out from the clients that you have seen but let me warn you that, while the Town Council will want your expertise, you'll run into roadblocks at every turn when it comes to the Mayor and the town's various department offices." Grinning, she added, "This will be interesting."

Her mind reeling, she realized that she had a lot of work to do to finish up several clients' files on her desk so that she could clear off her calendar to be able to work on the town's books. Thankfully, she had already hired another accountant to work with her and he would be starting soon.

She spent the rest of the afternoon in an epic battle between keeping her mind on her job and her thoughts off a date with Aiden. By the end of the day she had finished her files, in spite of the fact that her thoughts of Aiden had won out more often than not.

10

Friday evening, Aiden pulled into the driveway of Lia's house. Glancing down at his attire, he hoped the blue dress shirt and khaki pants were suitable for their dinner. Earlier, standing at his closet, he realized how much of his life was spent in casual clothes. Jeans and t-shirts for when he was at work, and the same for when he was out having a good time. Other than his friends' weddings, it had been a while since he had needed to dress up.

He walked briskly to the front door, barely knocking before the door was thrown open. Looking down, he grinned widely as Emily greeted him with a smile of her own.

"Mr. Aiden!"

He knelt down, opening his arms for a hug. She rushed into his embrace and he picked her up, stepping across the threshold. Leaning back so he could peer into her face, he asked, "How was your day?"

She immediately began to tell him of all that had happened in her first-grade class that day and he grinned at her enthusiasm. A noise on the stairs sent his gaze upward and he barely heard Emily say, "Isn't Mama pretty?"

His voice raspy to his own ears, he said, "Yes. She's beautiful." Hearing a little giggle, he looked back at Emily and added, "Just like you."

Emily clapped her hands and he set her feet onto the floor, standing just in time to greet Lia as she approached him. Her makeup was heavier but still subtle and her thick hair fell in waves down her back. He watched as she nervously ran her hands over her dress. The little black dress' V-neck did not show cleavage but fit snugly to showcase her breasts. It narrowed at the waist then flared out in a full skirt over her hips and down to just above her knees. Paired with black, high-heeled sandals she looked classy and delectable.

As his eyes were roaming over her, they made their way back up to her face and he realized she was doing the same to him. Hoping he measured up to her expectations, he waited nervously.

She blinked, as though embarrassed to be caught gawking, and said, "You look really nice tonight."

"Nice?"

"Yes, nice," she laughed. "And handsome, but I'm sure you knew that."

He stepped forward and placed his hand on her waist while leaning over to kiss her forehead. "With you, I'm never sure about anything, so it's nice to hear that I meet your approval." Her shy smile warmed his heart, but before he had a chance to say anything else, he heard a noise from behind him.

"Susie!" Emily called out her greeting.

Turning, he spied a young teenager he knew walking into the house. She stooped to greet Emily before calling out her hello to Lia, then, looked up at him and grinned.

"Hey, Coach McFarlane," she said.

He greeted Susie and watched as Lia got Emily settled before she walked back over to him, checking her small purse to make sure she had her phone. He took the black lacy shawl from her arms and draped it around her shoulders. Calling out their goodbyes, he escorted her to his truck.

He knew that she was nervous, considering this was her first date in years, but what he did not want to admit to her was that it was his first date in many years as well.

As they chatted on the short drive to the Sunset Restaurant, she commented that she had not been there yet but had heard wonderful things about the food.

"The restaurant changed hands several years ago and was bought by a New York businessman. We weren't sure for a long time what he was going to do with it and we were a little afraid he was going to just shut it down. But he's managed to run it well and it brings in good business to the town."

"Is it awkward to be going to a rival establishment?"

He shook his head. "Not at all. This place has a lovely view of the sunsets over the bay—hence the name

—and their menu is different than what we offer at the pub. Our closest competitor would be the Seafood Shack, over by the harbor. But they still close down during the winter months when there are not as many visitors to Baytown. Even during the height of the season, though, there's plenty of business to go around."

After giving his explanation of the restaurant business in Baytown, he asked, "What about the accounting business? When you were in Virginia Beach, was there competition among companies?"

She cocked her head to the side as she pondered his question, and said, "Not really. Like you, there was enough business to go around."

"What about in Baytown?"

She chuckled. "Well, you know here, I'm the only accountant in town now that Mr. Redding has retired. But I'm finding that I'm too busy, so I've hired another accountant to work with me."

Parking in front of the restaurant she peaked out the windshield and exclaimed at the beautiful view of the Bay.

"I made reservations and requested a window booth, so we should have a front row seat of the beautiful sunset tonight."

As they walked inside, he guided her with his hand on the small of her back. Such a tiny gesture but, with her, he found it so intimate, loving the feel of her underneath his fingertips. Approaching the hostess counter, his heart stuttered as he observed a long-ago fling. *Carlotta...fuck!*

"Aiden! I haven't seen you in forever!" The woman

strutted closer and threw her arms around his neck, offering a loud smacking kiss on his cheek, perilously close to his lips.

He had to remove his hand from Lia's back to give a slight push to Carlotta in order to encourage her to move back a step. Keeping his tone even, he said, "We have a reservation."

Carlotta's eyes widened as they jumped between him and Lia and she gave him a knowing wink. "Sure, honey. Just follow me." She grabbed two menus and began leading them toward the back of the restaurant where the booths facing the bay were.

Placing his hand on Lia's back again, guiding her along, he felt the tension now radiating from her. Hoping to move past the awkward entrance into the restaurant, he gave a curt nod to Carlotta as he assisted Lia into the circular booth. Not giving her a chance to sit on the opposite side, he moved in next to her, forcing her to scoot over a little bit to make room for him.

Carlotta smiled as she rattled off the evening's specials and winked at him again before she left, making her way back to the hostess counter.

Swallowing hard, he decided to ignore the past few minutes and plunged ahead. "What would you like to drink?"

"Just a glass of white wine," Lia said, keeping her eyes down, already studying the menu.

As the waiter came by, he gave him their drink order and they listened to the specials again. Once the waiter left their table, he decided to come clean, hoping to alleviate the embarrassing start to their dinner. "I'm sorry about the hostess. She…um…is an old acquaintance."

"Yes, she seemed to be," her eyes moving to his.

She offered him a tightlipped smile that did not reach her eyes. After the waiter returned with their wine and they placed their orders, he directed her attention to the setting sun, enjoying the way she had to twist her body slightly into his to view it. Hoping to ease her tension, he reached his arm around her shoulder, his fingertips lightly moving over her soft skin, and breathed a little easier as he felt her muscles relax.

As their meals were served, they began to chat again and he felt as though the earlier tension had left.

"Tell me about the American Legion and the ball teams," she said.

Enthusiastic to have a conversation he was passionate about, he said, "Historically, the American Legion was chartered in the early 1900s as a veteran's organization. It started as a group for the veterans of the first World War and has grown into one of the most influential nonprofit organizations in the United States."

Eyes wide, she continued to eat as she listened with rapt attention. He liked the fascinated look on her face and was proud to have such a wealth of knowledge about the subject.

"When me and the other boys were in high school, we made a pact to all go into the military. It was our way to escape this tiny town and see the world. We had big dreams that we would go out and conquer." He held her gaze as he sighed, adding, "But what most of us discovered was that the other side of the world is just that—another place. It wasn't where our hearts were. So we all came home after our various tours ended...all but one of us."

Her fork halted over her plate and she stared into his face. "Oh, Aiden, I'm so sorry."

"It was our friend Philip. Philip Bayles. He was actually Katelyn's fiancé."

Lia was stunned into silence, clearly not having realized that Katelyn had suffered such a loss before finding love with Gareth and having their new baby.

Giving a mental shake, he continued, "But I didn't mean to make this conversation a downer. It's just that when we all came back, we realized that we wanted to be able to share our experiences that bound us together. There was an American Legion chapter in the northern part of the Eastern Shore that had almost died out. Mitch took the lead and managed to bring the chapter to Baytown."

"I went to the Auxiliary meeting the other day. It was interesting and I've done the paperwork to become a member, but there's still so much I don't know," she said.

"There are lots of activities that the American Legion is involved in, but baseball is actually one of their most successful amateur athletic programs. Our goal is to educate young people about the importance of sportsmanship, citizenship, and fitness. We're also involved in supporting recovering wounded warriors and their families. And the Auxiliary helps us with all of those endeavors."

"Why is baseball so important?" She cocked her head and added, "For you, I mean."

He chewed silently for a moment, thinking of his response. Swallowing, he held her gaze and said, "I guess it all comes down to my memories." Seeing her rapt attention on him, he continued. "I grew up in this little, no-where town in America. Friends, family. Hell, the Baytown Boys were my life. Once I was in Afghanistan, I realized how much I missed it. The fun. The camaraderie. The sense of belonging. I came back to that, but started to notice how many kids in this area don't have it."

She nodded, her gaze never leaving his.

"When I was growing up, I never realized how poor this county was. We were big in agriculture, but by the time I was an adult, a lot of that was gone." Shrugging, he said, "I'm just hoping to give some of these kids a chance to have a little bit of what I had."

She reached over and touched his arm with her delicate fingers. "That's lovely, Aiden. Really lovely."

They finished their meals and pushed their plates back, both reveling in the nighttime sky over the bay and the good food and wine.

His hand settled across her shoulder again, fingertips soothing her skin, and he asked, "Do you think that Emily would enjoy being part of the team?"

She bit her lip, quiet for a moment, and he could see her thoughts churning behind her eyes. "Part of me wants her to feel normal and to do anything that she wants to do. The other part of me isn't sure how that would work."

"Why don't you let me—"

"Aiden!"

A female voice sounded from the side and he jerked his head around. A statuesque blonde in a skintight cocktail dress leaving little to the imagination stepped over to their booth. He did not know her name but recognized her face as one of the vacation-fucks he had had the previous year. *You have got to be kidding me,* he thought, once more feeling Lia's back straighten and her shoulders tense.

"I was back in town for the weekend and wondered if I'd have a chance to see you again. We had such a *memorable* time the last time I was here." Her voice slurred slightly, as though the effects of too many martinis had dulled her speech as well as her good sense.

Her behavior was rude, considering he was clearly on a date, and paired with his embarrassment over the whole thing pushed him over the edge. Deciding that he was no longer going to play nice, he said firmly, "I'm sorry, but this is not the time for a reunion. As you can see, I'm with someone."

The blonde blinked, her eyes narrowing slightly as it appeared to dawn on her that he did not intend to welcome her with open arms. "Well, well. I never thought to see the leopard change his spots, but I guess anything is possible. But, just so you know," she leaned in a little and mock whispered, the alcohol on her breath hitting him in the face. "If you change your mind, I'll be here through the weekend, staying at the

Baytown Hotel." Batting her lashes, she turned and sashayed away.

Closing his eyes at that horrible display, he sat with his arm still around Lia, feeling the negative vibes pouring off her. Letting out a sigh, he turned to her. "Lia, I'm sorry, I don't know what to—"

Without looking at him, she scooted to the other side of the booth and stepped out quickly. Not lifting her eyes to his face, she said, "I think I'll skip dessert. I really need to get home and check on Emily."

Dropping some bills on the table, he hastened to follow her out finding, even with his long stride, she was difficult to keep up with as she hurried out of the restaurant. Reaching his truck, he saw her standing facing the passenger door, still not looking into his face even as she heard him approach.

"Lia, please let me apologize. I never wanted our date to be interrupted like that."

Her shoulders slumped and a sigh heaved from her body. Softly, she said, "I'm sure that's true, Aiden. It happened nonetheless. Please take me home. I really do need to check on Emily."

He felt sure that that was just an excuse but could not come up with a plausible reason for her to give him more time. He unlocked her door and assisted her in and as he rounded the truck to get to the driver side, his mind was wracked with frustration.

The drive back to her house was short and the silence in the cab of the truck was deafening. Walking her to the door, he reached out, placing his hand on her arm and halting her forward movement. "Please Lia, hear me out. I wanted to be with you tonight and no one else. You're the only person I've thought about since I met you. The only person I want to be with. But I can't change my past. Right now, though, I wish I could."

Turning to him, she lifted her eyes to his, the dark chocolate holding his steady. She nodded slowly and with a sad voice said, "I believe you, Aiden. And it isn't the women though, to be honest, that was really uncomfortable." He opened his mouth to speak but she shook her head. "I know that I can't hold your past against you, that wouldn't be fair, and that's not what this is. But I think we're better off as just friends and nothing more."

His face fell and the air left his lungs in a rush. "Why do you say that? I want you in my life, Lia, and I thought you felt the same way. I'd like a chance to show you how good we could be."

"It's not just me, I have to think about Emily, too. She doesn't remember her father and I haven't dated since Carl's death. To start something more than friendship with someone who—" she cut herself off and he took a step back.

"Who what? What were you going to say?"

She took a deep breath, then said, "Who doesn't have a good history of commitment. That's a risk, and after tonight, I'm not willing to risk Emily's heart along with mine."

She turned and placed her hand on the doorknob, then hesitated. Looking over her shoulder, she blinked away the moisture gathering in her eyes, and said, "I'm sorry. Maybe I'm just a big chicken, but I just can't risk it."

He stood for a moment on her front porch, hearing Emily's excited greeting through the door when she saw her mother. Stunned, he walked to his truck, his heart heavy. Driving back to his small apartment, he was filled with the knowledge that ever since meeting the enigmatic Lia he had been drawn to her, even when he thought she was the complete opposite of what she turned out to be. Since learning who she really was, he had wanted something more than what he had ever wanted before. But, after tonight, he had no idea how to show her he could be the man she deserved.

Sitting on Emily's bed, Lia closed the storybook that they had just been reading. Bending over to tuck Emily in, she was surprised when her daughter looked up and asked, "Mama, do you like Mr. Aiden?"

Blinking at the question, she reached down to tuck the covers tightly around her, thinking of the best answer. "Yes. I think he's a very nice man."

"Susie told me that he's a good coach and is really fun to be with."

"I'm sure he is fun to be with," she responded, then winced at the slightly sarcastic tone of her voice. Clearing her throat, she added, "I think he's probably a very good coach and I think the kids enjoy being around him a lot."

Emily was quiet for a moment as she shifted over in

bed, tucking her hands up under her cheek. Her eyes lifted back up to her and she said, "I think maybe one day I'd like to play ball, too. I wasn't sure if I could, but I think Mr. Aiden would be able to teach me."

Smiling without saying a word, she leaned over and kissed Emily's cheek, turning out the light as she left her daughter's room. Moving across the hall to her own room, her thoughts were swirling. When she had entered her house after her date, she had considered what it would be like to live in Baytown and just be friends with Aiden as she had told him they could be, knowing it would hurt to see him with other women. She had wondered if it would be better to avoid him, but that idea seemed foolish. *He's a good man and he might be really good for teaching Emily.*

As she crawled into bed, her mind continued to roll over the events of their date. Being honest with herself, she realized that there was nothing about his behavior that was untoward and he appeared just as uncomfortable with the women who approached as she was. Grimacing at the thought of Carl's betrayal, she realized her own confidence had taken a hit when she and Emily were too much for him to handle. *So, do I have it in me to be with a man whose past might always rear its ugly head? And what if we get to be too much for him? Would he bail as well?* As she fell asleep, she had no answer to those questions.

11

Aiden awoke the next morning no more rested than when he had fallen into bed the night before. Frustration still hummed through his blood, occasionally mixed with irritation and anger. Unable to separate his swirled thoughts, he climbed out of bed and dressed quickly.

It only took ten minutes to drive to the small house set behind the dunes of the Chesapeake Bay, a crushed oyster shell driveway leading from the road all the way to the old, clapboard building. It was freshly painted, something that he and Brogan had finished the previous summer, and he admired the way it was holding up as he climbed out of his truck. Twisting his head, he watched the gentle surf as the early morning sun glistened on the water. This place was perfect. Taking a deep breath, he walked to the front door and knocked.

Not a minute later, the door swung open and he greeted the occupant with a wide smile. "Hey Pops."

Finn looked up at him, his blue eyes twinkling in the early morning light, and shook his head slowly. "Well, well, boy. You showin' up here this early means either you didn't go to bed last night or you got something on your mind that kept you awake all night. Reckon you want to come on in and tell me which one it is."

He followed his grandfather into his small house, the familiar scent of pipe smoke settling in the air. Finn did not smoke a pipe often, but occasionally he enjoyed the tobacco. He always said his wife had loved the scent. He had been a widower for over six years and had moved to the small beach cottage after she passed away, saying that to stay in the house he shared with Mamie would have broken his heart.

Aiden glanced around the small living room, furnished with a sofa and two chairs surrounding a coffee table, all facing Finn's pride and joy, his large, flat screened TV. *"A man needs something to watch his games on,"* his grandfather had proclaimed. The scuffed hardwood floor gave the room character, and the only decorations on the walls were a few family photos. *"When a man's got a view of nature outside his window, he don't need fancy decorations in his house."*

Shaking his head as he followed Pops into the kitchen, he grinned at the memories of the older man's simple life philosophies.

The small kitchen would never have been large enough for his grandmother, who loved to cook for their huge family, but for Pops it was the perfect size. He helped himself to a cup of strong coffee, throwing in a dash of milk, and they walked back out the door and settled into two Adirondack chairs facing the bay, the warm mugs in their hands.

Sitting in silence for several minutes, they watched the sun rise higher into the sky. The gulls flew over the water, calling to each other and diving underneath the surface to come up with their breakfast. A flock of black pelicans flew by next, low over the water as the tall seagrass surrounding Pop's small plot of land bent and waved in the breeze blowing from the bay.

He knew that Pops was not going to ask him what was on his mind, rather allowing him to unburden as he needed. The problem was, he had no idea where to begin.

After shifting in his chair a moment, he finally caught Pops' eyes and the older man said, "If you don't know where to start, then just jump in, even if it's the middle. Once you start going, you'll figure out what you need to say."

Grinning, he knew his grandfather was right. "I went on a date last night." He waited to see what Pops was going to say, but nothing came forth, so he continued, "A real date."

Pops turned his head and looked at him, saying, "Boy, if that's your problem, then I don't think you've got it too bad."

Chuckling, he continued, "It was a real date, Pops, with a woman that I really like."

"I'm still not seeing the problem, boy, but I'm gettin' from your tone of voice that the date didn't go so good."

Taking another sip of his now-cooling coffee, he said, "I took her to the Sunset Restaurant, where we ran into a couple of women I had...uh...known in the past. Both made a point to not only speak with me, but implied about our previous relationship while ignoring that I was with someone. I shut them down quickly, but it was embarrassing nonetheless. We were having such a good time, but that put a real damper on the date. By the end, Lia just wanted to go home. She said it wasn't the women that bothered her, though I know that's not entirely true. She said what bothered her was that my past indicates I can't commit longterm."

"Lia, huh? The pretty, new accountant in town? The one with the little girl you rescued?" Pops sat quietly for another minute, then said, "For you to be here this early in the morning, you must be serious about wanting to see her. She seems real nice and so does her little girl. Might not be your typical type, Aiden, but people change, grow up."

"Not going for my typical type anymore, Pops, you're right about that. At least, not since I've met her. But I don't know how to get her to trust me when my past says that I'm nothing more than a good-time guy."

"Nothing wrong with a young, single man having a good time. In my day we called it 'sowing our wild oats.'"

"I know, Pops. And I learned quickly that a casual hookup with someone that lived in town wasn't a smart move. Even if we said it was just for fun, it could be really awkward to run into that person again or to have them develop expectations that I didn't share. That was the first thing that threw me last night. One of my casual...uh...*acquaintances* was the hostess. She greeted me rather exuberantly, ignoring Lia in the process. I tried to politely move away, but I could tell it was uncomfortable for Lia."

Again, for a few minutes they sat sipping their coffee, watching the fishing boats head out into the Bay. Not usually one for rising early, he had to admit that when he did, it made him appreciate the water activity near Baytown even more.

Finally, continuing, he said, "I tend to meet up with women who are here on vacation or just passing through town. It's not hard to meet them, with the pub and all. But then, after Lia and I were finally having an enjoyable dinner, one of those types of women came up and remembered me. She essentially told me she was back in town and didn't mind a hookup. Right there, when I was having dinner with another woman."

Pops eyebrows snapped down in a scowl and he looked toward him. "Now that just seems rude to me," he said. "I don't understand why any person would do that."

"I thought the same thing. I've never made it a secret to any woman I've hooked up with that it was nothing more than a couple of hours of fun. I never promised to call. I never promised to see them again. At the time, I always made sure that they were on the same page that I was. A one-time thing, just for fun. And, honest to God, with most of the women I had been with, I figured they would be very decent if I ever ran into them again. Thought most would offer me a smile, but not say anything, even if I was alone. But fucking hell, Pops, two in one night, right in front of

Lia, was more than she could take. It was more than *I* could take."

Pop nodded his head slowly, finishing the last of his coffee before setting his cup down on the wide arm of the Adirondack chair. "You came back different, boy."

Jerking at the sudden change of conversation, he asked, "Different?"

"You were always a fun kid to be around. Brogan? He was the oldest and took his responsibilities very seriously. Katelyn? She was such a combination of tomboy and princess. But you? You loved life, you loved hanging out with your friends. You seemed to enjoy everything you did, whether it was fishing off the pier with me or hanging in the kitchen baking cookies with Mamie. I worried about you, when you decided to follow Brogan and joined the Marines. I was afraid that the Marines would take the fun spirit out of you, boy."

He sat in thought for a moment, before responding, "Boot camp was hard, but I loved the camaraderie. Met some great guys and was proud of what we were doing." He turned and looked at his grandfather's profile, seeing the deep wrinkles set in his face. His snow-white hair was thinning a bit on top, but his jaw was just as firm as it ever was and his eyes just as sharp.

"When Brogan came back, it was as though the devil was chasing his heels. I saw deep hurt in your brother, and my heart ached for him. I was glad when Ginny came into his life. They're good for each other." Pop clasped his hands together, resting them on his stomach as he continued to stare out over the Bay. "When you came back, everyone saw the same fun-loving boy who had now grown into a fun-loving man. But not your family...we saw someone who was also running, but with a different devil chasing his heels."

He felt the muscle in his jaw tick as he ground his teeth together. He had no idea his family had seen what he did not understand himself. Swallowing deeply, he said, "Just learned over there that you gotta appreciate life while you have it. Came back and decided to enjoy it the best way I knew how at the time."

"Don't reckon that's a bad thing, son, but chasing women when you've got a devil at your heels ain't a good thing. I'm going to give you the same advice I gave your brother. You better do something about that so that you don't lose your chance at happiness. I hear them talking about the Mental Health Group at our American Legion meetings. Wish I'd had something like that when I came back from Korea. I know your brother wouldn't be the man he is today if he hadn't started talking to someone. Now you know, boy, you can always talk to me, just like we're doing here, but I can't swear to know how to get after that devil. But I reckon at the Mental Health Group, they can help you."

"Just that easy, huh?"

Finn's head jerked around toward him, his blue eyes flashing. "Boy, you didn't hear me say nothing about easy. Most things in life aren't going to be."

He dropped his chin, staring at his hands still wrapped around his coffee mug. He sat silent for a moment, and then nodded before lifting his head up to hold his grandfather's gaze. "You're right. I hadn't really thought about it in those terms, but I do have a devil nipping at my heels. And if I want to be the kind of man that I think Lia and Emily deserve, then I need to do something about myself."

Standing, they walked into the kitchen, rinsing their mugs out before placing them in the drying rack. Pops walked him to the door and they embraced. His grandfather was not one to often give out hugs but, right then, it was exactly what he needed. With a grin and a wink, he walked to his truck, pulling out his phone to make a call.

1 2

Lia walked along Beach Road, staring up at the large, red brick, historic home that she had been told had been the location of the Sea Glass Inn for many years. Originally bought and used as a bed and breakfast by Tori's grandmother, it had been passed along to Tori who continued to welcome guests to Baytown with a marvelous stay at her inn.

The three-story home boasted a wide front porch with white columns and a red front door, the latter of which flung open before she even had a chance to ring the bell, and she was greeted by a smiling Tori, waving her inside.

"Come on in!"

Stepping across the threshold, she greeted Tori with a hug before being led back past a massive living room on the left and a beautiful dining room on the right. Moving down the hall with its warm wooden floors, Tori led her into the kitchen.

"We're all outside," Tori said. "I had just come inside to gather another tray."

"Can I help you?" she asked.

"Absolutely. I never turn down any help," Tori laughed.

After grabbing the tray filled with pastries, she followed Tori out the back door and onto a large stone patio where she saw the gathering of friends. Jillian, Katelyn, Jade, Belle, and Madelyn all sat in comfortable lawn chairs. She and Tori joined them, the conversation lively as they sipped their tea and enjoyed Tori's munchies.

It did not take long for their chat to move to the topic of children, and Katelyn asked about Emily.

"How is Emily handling the move to Baytown?"

She smiled, always loving to talk about her daughter. "She's done really well. She's making some friends and," smiling at Jade, "she loves her teacher."

Jade laughed, and said, "She's an absolute delight to have in class."

"I'm glad she's making friends," Belle said. "It's always so hard in school for anyone who feels the slightest bit different."

She could tell by the wistful tone in Belle's voice that she must have faced some challenges when she was in school. Nodding, she agreed. "I used to worry about that so much, but she always seems to migrate toward other children who have such empathy."

"Even though she speaks well, I have a number of students who are in speech therapy, so she does not feel self-conscious about having that accommodation," Jade said. "And the other students in the classroom are very good about allowing her to see their face when they speak. Several of them are even learning some basic sign language just because they're interested."

"And how are *you* handling the move to Baytown?" Jillian asked. "A little birdie told me that you and Aiden had a date the other night."

Before she had a chance to think of a response, Katelyn added, "I'm so glad you took a chance on Aiden. I feel like my brother's been looking for something special for years, but not having a clue where to look or how to find it."

Madelyn smiled, and said, "Zac says that Aiden is one of the best volunteers he has with the fire department and emergency services. Anytime, day or night, when a call goes out, he knows he can count on Aiden to be right there helping."

Unable to keep the surprise from her face, she stammered, "I...I...had no idea he did that. He never mentioned anything about that."

Belle added, "Don't forget, he also coaches for the AL ball teams."

Looking around, she noted the other women's eyes pinned on her, their expressions ranging from amused to concern. "We had a nice time, but we just went to dinner. We're just...uh...friends."

"You know, I don't think everyone gives Aiden the chance he deserves," Katelyn said. "He can be such a Peter Pan sometimes, but I've often wondered if that's just because he's had no idea how to find what he really wants."

Jillian, her eyes pinned on her, agreed. "He was always the fun kid and Brogan was always the serious one. But if any of us ever needed anything, Aiden was always the first one to volunteer."

"I think all the boys came back a little changed," Katelyn said, drawing her attention back to her. "In different ways, some good and some not so good. Aiden went into the Marines as a fun-loving guy but came back from Afghanistan almost desperately searching for the next good time." She lifted her shoulders in a little shrug, and added, "He has such a capacity for love and loyalty. I know we all think of him as a big flirt, just out for some non-committal fun, but I know when he finds the right person, he'll give everything he has to them. All the women before mean nothing to him, but it will take a very special woman to know what she has, once he's given her his heart."

Feeling the weight of Katelyn's gaze, she looked to the floor, letting her words sink in. Aiden must really be a wonderful man to inspire such loyalty from his sister. *Loyalty.* She thought about the conversations that she and Aiden had enjoyed. He had made it obvious that he had no interest in the women in the restaurant, keeping his fingers on her, pulling her close, staring into her eyes as she spoke. Sucking in her lips, she stayed lost in thought as the conversation around her moved in many directions.

After her impromptu brunch with her new friends, she walked back down Beach Road on her way to her office. At the end of the road, she came to the Baytown pier. As though having a will of their own, her feet took her toward the long, wooden pier. Being fall, the beach was no longer filled with the shouts of children and harried parents loaded down with lawn chairs and umbrellas. Instead, there were several walkers along the shore and as she looked straight ahead, she could see a few fishermen standing near the end of the pier, their lines tossed into the surf.

Walking past them, she made it to the very end and propped her elbows on the wooden railing, rested her chin on her hands and staring out into the Chesapeake Bay.

"Pretty sight, isn't it?"

Startling, she turned around, seeing Finn McFarlane setting his bucket and tackle box nearby and propping his fishing line against the railing. He stood and faced her, his snow-white hair partially hidden underneath an old, faded ball cap, but his blue eyes were startling in their sharp gaze.

She could not help but smile back at him and agree. "Yes, it is."

"It's a good place to let your mind go or just to ponder over life." Bending over, he popped open his tackle box and soon had his pole and line ready. With an efficient snap of his wrist, he sent the hooked line into the water before propping it against the railing.

Unsure if she should speak while someone was fishing, she remained quiet. It did not take long though for Finn to fill the silence.

"Always did like the fall. Don't mind the summer, but it's nice when the crowds are gone and the only people on the beach are the sea glass hunters. My wife used to search for sea glass all the time. She'd fill jars and jars and jars with it and set them around the house or give them to the grandchildren or the other kids who would come and play."

"I've seen some of the sea glass art displayed at Jillian's Galleria," she said. "But I had no idea that people just collected it."

"My wife always said it reminded her to look for the best in people."

Her brow creased in uncertainty and her head tilted slightly. "I'm sorry?"

He shoved his hand into his pants pocket. Pulling his fist out, he opened his hand, palm up. She leaned over and spied a smooth, shiny, oddly-shaped piece of green glass.

"I guess it's just habit, but every morning I stick a piece of sea glass in my pocket. I suppose it's my way of keeping my dear wife with me."

"It's lovely," she said honestly, lifting her gaze up to his face, seeing a twinkle in his eyes.

"You know where sea glass comes from, don't you?"

"Um...the sea?"

He chuckled and nodded. "That's partially right. But it first came from all those ships you see out there in the Bay. They come from all over the world and as they sit anchored right outside of Baytown, waiting to get permission to head on up to the Baltimore port, they often throw out their glass bottles and plates. The glass gets broken and churned in the surf, tossed by the waves, and ground by the sand before it floats up onto the shore. And this," he shook his hand to draw her attention back to the green piece in his palm, "is what's left for us to find."

Her eyes widened, and she smiled. "It's kind of like the ocean has its own way of turning glass pollution into something beautiful, isn't it?"

Finn nodded, his smile spread across his face. "That's exactly right, Ms. Smith. That's a perfect way to describe it. And of course, my dear wife always used to say sea glass is just like people."

"Just like people?" she asked, looking up to see him nodding emphatically.

"We get tossed and turned by life. Sometimes the bad things that happen to us feel like they are grinding us up, turning us over, beating us down. We feel broken and feel like we have nothin' but jagged edges exposed."

She sucked in a quick breath as his words shot straight to her core. She loved her daughter, but hated the struggles she faced. Carl's inability to weather the storm, deciding to leave their family, had angered her, but had also left her feeling broken. Early on, she had often looked into the mirror and tried to find the confident young woman that she used to be. Sucking in her lips, she breathed through her nose, willing her spirit to calm. Finally, she admitted, "Yes, I know what you mean."

His blue eyes appeared to soften as he stared back at her, his lips curving in a slight smile. "It's okay, you know. Most of us have felt that way, at one time or another. But we don't have to stay jagged."

Unable to speak, she waited, silently willing for him to explain.

"You see, my dear, all of those things that happen to us in life are simply polishing us so that when we finally come out of the storm, we're smooth and beautiful." He turned and grabbed his pole, giving it a little jerk and looked over the railing to check to see if he had caught anything yet.

She leaned against the railing as well, both of them giving flight to their inner thoughts. She did still feel beat down at times, that was true, but she knew that over time, since Carl's death, she had come out stronger. She was not broken, she didn't live her life that way. She was happy with Emily and happy with her job. She just hoped she was showing her daughter how to be strong as well. She had spent so much time moving forward, making sure her and Emily were going to be okay, that she had not realized that her edges were smoothed out in the process.

Interrupting her musings, Finn said, "I hope you can see my grandson, Aiden, as a piece of sea glass."

Blinking in surprise, she jerked her head around and stared at his wizened profile.

He kept his eyes facing the water, but said, "People often underestimate him when they first meet him. Sometimes I think that comes from being the younger son. And by the time he came back from the war, he seemed determined to not let people see any pain inside. But I look at Aiden and I see a man who may have been tossed and turned, but has come out a good man with a kind heart. I know he's seen as someone who's not serious, but that's just not true. He's dedicated to his friends, his family, his job, and, with the right woman, he'll be dedicated to her too. There's no better man around."

Letting that sink in, neither spoke for a few minutes as they stood side-by-side, forearms resting on the wooden railing.

Seeing his pole jerk, Finn grabbed it and began to reel in the fish. She had no idea what kind of fish it was, but it was certainly big enough that he was cackling about having caught his dinner. She laughed at his antics and for a second could see an older version of Aiden.

He unhooked the fish and placed it in his bucket, before facing her again. "Well, I reckon I ought to head home. Thanks for spending time with an old man."

Her smile came from deep inside and she leaned forward, placing her hand on his arm. She moved in closer and kissed his rough cheek, saying simply, "Thank you."

With a nod, he turned and picked up his pole, tackle box, and bucket. "You should take time and find some sea glass." Winking, he walked back down the pier leaving her wondering if he was referring to the actual glass or Aiden.

13

That afternoon, Aiden sat in the counselor's office at the Eastern Shore Mental Health Group's clinic. He was stunned when, after confiding in Brogan that he was going to see a counselor today, his brother grabbed him in a bear hug, clapping him on the back.

He could have sworn Brogan had tears in his eyes when he had proclaimed, "Charles is the best, man. If not for him, I don't think Ginny and I would be together."

So now, here he was, sitting in the office, his eyes darting around. He noticed the seascape pictures on the wall and simple furnishings. Charles had a desk but was sitting in front of it facing him. It gave off a more casual vibe than talking to someone with a large desk in between them, making it feel almost like two friends having a chat.

Glancing down, he noticed his leg was jiggling, his

knee bouncing up and down. Lifting his gaze, he said, "I guess I'm kind of nervous."

"That's not unusual," Charles said, leaning back in his chair. "I'm just here to listen to what you have to say. My job is not to tell you what to do or what to change about your behaviors or your emotions, but to listen, to see where you are and where you would like to be. Then we'll work out together how best to help you move forward in life."

"So you just want me to start talking?" He chuckled, then winced, embarrassed to be laughing in the counseling office.

Charles grinned widely, and said, "Don't worry about laughing. In here we can laugh, talk, cry…whatever you need. In fact, I have to say that laughter truly is some of the best medicine."

Feeling his breathing ease, he leaned back in his chair, gathering his thoughts. "I was always the lighthearted kid. I liked to make people laugh. I even got a kick out of driving my parents crazy. If there was a dare, I did it. If there was a tree to climb, a fence to jump over, a bigger wave to ride, I did it."

Charles remained quiet, a slight smile on his face and his hands clasped gently in his lap. His unassuming demeanor eased the way for him to continue to speak.

"My grades in high school were okay, but they were never going to be good enough for me to go straight into college. Me and the other Baytown Boys were pretty good at football and baseball, but I was never going to be the talented athlete that was going to get a scholarship. Everybody always asks when you're younger, 'what do you want to be when you grow up', but honest to God, I never really had much of an idea. Dad worked in the cement factory and my Pops owned his pub. I suppose of the two, I felt like Pops had the cooler job."

"And the military?"

He shook his head, and said, "I could lie and tell you that I had an overwhelming calling to go into the military. I could tell you that I was a flag-waving patriot who felt like it was my duty to go and serve." Lifting his shoulders in a slight shrug, he looked up at Charles, and confessed, "But the truth of the matter is, my friends and I just talked about how much we wanted to escape this little town. We wanted to see the world and we all made a pact that as soon as we finished high school we'd join up. My brother, Brogan, joined the Marines and when I graduated a year later I followed suit."

"Did you find it hard to acclimate to the rigors of the Marines?"

Chuckling, he replied, "Surprisingly, no. I guess that sort of shocked everyone. But I had always been really close to my friends and my brother, so it was not hard to transfer that loyalty to my fellow Marines. A tour in Afghanistan made me long for this little town and when my tour of duty was up, all I wanted to do was come back home."

"I think you'll find that for most servicemen and women, that's a very common emotion."

He agreed. "Yeah, I've heard that from all my friends. Hell, I've even heard that from the older men who served in the military in prior wars when they tell their stories at the American Legion meetings."

They were quiet for a moment, then he added, "I never had anything really bad happen to me over there, though. I know some of my friends did. I know my brother, Brogan, did. But I'd feel like a real pussy if I acted like my time in Afghanistan was more horrible than anyone else's. I never lost a close friend. I was in some difficult situations but didn't have an entire team wiped out. I mean, mostly we did what we were told to do and everybody in my squad came home unscathed."

"So," Charles prodded, "what is it that has brought you here today? What is it about your life that you think might need to be changed?"

"Ever since I came back, it's been really important to me to make sure I'm living life to the fullest. Our grandfather deeded over Finn's Pub to me, Brogan, and our sister Katelyn. It's a job I like and I take the business seriously. Katelyn has always been the brains, so she handles most of the finances. Brogan has always been the steady one, so he handles the personnel. And me? I serve drinks, laugh with the customers, and flirt with the ladies. Well, I used to flirt with the ladies," he corrected.

He cast his gaze upward, watching Charles' face, but observed nothing more than a professional interest. Glad that he did not see a derisive expression, he continued. "Shortly after I came back, I quickly learned that a fling with someone living in town was not a good idea. All I wanted was fun and, even though I thought we were on the same page, eventually someone would get clingy. So," he shrugged, "I found that the single women who vacation here made for the perfect one-nighter. I saw myself as just being young, unattached, and out to have fun."

"If you're looking for censure over your sex life, I'm afraid you're not going to find it here," Charles said. "But I get the feeling that there's more to it than you just wanting to have fun."

He leaned back in his chair, his memories tumbling and, as usual, he tried to battle them back to the recesses. "It was actually my Pops who told me that he felt like I was a very different person when I came back from the military. It's true, I wake up with an occasional nightmare sometimes, but I just figured we all do. I never associated anything that happened over there with my...well, I've been called a Peter Pan by someone recently, implying that I didn't want to grow up and just wanted to have fun. I guess that really stuck with me and got me thinking."

"Do you see yourself as a Peter Pan?"

Scrunching his face as he pondered the question, he said, "Not really. I just never found anyone I really wanted to grow up for. I guess that sounds stupid, but as long as I was just having fun with the ladies, I didn't think my behavior mattered."

"And now you've met someone," Charles stated.

His lips curved into a smile as he thought about Lia and Emily. "Yeah, I have. But she knows of my reputation and is naturally concerned about being with someone that she sees might not be serious. And for the first time, my previous behavior really stings."

"Stings?"

"Yeah. What if everybody's right about me?"

Charles nodded, then asked, "Let's talk about the nightmares. Are you ready to talk about what happened over there?"

His voice low, he said, "I've never told anyone, 'cause it didn't really happen to me, I was just a witness." They sat in silence for just a moment, before he added, "But yeah, it's time I faced the connection between what happened there and who I am now."

Clearing his throat, he began, "I was with my squad and we were doing what was supposed to be a routine check on a village. We had heard that there were insurgents nearby, but we were escorting some Red Cross volunteers to check on a village where illness had swept through. We entered the village, all was normal. They did what they needed to do and then we were escorting them back to base. Not difficult…no problems. It was then that we came across a freak accident. Another squad's truck had hit a landmine and it had been blown to the side. Amazingly everyone seemed okay, except the driver. I happened to get to him first and could tell it was bad."

Closing his eyes, he could see the events playing out in his mind as though watching a movie. "I wasn't a medic, so I backed away, giving our medic and the Red Cross volunteers a chance to get to him. We called for a medivac, but knew it was going to take about twenty minutes for them to arrive. Our medic told me to stay up by the guy's head, keep him calm, and just talk. Guess he knew me well enough, he figured the one thing I could do in any situation was talk. So I moved up next to his head and stayed close."

He opened his eyes and looked at Charles, his breathing heavy, and realized it had been a long time since he had faced the events of that day and remembered them clearly.

"What did you talk about?" Charles asked

Shrugging, he said, "Just shot the shit. You know… sports, girls, what we wanted to do when we got out."

"Tell me about that. Tell me about your conversation."

He chewed on his lip for a moment, the memories slowly coming back to him. "I found out he came from Cincinnati, so we talked baseball for a few minutes. Said he loved to go to the Reds games. I told him I'd played in high school but wasn't all that great. He tried to laugh through his pain and confessed that he wasn't either. He told me he didn't have a girl to go home to and I told him he was a lucky fuck to be able to go home and play the field. He grinned but I could tell it hurt. We talked about some of the shit we wanted to do when we got home. Hit the bars with our friends and go drinking. Pick up girls and run through as many as we could before we ever decided to settle down. Eat what we wanted, drink what we wanted, fuck who we wanted."

Charles made no comment, but as he listened to himself, he shook his head in derision. "Jesus, listening to myself right now, what a bunch of stupid shit he and I talked about."

"Did it seem to take his mind off his injury? Did it

133

seem to take his mind off the fact that it sounds like he was dying?"

Charles' questions had him sucking in his breath quickly, his eyes darting to the counselor's. Letting out a long sigh, he nodded. "Yeah, he was dying. I didn't realize it at first, just thinking that the medics were working to save his life, but after about ten minutes, I realized they were just trying to keep him out of pain." He blew his breath out in another long sigh, suddenly feeling tired, as though he had run a long race.

"I think our conversation made him feel better," he said. "Honest to God, if I had known he was dying, I probably could've thought of something a helluva lot more profound to talk about."

"I don't know. I think it sounds like what you and he had was a normal conversation between two men stuck together in time. As you say, just shooting the shit. Maybe the kind of conversation that you would have had if you had been stuck on a plane together or waiting in a long line for something. What you gave him, Aiden, was a few minutes of *normal* in a very abnormal time. What you gave him was actually very precious."

Suddenly, tears stung the back of his eyes and he looked down at his hands and blinked furiously to keep them at bay. Unsuccessful, one dropped from his cheek and landed on his jeans. Without looking up, he accepted the proffered tissue that Charles held out. After a moment, he pulled himself together and looked up, the stain of blush heating his cheeks.

Charles threw up his hand, and said, "Before you

apologize, don't. It's actually very important that you remembered and faced the traumatic incident from when you were in the Marines." After another moment of silence, Charles asked, "How did things end with him?"

He inhaled deeply before letting out a long, slow breath. "I heard the sound of the medivac coming and knew they would be there in a moment. I bent closer so that he could hear me and told him he'd be going home soon. He looked up at me, held my gaze, and asked me to promise that when I got home, I'd do all the things that we talked about doing. And then he took his last breath just as the helicopter landed."

"I'm very sorry that happened."

Silence filled the room and he appreciated the time of quiet reflection that Charles was giving him. Blowing out another breath, he allowed himself to remember the young Marine.

"How did that experience parlay into your attitude when you returned home?"

"I swear this makes me sound like a prick," he replied, "but I just felt lucky. That experience stayed with me for a while, but it slowly eased from my mind and by the time I came home, I was just glad to be home in one piece. I don't remember consciously making the decision, and yet from the moment I got back to Baytown, I just wanted to do all the things he and I talked about doing. I felt lucky to be back home, in a place that I loved. I felt lucky to be back with my family. I felt lucky to be young and single and free so...I spent a lot of time drinking and fucking, figuring that was what I was supposed to do. I mean, it's not that I didn't enjoy it, don't get me wrong. It wasn't pressure or anything. I just think I put myself in a box and didn't stop to question if that box still fit, if it ever really did in the first place."

Charles leaned forward in his seat, his forearms now resting on his knees as he held his gaze. "If you had felt overwhelming guilt instead of luck, I would think that would not be very healthy. I think deciding to live your life fully is a much healthier choice," he empathized. "Do you feel that you have been living life to the fullest?"

His brows snapped down and he shook his head slightly. "Well, I thought so. Or I used to think so. At least until recently."

"How do you view your lifestyle now?"

Shaking his head, he said, "I now look back and it all seems like I was just running away. That all those meaningless flings were nothing more than immediate sexual gratification, but they weren't making me happy. Not really, not for long."

"Meaningless can keep you from feeling. No feelings keep you from being involved and not being involved keeps you from feeling hurt when the ending is not what you'd hoped it would be or what you feel it should have been."

Eyes wide, he nodded. "Exactly. I'd never considered that, but that's exactly what I've been doing. I haven't wanted to risk feeling so…out of control again." He chuckled. "Ironic right? Most people would probably say my moving from one girl to the next is pretty out of control."

"You know, Aiden, a lot of people seek counseling because their feelings are rather jumbled up inside of them. For many they need a lot of help detangling those feelings. But I think you have the solutions inside yourself, you just hadn't verbalized them. You suffered a life-altering event while in the Marines. But I think that event is one of the reasons you decided to come back to your hometown, work with your family in a business that you enjoy and spend time with your family and friends. Part of living life to the fullest has been becoming involved in the American Legion and I know you work with the youth baseball teams. So, don't forget all the wonderful things that you're doing to live life to the fullest. That's not being a Peter Pan. That's truly enjoying a productive life."

He leaned back in his chair, feeling like all his thoughts had been untangled. He had always been a a genuinely happy person, for the most part, even after Afghanistan, but there had been an unnamed tension when he got back that he just could not ease. Finally, he could breathe freely again. Charles was right. He just needed to name it, voice it, in order to let it go.

A vision of Lia's face moved through his mind and he winced when he remembered her expression of disappointment by the end of their date. Lifting his gaze back to Charles, he said, "I'm no longer interested in meaningless flings but have no idea how to move forward with a real relationship."

Charles said, "In just the hour that we spent together today, Aiden, I can tell that you do know how. So now, tell me about the relationships in your life you are good at and why."

Smiling, he said, "That's easy. My family is fabulous. My parents have been married forever, so were my grandparents. They raised me and my brother and sister to be close. We watch out for each other, work together, sometimes fight together, but always laugh together. The Baytown Boys were my closest friends growing up. I would drop anything in an instant to be there for any one of them. And that includes the women that many of them have fallen in love with now."

"Okay, so what I hear you say is that you have the ability to be loyal, dedicated, loving, and put those people you care about ahead of your own needs. Does that sound about right?"

He grinned, and said, "Man, when you put it that way, I feel like a pretty decent guy."

Charles threw his head back and laughed. "Yeah, I'd say so too." Sobering, he held his gaze, and said, "And now for the hard part. If you have the capacity for all that, what were the most important things with a fling?"

Blushing, he responded, "Uh...I guess easy. No commitment. Preferred not to see them again. Definitely not spending the night with someone. God, it does make me sound bad, but really it was just about sex."

"I think while the physical act of sex, without an emotional attachment, might be very normal for some people, it ended up making you feel as meaningless as the non-existent emotions. Thinking about how you are with your friends and family, I think the answer for how to build a true relationship lies within you."

As self-doubt slid away from him, he sat up straighter in his chair. "I know it won't be easy, so I have to be willing to work at it. I have no problem being loyal, but I have to be able to convince her that I'm in for the commitment. It's been a long time since I've ever spent the entire night with a woman, but for Lia, the idea of holding her all night is exactly what I want to do. And while I think she's beautiful, and I'd be a liar if I said there were no sexual feelings, what I really want to do is just *be* with her."

"Then my suggestion is to do just that. Just *be* with her. And while it might take time for her to learn to trust you, that will come."

Standing, they shook hands and, afterwards, he tilted his head to the side and said, "This seemed too easy. I thought counseling was going to be a long, agonizing process."

Charles laughed again. "Well, not every counseling session is quite so straightforward. I would like to see you again, though. Because you do have some nightmares, I think it would be healthy to explore a little more about what happened to you in Afghanistan, if you are amenable to that."

He nodded his head slowly. "Absolutely. I think that's definitely something that would help."

After setting up another appointment time with the receptionist, he stepped out into the sunshine, sliding his sunglasses onto his face. The warmth penetrated and for the first time in a long time he felt confident. Smiling, he walked down the road toward the pub.

Entering, he observed the usual afternoon crowd with Brogan behind the bar. His brother looked up, catching his eye and holding his gaze, Brogan's curiosity and concern evident. With a smile and a nod, he silently communicated that he was fine. Brogan grinned and nodded before pulling another beer for one of their customers.

"It's kinda quiet in here," he called out loudly. "Why don't we crank up the music and get this place hoppin'?"

As he walked behind the bar grinning widely Brogan popped him on the back of the head. "Why do you gotta be so loud in front of the customers?"

He answered with a continued grin and was met with Brogan's wide smile in return. Moving to the back of the bar, he recognized the wonderful feeling of coming home.

14

"Mrs. Markham?" Lia called out. "I think the new accountant, Mr. Redding's grandson, is supposed to show up this morning. I'm trying to get ready to meet with the Town Council after lunch, so as soon as he comes in please show him back."

Receiving acknowledgment from Mrs. Markham, she finished her preparations for meeting with the Town Council. She had read the audit that was provided to her by the Mayor and had concerns. She hoped that the members of the various departments in the town would cooperate, but she knew that most people who knew that they are being investigated would not welcome her with open arms.

Her mind began to wander and visions of Aiden filled her head. After hearing what his family had to say and considering how things had been between them after they had cleared the air and started fresh, she realized she had been unfair to him the other night. Her original impression of him was so wrong and rather than put that aside and see him for who he was, she had let her own insecurities get the better of her and had laid such judgement at his feet because of it.

The reality was he made her laugh. He made her comfortable enough to share about her marriage with Carl and the difficulties she had had with Emily. He treated her with kindness and respect, and she had repaid him with criticism and suspicion. Embarrassment flooded her and she determined to make amends. She started to send him a text, but then decided she preferred to talk to him face-to-face.

Closing her notes, she carefully put them in her briefcase just in time to look up as the new accountant arrived. Following Mrs. Markham into her office was a tall, dark-haired man. She rose from her chair and made her way around her desk to shake his hand. She had pictured a young man barely out of college, but this man was obviously closer to thirty years old.

"Welcome, Scott. I see you met Mrs. Markham."

His handshake was warm and firm and as he smiled down at her, she was immediately relieved. Waving him to one of the seats, she sat down at her desk, eager to get acquainted.

"I have to confess that I'm very excited about you joining our firm. As you know, I only took over for your retiring grandfather a couple of months ago. Tax accounting is not my forte. I can certainly handle the basics but am not comfortable making that the full practice. My specialty is forensic accounting, but of course I know that there's usually not enough work for me to do that full-time. On a normal basis, I'm sure we'll have enough work for both of us to stay quite busy. As it turns out, right now, the Town Council has asked me to take a look at their books."

Scott's eyebrows lifted, and he said, "That's interesting. Did something come up in their audit?"

Nodding, she confirmed, "Yes, and it made the Mayor concerned enough that he was forced to take it to the Town Council. In fact, I have to meet with them right after lunch today."

They chatted for a few more minutes and he told her of growing up in Accawmacke County and visiting his grandfather in Baytown when he was a child. He glanced around the office and smiled saying, "I like your decorations much more than my grandfather's stuffy diplomas on the wall."

She laughed and replied, "There's still more I'd like to do, but I've been so busy since I got here. Unfortunately, as you know, we don't have another office, but the conference room is so rarely used, I'm going to suggest that we make that your office."

"That's perfect," he replied. He looked at his watch, and said, "Do you have time for lunch before your meeting? We could grab something, chat a little more, and then you'll be ready to meet with the Town Council."

"That would be lovely."

"We could always go to the pub," he suggested. "They have great lunches."

Blinking in surprise, she quickly rallied. "I think

perhaps I'd prefer the Seafood Shack, today, if you don't mind."

Standing together, he allowed her to walk out before him, saying, "It's been a long time since I've been there. That sounds great."

Walking out with her new employee, she breathed a sigh of relief knowing she would not run into Aiden.

Aiden walked out of the Seafood Shack manager's office, having taken a few minutes to stop by and say hello. He had been killing time as he waited for the Carson & Sons fishing boat to come back into the harbor. Purchasing the fresh fish from local fishermen was one of his favorite duties at the pub.

With a chin lift, he said his goodbyes to the bartender and moved toward the front door. Looking around as he went, he did a double take when he glanced to the side and observed Lia sitting with a man he did not know. Instantly alert, he leaned over to get a better view. The man was tall, dark-haired, and wearing a business suit.

A strange feeling hit his gut and he realized he was staring jealousy in the face, an emotion he was unused to. Keeping his eye on the couple, he noted they were not holding hands, nor did the man touch Lia in any way. *Which is good, or I'd have to break his hand.*

He continued to watch for a moment as the two of them chatted. Then, unable to stop his feet, he found himself heading straight for them. She looked up as he approached and blinked in surprise. He could have sworn a flash of uncertainty moved through her eyes before her smile widened as she greeted him.

"Aiden," she called out.

"Lia," he said, barely recognizing his rough voice. He watched her blink again before she glanced to the side at the man she was with.

"This is Scott. Scott Redding. He's Thomas Redding's grandson and has joined the accounting firm."

Fighting the ever-growing feelings of jealousy at the thought of the college educated, business suit wearing man being around Lia every day, he accepted the handshake offered to him. He was so focused on Scott, he did not realize Lia was speaking to him until he felt a slight squeeze on his arm. Jerking his eyes back to her, he tilted his head in question.

"I have a meeting with the Mayor this afternoon and I have a feeling it's going to take the rest of the day. But...uh...I had planned on calling you later...if that's all right. That is, if you're not busy or have plans or something."

As though his world tilted on its axis, falling into place, he met her nervous gaze with a wide smile. "Lia, you can call me anytime. I'm always available for you." The words were true, but he hoped she realized there was meaning in them.

She and Scott stood, and he observed their meal was finished. Holding out his arm for them to lead the way, he followed behind. Walking out, he looked over to the harbor and saw that the fishing vessel had returned. He watched Lia and Scott walk across the parking lot, heading back toward Main Street and he sighed.

Within the hour, he had the ice chests of fresh fish and seafood loaded into the back of his truck. Needing to get back to the pub, he climbed into the driver seat, his mind full of Lia. Slumping down, he thought back to his conversation with Charles. *I know it won't be easy, so I have to be willing to work at it.* Finally cranking his truck, he put it in drive and headed toward the pub, more determined than ever to show Lia he could be the man for her.

Lia fought to keep from rolling her eyes as Mayor Banks droned on to the Town Council. Silas Mills, the town manager, was also in attendance, but his mannerisms were far from welcoming. Slender, with a thin, weasel-like face, it was hard to imagine that he had been rumored to have had an affair with Corwin's secretary while being engaged to another woman. Shaking the musings from her mind, she brought herself back to the matter at hand, realizing that Corwin had finally stopped talking and was turning the meeting over to her.

She pointed out the areas of the audit that had brought out the discrepancy and outlined the steps she would be taking to try to identify the missing money and the person responsible. The Town Council consisted of six members, all appearing concerned, and promised her the town departments would work with her.

After she had answered their questions the meeting was adjourned, each member shaking her hand. As they filed from the room, she turned to Corwin and said, "Thank you for the records that you have already sent to me and I would like to go ahead and meet whoever I can today. When I am ready to formally interview them, I will set up my own appointments for that."

"Fine, fine," Corwin said, turning and moving toward the door. Looking back over his shoulder, he called out, "Silas, come on. You need to be a part of this too."

She cast her gaze to the side and saw Silas' blatant irritation as his lips pinched and eyes narrowed. Her curiosity grew but she left her face studiously blank. She found it easier when interviewing people if they were unable to see what she was thinking.

They stepped from the Town Council conference room into a hall that led to the back of the Municipal Building, bypassing the lobby and continuing to where the main offices were. Corwin's secretary was sitting at a desk right outside of his office, situated where she could also see into Silas' office. Celia Ring jumped to her feet as soon as Corwin and Silas came into view, her eyes darting between the two men and Lia.

Lia wondered if she imagined that, for an instant, Celia's eyes narrowed on her. *Nervousness? Jealousy? Insecurity?* She also noted that Celia's desk was a large, highly polished oak desk and her chair was a thick, comfortable leather chair. Odd, considering the furniture in the Town Council's conference room had been more utilitarian and, from a previous visit to the building's lobby, she also knew the receptionist's furniture was a plain, metal desk. She was trained to not make hasty judgments, but simply to pay attention to her surroundings whenever she was investigating possible fraud so she simply filed that little observation into the back of her mind.

"Celia!" Corwin barked. "Get me Sandra and Mark. While you're at it, get the others into my conference room as well."

"Absolutely," Celia purred, sitting back into her chair and immediately picking up her phone.

As she walked into the Mayor's office, she watched Celia's gaze slide over to Silas, her lips curving in a smile.

Corwin's office was also understated opulence for a tiny town, consisting of heavy wooden furniture paired with thick leather chairs. Artwork on his paneled walls indicated that he liked to surround himself with the accoutrements of what he considered his position to be.

Silas darted through the door to the right, saying, "I need to make a quick call. I'll be right there."

Corwin led her through the door on the left and into his nicely appointed conference room, with a huge wooden table in the center, and she settled into one of the comfortable seats at the end of the table. Corwin sat at the other end and she watched as he fiddled with his phone, as though he wanted to limit his time making conversation with her.

Within a moment, several other people walked into

the room, some smiling, some not, and she nodded politely at each of them as they took seats. Silas had made it back into the room and glowered as he took the only seat left, the one next to her.

She took notes as they each introduced themselves to her. Sandra Toski, the elected town treasurer. Mark Weber, the accounting clerk. Silas Mills, town manager. And rounding out the table was Celia Ring, the Mayor's secretary.

She knew there were many other departments in the town's staff and would be looking over their finances as well, but all checks and purchases went through the finance department represented at the table, so they were a good place to start.

Used to this type of meeting, she launched into her explanation of what she would be doing in her forensic accounting investigation and what she would need from each of them. All eyes were on her, some heads nodding in acquiescence, some jaws clinched, some eyes wide in surprise and others narrowed in irritation.

At the close of the meeting, she indicated for Sandra and Mark to wait behind. She gave each of them a list of the reports that she would need from them and asked that they would send them electronically to her. Gaining their agreement, she smiled as she said goodbye and watched them file out of the room.

Alone in the room, she breathed a sigh of relief. She loved delving into the numbers and tracing where money came from and where it was spent. It was like a puzzle and she enjoyed fitting the pieces together and finding out which ones were not right.

Standing, she was surprised when Silas stepped back into the conference room. He approached her, his face pinched as he asked if he could speak to her privately.

"Of course," she replied.

He glanced behind him at the closed door that led to Corwin's office, and said, "I know that Corwin is trying to do the right thing by bringing you in. I, personally, don't see that there's a problem. Certainly not a problem worth making a big deal about. But you've got to understand, this is an election year. He's been the elected mayor for almost eighteen years and has done a wonderful job for this town. He and his wife support lots of different activities and benefits for Baytown. I would hate to think that news of your little investigation would get out and harm his chances of being re-elected."

"Mr. Mills, I assure you that I treat every investigation with the utmost professionalism. My goal is to discover if there has been financial wrongdoing on someone's part. I would think, if you have the town's well-being first and foremost in your mind, you would want that to happen."

"Of course I do," he bit back. "I just want to make sure everything is done as quickly and discreetly as possible so that nothing interferes with Corwin's re-election."

Bending, she gathered her files into a neat stack and placed them into her leather briefcase. Slinging it, and her purse, over her shoulder she turned and faced him once again. "I will do the job that I've been hired to do. It will take as long as it needs to take to be an accurate representation of what is happening. Good day." With that, she pushed past him and moved into the hall, noting Celia had been standing right next to the door. The secretary jumped, before hurrying to her desk.

Walking down the hall she noted Sandra and Mark in one of their offices, heads bent as they talked. She gratefully stepped out of the building into the sunshine and sucked in the fresh air.

As she walked back to her office, she sighed, knowing that she wanted to talk to Aiden but had hours of work that needed to be accomplished first.

15

"Hello."

Aiden turned toward the sultry voice, eyeing the customer sitting at the bar. Makeup applied for maximum effect. Hair teased out for maximum volume. Clothes, tight and revealing, but not over the top slutty. Just the type of woman that would have caught, and held, his eye not that long ago. But no more. Moving down toward her, he nodded toward her half-empty glass, and asked, "Need a refill?"

She smiled and tapped a long, painted fingernail on the side of her glass. "My drink is fine, for now. But I was wondering about later."

Pretending to not understand her flirtatious invitation, he replied, "Well, if you need a refill on your drink later, you just have to ask." With a polite nod, he moved back down the bar to check on another customer.

Brogan approached and, with a low voice, asked, "Are you okay?"

Tilting his head, he looked into Brogan's quizzical face. "Yeah."

Brogan jerked his head in the direction of the other end of the bar, and asked, "Not interested?"

Shaking his head, he replied, "Nope."

"Lia?"

Sighing, he grabbed the beer he had just pulled and set it in front of a customer. "I'm just not interested. Well, at least not interested in anyone other than Lia, so yeah, I guess you're right. I've got to prove to her that I'm more than just what everyone thinks of me, you know?"

"Aiden, everyone thinks you're a great guy."

He turned and faced Brogan, his hands on his hips. "You know as fuckin' well as I do that everyone thinks I'm just out for a good time."

Brogan held his gaze for a long time before slowly shaking his head. "Your friends know who you really are. The man deep inside…the one who cares about everybody."

Dropping his chin to his chest, he stared at his boots for a moment, letting Brogan's words sink in. Looking back up, he said, "That may be, but I still need to prove to her that I'm not just out for a casual night. As far as I'm concerned, those days are over."

Hearing the female customer call out again, saying she was ready for a new drink, he sighed. Starting to move, Brogan stopped him with his hand on his shoulder. "No worries, Aiden. I got this."

He watched Brogan walk over and refill the

woman's drink, while she glowered at both of them. Grinning, he headed to the back toward the kitchen.

A few minutes later, he felt his phone vibrate in his pocket and he pulled it out. Seeing the call was from Lia, he answered it immediately. "Hey," he said, finding his heart beating faster at the anticipation of hearing her voice.

"Hi," she replied.

That one word was filled with nervousness and he rushed to reassure her. "I'm so glad you called. I've been hoping you would."

"I didn't know if this was a bad time," she said. "I'm sure there's a crowd at the Pub—"

"Don't worry about it. I always have time for you."

"Oh, okay…uh…well, I wanted to talk to you about something."

"Can I come by your house?" She was silent for a few seconds, so he pressed, "It's kind of loud here, but I can leave anytime. I could swing by your place and we could chat there."

"Sure. Yeah, that'll be fine. We'll be home whenever you want to come."

Pleased that she indicated Emily would be there as well, he breathed a sigh of relief. Somehow knowing that her daughter would be present made him feel better…as though she trusted him. "I just need to check on some things in the kitchen, so I can be there in about thirty minutes."

Disconnecting after saying goodbye, he headed back to the bar to tell Brogan he would be leaving soon before returning to the kitchen with a huge grin on his face.

———

Lia heard her cell phone vibrate on the kitchen counter and quickly set the glasses in her hand down. Grabbing her cell, she answered, "Hello?" No one spoke. Wondering if the connection had been delayed, she repeated, "Hello?" While confused at the prank call, she was glad it was not Aiden calling to cancel. Disconnecting, she tossed her phone down at the interruption. Turning back to her preparations, she heard Emily call out.

"Mama! I see him. It's Mr. Aiden. Can I open the door?" Emily ran back from the living room to the kitchen and looked up at her.

Taking a pan from the oven, she smiled at her daughter. "Yes. You may open the door for him."

Emily turned and ran back toward the front, throwing open the door before the doorbell rang. "Hi, Mr. Aiden!"

She placed the hot dish onto the trivet and pulled off the oven mitts, tossing them to the counter. Walking down the hall, she saw Aiden smiling as he squatted in front of Emily.

"Hey, darlin'," he greeted. "Did your mom say it was okay for you to open the door by yourself?"

A warm feeling slid through her as she heard the concern for her daughter in his voice. Before she had a chance to speak, Emily was telling him that she had seen him from the window and had been given permission to open the door.

Stepping into the room, she watched as his gaze slid beyond Emily to her, his smile widening. Standing, he allowed Emily to escort him into the room. As he reached her, he leaned forward and placed his hand on her waist, bending to kiss her cheek. "I'm glad you called. It's really nice to see you again. I know it's only been a couple of days, but it feels like so much longer."

Rolling her eyes, she said in an exaggerated voice, "I'm sure."

He held her gaze, and said, "I'm being honest, Lia. I understand your concerns, but I really missed you."

His blue eyes burned into hers, sending warmth throughout her entire body. Unable to speak, she stared into his handsome face, fighting the urge to lean up on her tiptoes and kiss him.

"Mama, is Mr. Aiden going to stay for dinner?"

Emily's voice jolted through her, jerking her back to reality. She felt the heat of blush hit her face and was unable to keep the smile away. "We have plenty and were just getting ready to sit down. Would you like to join us?"

If it was possible for his smile to widen even more, it did. "I can't think of anything I'd rather do," he replied, "than have dinner with you two lovely ladies."

Emily giggled and she sent her into the kitchen to set another place at the table. Before following, she leaned toward him, and said, "What I want to talk to you about has to do with Emily. But I'd rather we talk privately."

"Absolutely. You just let me know when and I'm all ears."

With that out of the way, she nodded and led him back to the small table in the eat-in kitchen.

As she served the homemade chicken pot pie casserole, she noted the ease with which he communicated with Emily. He did not over exaggerate his speech, nor did he speak too slowly. He made sure that he was facing her when he spoke and appeared to be careful to make sure she was understanding. And from the laughter elicited from Emily, he was communicating successfully, without making her daughter feel different.

Walking back to the kitchen counter to grab the plate of dinner rolls, it struck her. What Carl was unwilling to learn with his own daughter, Aiden was doing with ease. Setting the rolls on the table, she took her seat and smiled up at him, entering their conversation.

He ate with relish, obviously enjoying the meal. "This is really good, Lia."

"I consider that high praise, since you own a restaurant."

He nodded and wiped his lips with his napkin. "There are a lot of benefits to owning my own restaurant and tasting what comes out of the kitchen is one of them. But at the same time, I sometimes get tired of that. Honestly, I practically never have a home-cooked meal unless I stop by my mom's, or Katelyn's, or Brogan's house. So to me, this is a real treat."

"Then you can eat with us every night," Emily said. "That way you'll always have a good dinner."

Chuckling, he nodded. "I wouldn't mind that at all, darlin'. But I'm not sure your mom's up to having company every night."

The idea that he might not be talking just about dinner rushed through her mind, sending tingles throughout her body. Forcing her mind back onto the topic, she said, "Anytime you're hungry, you're welcome to dinner. Although sometimes, it might just be take-out pizza."

Before he had a chance to respond, Emily asked if she could watch TV before going to bed. She agreed and watched as her daughter skipped out of the room.

"I'll help you clean up," Aiden said, but halted when her hand snaked out and grabbed his arm.

"I thought maybe we could talk now, since Emily's out of the room."

"Sure," he responded, his brow lowered in concern. "What's going on?"

She sucked in a deep breath, exhaling slowly. "It's just that...and I've done a little research, so I know it can be done...but I just don't know quite how it works...and I'm not even sure it would be a good idea—"

"Jesus, Lia," he said, leaning forward to cover her hands with his own. "You're making me nervous here. Just tell me what you're thinking."

"Emily wants to learn how to play baseball with your team," she blurted.

He blinked. Slowly. Twice.

Watching him, she scrunched her forehead, and said, "Is that bad? Would it work? She's never wanted to play a sport before and, quite frankly, I'm not athletic either, so it never bothered me that she didn't want to participate. But, now she wants to, and I just thought that maybe you could…I don't know… uh…help her somehow." After having rebuffed him at the end of their date, she worried that asking him to help Emily might not be the right thing to do. "It's fine for you to say no. I probably shouldn't have even asked—"

"Lia, I think it's a great idea." He squeezed her hand, bringing her gaze back to his. "Honest to God, I'm so honored that you asked me. This is going to be great," he enthused, his eyes shining and his smile firmly back on his face.

"Really?" she asked, hope burning in her chest.

"Absolutely." He leaned in closer, his hands still holding onto hers. "There are deaf baseball players… hell, deaf players in all sports. With her partial hearing and ability to read lips, coaching her in a game would just be a matter of making sure we are right in front of her. Other than that, she can easily learn signals and we can learn some basic sign language. And until she's ready, I can give her private lessons, so she'll learn how to throw and hit the ball."

She felt tears sting the backs of her eyes and she tried to keep them from falling. Her voice raspy, she asked, "You'd really be willing to do that for her?"

She watched as the bright blue in his eyes dulled slightly. "You think I wouldn't?"

Unintentionally she had insulted him with her

concern, so she rushed to explain, "Oh, no! I know you're a good person and that you would want to do that for her. I just meant, it's a huge commitment. I didn't know if you had the time, if it was too much to ask of you." Inhaling deeply, still battling tears, she continued, "She really wants you to teach her. And, so do I."

His smile returned and he lifted his left hand to gently wipe away a tear that had fallen over her cheek, continuing to cup her face after the tear had been captured. "Please believe me when I tell you that I really want to do this."

"I owe you an apology, Aiden," she began, wanting to make things right. "I wasn't trying to judge you at the end of our date but, I've come to realize how Carl's behavior has tainted how I look at other people. You gave me no reason to believe that you had any other interests on our date other than me or that you were unreliable or not ready for a commitment. I allowed my own insecurities, my fear that you would get tired of us and walk away, to be foisted upon you."

Shaking his head, he said, "I accept your apology, but only if you'll except one from me, too. I've gone through life since I got back from the war pretty much living the way I wanted, without giving any real consideration to how it might affect others. I certainly never gave any consideration to how it might affect a future relation-ship. That was a mistake I made, and unfortunately one that I can't go back and change. But I've decided to take steps to look at my past behavior, figure out why I acted in certain ways, and decide how I want my future to be.

So, my apology to you is for any previous behavior of mine that causes you to be embarrassed or doubt me."

A smile slipped across her lips as she nodded. "Another fresh start...for real this time?"

"Absolutely," he said, leaning forward to kiss her forehead. "Now, how about we go tell Emily about her new baseball lessons?"

Giving her cheeks a quick swipe to rid them of any remaining tears, she stood, feeling so much lighter than she had in a long time.

16

Aiden stepped into his parents' house, the familiar scent of beef stew and buttered bread filling the air. With their schedules, weekly family meals were a thing of the past but his mother insisted that they still eat together at least twice a month. Their family had grown, but it only added to the fun.

Coming down the hall, his father greeted him with his arms full of little Finn. He tickled his nephew's tummy before walking over to say hello to Pops. Brogan walked out of the kitchen with a beer and handed it to him before settling in next to their grandfather. Thanking him, he headed into the dining room where Gareth was setting up the highchair. Moving to Ginny, who was setting the table, he gave her a quick kiss on the cheek.

"How are you feeling?"

She rolled her eyes, but then smiled and rubbed her

stomach. "I wish everyone would stop asking that. I'm pregnant, not terminal."

Laughing, he put his hands up in surrender and stepped into the kitchen to greet Katelyn and his mom.

Soon, with everyone seated around the table, the conversation was as lively as he had remembered it being his entire life. Laughing and talking was now interrupted with intermittent screams of delight from his nephew, vying for the attention of the crowd, but that just made him smile.

His mom passed him the plate full of bread, and asked, "So, Lia?"

His spoon halted on its way to his mouth as the table went suddenly quiet, all eyes on him. "Lia?"

"Now Aiden, don't play dumb with me. From what I hear you were seen out with her, dining at the Sunset Restaurant, and have now spent the past week at her house every evening."

Looking at his siblings for help, Brogan and Katelyn just stared at him, both fighting a grin. His dad leaned back in his chair, and said, "Don't know how you thought you were going to keep a secret from your mom."

Gareth shot him a sympathetic look, before turning his attention back to his son, and Ginny grinned widely. Finally looking toward Pops, he saw the twinkle in his grandfather's eyes. Sighing, he laid his spoon down and turned toward his mom.

"I wasn't really trying to keep it a secret," he said, shrugging slightly. "We got close after the music festival, when I took her and Emily home. We spent a little time together and I really wanted to take her out, so we went to dinner." Shooting Pops another glance, he admitted, "But I'm afraid my past, somewhat indiscreet, behavior bit me in the…uh…backend. I can't really blame her, but that night she told me she didn't think we should go out again and that we should just be friends."

The expression on his mother's face cut into him, not because she was staring at him with any censure, but because she looked like a mother who hurt for their child. Shaking his head, he said, "Don't feel sorry for me, Mom. I never saw a reason to not enjoy myself however I wanted, so I gave no thought as to how it might look to someone that I really wanted to be with."

"I can see where that would be a tough lesson to learn," she said. Holding his gaze, she asked, "But now? You've been going to her house every evening, right?"

A smile slid across his face as he nodded. "I'm not quite sure what all happened to change her mind, but she invited me to dinner and we had a good time. Then she asked me if I would work with Emily, to teach her how to play baseball. Emily wants to play, but Lia is really nervous because of Emily's hearing impairment. I told her that lots of people with hearing impairments play sports, including baseball, and I'd be honored to work with her."

Pops winked at him, but as he stared at the rest of his family, he was taken aback by their smiles.

His mom spoke first. "Aiden, honey, you've always been someone who enjoys life. That's nothing to be ashamed of."

"You're my mother, you have to say that. But then,"

he added, "I also know you wondered if I was ever settling down."

Grinning, she said, "Well, now that you mention it..."

Brogan looked over, and commented, "Lia's got a six-year-old daughter."

He looked over at his brother, not understanding why Brogan was stating something he obviously knew, and said, "Uh, yeah. I was just talking about her."

"You ready for that?"

"Brogan!" His mom and Ginny said at the same time.

"No, no," he shushed them. "Brogan's right. For the man I've been in the past, this absolutely would give others pause." Facing Brogan, he explained, "I've been doing a lot of soul-searching, figuring out why I've been avoiding any type of entanglement. And the truth is, I've been doing this searching because of Lia. I don't know what the future holds, but if all she's willing to offer me right now is friendship and a chance to coach her daughter, then I'm going to take it."

Brogan held his gaze, and asked, "And if it leads to more?"

He smiled. "Then I'm going to be one lucky man." He picked up his spoon and began to eat again, missing the smiles bouncing around the table between all the members of his family.

Lia rubbed her forehead and sighed. The slight ache that had been threatening since the early morning was now blossoming into a full-blown headache. It had been a few weeks on this case now and it was starting to take its toll. She had spent most of her time in her own office going over the many records that had been sent to her from the town treasurer, but now she sat in a small room in the Municipal Building, facing an irate town manager.

"I can't believe it's taking this long," Silas growled.

"You may not know it, but many investigations take a year to complete," she retorted. "I have set everything else aside and given it to my partner so that I can devote my full-time attention to this one investigation. I am working as fast as I can, while making sure to not make any errors."

"I'm concerned about Town Council members, who might run their mouths to the press before the election."

"That, Mr. Mills, is not my concern. The only thing that is my concern is making sure that I find out where the missing money is and who took it." Looking back down at the files in front of her, she finished, "If that is all, I'll get back to work."

By the way he stalked out of the office, slamming the door behind him, it was obvious he hated being dismissed. Groaning, she battled the urge to throw something at the closed door. Reaching into her purse, she pulled out some Ibuprofen and swallowed it with the last sip of her now-cold cup of tea.

A knock sounded on the door and she pulled herself together. Having asked Sandra for an interview, she expected that's who it was. "Come in, please."

Sandra Toski entered the room, a tight smile on her

face. Sitting in the chair across from her, she placed her forearms on the table, her hands clasped together. She appeared to be in her early forties, simply dressed in a button-up blouse and slacks. Her hair was neatly trimmed in a blonde, chin-level bob.

After greeting her in a friendly, professional manner, she began her interview. "In going over the records, it takes quite a while to check all of the receipts, compare them to the purchase orders, and then compare them to the check that is cut. I just want to double check the procedure as it has been explained to me. All of the department heads send in their purchase orders to you and it is your job to approve them or send them back to the department head to be revised."

Her posture still on guard, Sandra nodded. "Every year I hold a meeting with all of the department heads in town and go over the new rules for getting bids, purchase orders, and any other information they need to have. But, of course, some of them still get things wrong, so if I see that the regulations have not been followed when I receive a purchase order, then it goes back to them along with an explanation of what they need to do to correct it. Those are sent to me electronically, and so is my response, so that I have a record in case there was ever a question."

"Excellent," she said, smiling slightly at Sandra. "In looking at the actual checks, you prepare them and the Mayor signs them, correct?"

"Yes."

"And if he's unavailable?"

Sandra blinked, her brows lowering, a question

crossing her face. "Unavailable? He's never... I don't know what you mean."

"If he's not available to sign the checks at the time that you are ready for him," she explained.

Shaking her head, Sandra replied, "I usually do checks toward the end of the day and take them for him to sign. If he's in a meeting or unavailable, Celia locks them in her desk until he is available. He signs them as soon as he is able and either he or she brings them back to me. If he has a question about one, then he and I discuss it."

"I see. And you have been in this position for quite some time, haven't you?"

"Yes. I've been the elected town treasurer for the last ten years. I take my job seriously and can assure you that I was unaware of any problems until the audit was finished."

"Thank you for your time and I'll let you know if I have further questions."

Sandra stood quickly but hesitated before leaving, as though uncertain she was truly dismissed. She offered her a polite nod before looking back down at her computer and heard Sandra leave the room. She believed that a financial investigation involved peeling the layers back slowly and never giving away more information to an interviewee than she was ready to at the time.

Several minutes later, there was another knock on the door she looked up to see Mark Weber standing there. The young man appeared anxious as she waved him in, having him sit in the same chair that Sandra just left.

"Hi, Ms. Smith. I was told that you wanted to talk to me this afternoon so as soon as I saw Sandra leave, I thought I would jump in."

"It's nice to see you again. What I'm doing today is getting some preliminary information. As I'm sure you know, I have been reviewing the records, but it's helpful for me to hear from people exactly what their particular duties are."

"Okay, gotcha. Well, I guess my job covers a lot of different things. I only have an Associate's Degree in Finance, but hope to be able to go back to school to get my Bachelor's in Accounting. I've been at this job for a year to get some experience."

Nodding, she could not help but smile at his enthusiasm. "What specifically are you in charge of?"

"When I was hired, my job description sounded pretty broad. I'm supposed to help with the Treasurer, when she needs it. I'm also in charge of maintaining the accounting records and reports for payroll and time-keeping. Most of the department heads keep track of their own employees, but then they all have to send their timekeeping and payroll to me. The bookkeeping is pretty basic and I mostly just enter the figures into the computer so that they will be there for the Treasurer."

"Do you ever fulfill any of her duties, if she is not available?"

Eyes wide he swallowed audibly. "Oh no, ma'am," he said with an emphatic shake of his head. "I do exactly what my duties tell me to do and not one thing more. Not that I don't want to be helpful," he rushed, "but I'm not about to do something I shouldn't do."

After a few more questions, she was ready to call it a day and thanked him. Once he left, she continued jotting down a few notes, compiled a few more records, saved everything to her laptop, and shoved all the papers into her briefcase. Glad for the day to be over, she walked out into the lobby of the Municipal Building. Celia and Sandra were standing near the Mayor's door, deep in discussion. Both stopped talking as she walked by and she chose not to look their way as her phone vibrated an incoming text. Stepping outside, she pulled her phone out of her purse and for the first time that day smiled.

Come to town field. We have a surprise.

Aiden and Emily had been practicing in her back-yard for the last several weeks so she was anxious to see what surprise they had for her.

She drove over the train tracks and parked in the lot near the town baseball field. Climbing out of her car, she noted the other vehicles around and was barely able to hear some voices coming from the stands. Mind on her daughter and Aiden, she hurried past the bleachers to the fence where she saw them gathered with several others. A quick glance over her shoulder gave evidence that Tori, Jade, Belle, Jillian, and Ginny were the ones she heard on the bleachers.

Drawing closer, she observed all the coaches. Brogan, Jason, Mitch, Grant, Zac, and Katelyn. Also, Emily's teacher, Jade, was on the field as well.

Her stomach clenched in nerves, but one look at Emily's wide smile and she relaxed. "Hey, baby. What's going on?"

"Mama! We've been practicing and Coach Aiden wanted me to meet with the other coaches. He's teaching me and them how to play."

Catching her daughter's excitement, and also understanding her meaning, she lifted her gaze to Aiden.

"She's getting better with hitting and understands the rules of the game. She'll be playing on our younger team of kids from five to seven years old and should be ready to play with us. But," he shrugged, "the other coaches wanted to make sure they understood the best way to communicate. So, we all decided to come out and have some practices with her."

Heart pounding, she sucked in a quick breath as she twisted in a slow circle seeing everyone who had come out, just for her daughter. As Emily chattered away with Katelyn, Aiden stepped closer to her.

"I can't believe what all you've done for her," she said, her voice shaky, staring up into his blue eyes.

With his hand on her waist, he leaned forward in a gesture that was becoming not only familiar, but so welcome. He kissed her forehead, his lips lingering. "I'd do anything for her," he said. Leaning back, he held her gaze, and added, "I'd do anything for you."

The desire to kiss him was overwhelming but, aware of their audience, she settled for a heartfelt smile.

"Mama, watch me!"

Turning, she gave her full attention to Emily and nodded. The coaches spread out and Katelyn threw a gentle toss toward Emily. She swung and missed the first two, but she was so proud that she did not get frustrated. On the next pitch, Emily hit the ball toward third base. She ran to first base, where Jason was waiting, giving her a simple hand signal to stop on-base. He then bent and talked to her once she was safely there.

Aiden batted next, sending a ball toward first base, but Jason had already given Emily the signal to run to second, where she was met with Mitch. Once again, using simple hand signals and making sure she could see his face, she halted. They continued this until she ran to home plate, where she met her with open arms and the cheers from the bleachers met their ears.

Thanking everyone, she offered hugs as Emily ran around and high-fived all of her coaches. As the gathering dispersed, Aiden walked her and Emily back to her car. As his hand lightly rested on her back, there was a familiar tingle that she felt every time he touched her.

As Emily climbed into the back seat and buckled in, she turned and smiled to him. "Coming to dinner?"

He chuckled, and said, "I've been to dinner every night for the past two weeks. Are you sure you're not getting sick of me yet?"

She shook her head and rested her hands on his chest, her palms feeling his heartbeat. Tipping her head back to stare into his face, she said, "No. It's hard to think of anything without you now."

His smile curved his lips, transforming his already handsome face into one that was breathtaking.

"Nowhere I'd rather be. Tell you what, I'll grab a pizza on the way."

Driving home with the sounds of Emily chattering in the back seat and the thought of Aiden bringing pizza to her house, the cares of the day floated away. Knowing that life held no guarantees, and this happiness might not last forever, she was ready to accept it, for whatever it was, for as long as she could have it.

As soon as Lia and Emily got to their house, she sent Emily upstairs for a bath, knowing they had a little bit of time before Aiden returned with the pizza. Once Emily was splashing happily in the bathtub and her hair was washed, she ran into her own bedroom to change. Stripping off her work clothes, she ran to her dresser and stood, trying to figure out what to put on. It had been a long time since she had worn anything to capture a man's attention. *Well, other than the date we had a few weeks ago where I let my insecurities get the better of me.*

"Okay, okay, I can do this. It's not a big deal," she muttered out loud. Grabbing a pair of black yoga pants that she hoped did not make her ass look too big, she searched her closet for an appropriate shirt. *Not too tight, not too baggy, not boring...*

"Mama!"

Hearing Emily call out that she was ready to get out

of the bathtub, she jerked a light blue, stretchy knit top off the hanger and pulled it over her head quickly, letting the soft material settle over her hips. It might not have been her best choice, but she was in a hurry.

Running across the hall she darted into the bathroom and grabbed a towel just as Emily was climbing from the tub. As the water drained and Emily toweled off, she helped her to her room so that she could get into her pajamas.

Looking at her daughter, she said, "I need to finish getting ready and then I'll be downstairs."

Emily grinned widely and nodded. Just as she was about to leave her room, Emily called out, "Mama!"

Turning, she cocked her head to the side.

"I like Mr. Aiden," Emily said, staring up at her. "I like him a lot. Do you?"

She heard the wistful tone in her daughter's voice and walked back over, kneeling in front of her. Placing her hands on Emily's thin shoulders, she said, "Yes, baby, I do."

"I like having him around. He makes me laugh." Emily's large eyes stared up at her, and her breath caught in her throat as her daughter continued. "I like the way he makes you laugh, too."

Her breath left her lungs in a rush as she stared at her daughter's hopeful face. It was like looking in a mirror. Nodding slowly, she said, "I do too."

Emily dropped her eyes to the floor as she fiddled with the towel still wrapped around her body. She lifted her daughter's chin with her fingers so that she could stare into her eyes and asked, "What are you thinking?"

"I think that he would make a good dad."

Tears stung her eyes as she realized how much her daughter had been thinking of this. She knew that Emily only had the barest memories of Carl, born from looking at photographs instead of actual remembrances. Hating that her daughter wanted something that might be out of her reach, she thought carefully on how to explain it to her. "I'm not sure that will ever happen. I know he likes being our friend. And you can never have too many friends. So, maybe we have to be satisfied with Aiden being our friend."

She watched the wheels turning in her daughter's head, when they were suddenly interrupted by the sound of the doorbell. "He's here, Emily. Run and go get dressed and I'll let him in."

Emily's face broke into a wide smile and she emitted a little scream as she darted into her room to get dressed. Moving to shut the light off in the bathroom, she caught a glance of herself in the mirror. She had wanted to freshen her makeup and run a brush to her hair, but there was no time. Jogging down the stairs, she called out, "Coming!"

Throwing open the door, her smile widened as she saw Aiden standing on the stoop, his hands full of two large pizza boxes, a plastic bag containing whatever else he decided to grab, and a two-liter bottle of soda.

"Good grief," she called out, reaching out to grab the bag.

He came in, a sheepish look on his face, and said, "They were having a special. For the price of two pizzas, I also got a container of salad, which I figured would be good for Emily so that she could have her green vegetables. They also had breadsticks, which I figured would be good to have with a meal another day. And the special included the soda, which I know you don't want Emily to drink tonight since it has caffeine in it, but maybe she could have some tomorrow."

She stared, amazed not only that he bought the special, but that he had given consideration to Emily's needs while doing so. Before she had a chance to thank him, he held up another small bag.

"And, they also had homemade cookies for dessert." His boyish face scrunched in concern when he added, "Well, I suppose they're not homemade since they were made in a restaurant. But their sign said they were made from scratch, so that's kind of like homemade, right?"

She giggled. "You're such a goof." Shrugging, she added, "But a lovable goof. Come on back. Emily will be right down."

She turned to lead the way to the kitchen, but his hand reached out and grabbed her shoulder. Turning around, she was mesmerized by the look in his blue eyes as he drew her closer.

"Just want to say that you're beautiful tonight," he said, his eyes never wavering from hers.

Her mouth opened slightly as she melted, moving closer to him. "I… I wanted to freshen up more before you came, but…uh… Emily needed help with her bath…"

He leaned down and kissed her lightly on the lips.

Murmuring against her soft skin, he said, "I think you're perfect, just the way you are."

With their faces barely apart, they stared into each other's eyes. Doubts, concerns, fears, insecurities all fell away. Her heart raced and she could not remember the last time she felt such a rush of desire.

"Mr. Aiden!" Emily called as she raced down the stairs.

He grinned widely, winking at her before moving over to greet her freshly scrubbed little girl. Shaking herself out of her stupor, she hurried into the small kitchen and called out, "Let's eat!"

The meal was fun, laughter abounding as they talked about baseball and Aiden shared antics from when he was young. As he described the Baytown Boys, she could see that Emily was not only interested, but a little wistful. Emily was starting to make friends in Baytown and she hoped this would continue now that she had decided Baytown was where she wanted her daughter to grow up.

Soon, the salad was consumed, the pizza was decimated, and the homemade cookies with milk had completed the meal. Emily usually begged to stay up a little later, but tonight she was tired. Her eyes were starting to close even sitting at the table.

"Can Mr. Aiden tuck me in?" Emily asked sleepily, her words interrupted by a large yawn.

She hesitated, not sure how Aiden would feel about that request, but before she had a chance to speak, he stood and scooped Emily up in his arms. With a wink at her, he stepped to the bottom of the stairs.

Jerking out of her stupor, she called out, "Brush your teeth!"

"We got it," Aiden called back.

She hurried to clear the table and put the leftovers in plastic containers, shoving them into the refrigerator. Giving the counter a final swipe with a wet sponge before tossing it into the sink, she raced around the bottom of the stair rail and took the stairs two at a time. Stopping for a second to catch her breath so it did not look like she had been running, she heard voices coming from Emily's room.

"I like the taste of toothpaste, don't you?"

"I don't know, I guess I never thought about it," Aiden replied.

"At the dentist, sometimes they use stuff that tastes like bubblegum. Or it's supposed to taste like bubblegum, but I think it's yucky. I like the minty stuff Mama buys."

She stuck her head around the corner and peered into Emily's room. Emily had crawled under her covers with her favorite doll and favorite stuffed animal on either side. Aiden was kneeling on the floor by her bed, pulling the covers up. Emily yawned widely again.

"You did really good today," Aiden said. "You should be proud of yourself."

She watched as Emily held Aiden's gaze and a nervous expression crossed her daughter's face. "But what if I don't do so good when I play with everybody else?"

"Sweetheart, I've struck out lots of times. I've fouled out lots of times. Nobody hits the ball every time they're at bat, so it's fine if you miss. It should always be about having fun and trying your best, no matter what happens. I just think you're amazing for trying."

She blinked as tears filled her eyes, lifting her fingers to press against her lips to keep the sob from bursting forth. Emily yawned once again and smiled up at Aiden.

"Sleep tight, little darlin'," he said softly, bending over to kiss Emily's forehead. "I'll send your mom in to say good night—"

"I'm here," she said, walking into the room. Bending over, she held her daughters gaze as she said, "I love you."

"I love you too, Mama."

With a final kiss goodnight, she stood and followed Aiden out of Emily's room, flipping the light off as she left.

They walked silently down the stairs, but as soon as they entered the living room, Aiden turned to face her. He immediately reached out, snagging her waist and pulling her close. She went willingly, her hands reaching up to clutch his shoulders.

She stared up at his face, seeing longing mixed with uncertainty. She wanted to give into the first and wipe away the second. Lifting on her toes, she moved closer, feeling his arms band tightly around her waist.

"I want to kiss you more than anything else, but I want to do the right thing, here," he said, his gaze searching hers.

"Then kiss me," she said, her words sure and steady.

Without hesitation, his lips met hers, scorching in the intensity of her overwhelming desire. One of his arms still held tightly to her waist, pulling her against his body, while the other slid up her back, pulling the clip from her hair. As it tumbled over her shoulders, he clutched the back of her head, his fingers tangled in the tresses. Angling her head, he slid his tongue through her lips, delving into the warmth of her mouth.

Stepping backward, pulling her with him, he moved until the back of his legs hit the sofa. With his arms banded tight around her, he tumbled them down so she lay atop him, keeping his lips on hers. The feel of him, the taste of him, the sensations rocking through her…all combined into a lust-filled flame. She felt as though she had been holding back forever and now the dam had broken.

Aiden sensed the change in Lia as her body yielded, her soft curves aligning with his hard planes. He slid one hand down to cup her ass, kneading the soft flesh as he pressed her closer to his erection.

Forcing his mind to stay on her pleasure, he slid his hand up over her hip, past the dip in her waist, and up her back, finally cupping her face. Taking the kiss deeper, he swallowed her moan as he plundered her mouth. His thumb swept over the soft, apple of her cheek and focused on the delectable taste of her tongue tangling with his.

She groaned and spread her legs so that her core was pressed against his upper thigh. She ground herself against the coarse material of his jeans, seeking all the friction she could gain.

Moving his hand from her face, downward, he felt her pulse beating wildly at the base of her neck. Skimming his palm over her breast he slid his hand further down until he was able to sneak it under the bottom of her shirt. He tried to tell himself he just wanted to touch her bare skin but he knew that was a lie. The instant his fingers touched her warm, silky skin, they slid upward to just underneath her breasts.

His cock was painfully aware of how close her core was as she continued to press on his upper thigh. Ignoring the desire to rip her yoga pants down her legs and take her on the sofa, he reigned in his desire, wanting this to be about her...all her. He could not remember the last time he was determined to give everything he had to a woman's pleasure, without any thought to his own, but this was the gift he wanted to give Lia. Only Lia.

With that in mind, he shifted her slightly so that his hand was able to skim up over her lace covered breasts, filling his palms.

Lia groaned, the electricity jolting from her nipples to her core causing her to grind harder against Aiden's thigh. She had not had sex since Carl and considering that he had been away for much of their marriage, it had been almost four years since she had been with a man. For a brief second, she wondered if she should be afraid, or hesitant, or even filled with doubt. But, remembering who she was with, she was never more sure of anything in her life. She wanted to be with him.

Leaning back slightly to see his face, she instantly missed the feel of his lips on hers. Meeting her gaze, his hand stilled on her breast. Seeing the question in his eyes, she smiled. "I want this. I want you," she whispered. She turned her head toward the stairs and sighed. "Emily. We have to be quiet...and careful, in case she wakes up."

"We can stop," he said immediately. "I don't want you to feel awkward and I certainly don't want Emily to be upset."

She settled her gaze back on his face and her heart melted that he cared so much about her and her daughter that he would halt what they had begun.

"If we're quiet, I can hear her, although she sleeps so soundly every night."

His lips curved in a smile that matched her own and his fingers gently slid the cups of her bra down, exposing her rosy-tipped nipples. He shifted her again, this time allowing him to kiss his way down to her breasts, his mouth latching onto one aching nipple. He sucked deeply, tugging and pulling, causing her to groan once again.

She clung to his hair, holding him to her breast as he slid his fingers down to the front of her pants, slipping them underneath the waistband. Dragging them through her wet folds, she had to stifle her cry of pleasure, not wanting to wake Emily.

Aiden plunged his fingers inside Lia's sex while continuing to suck her breasts, moving from one nipple to the other. He concentrated on the amazing way her body was responding to his touch and, like tinder to a flame, she quickly blazed hot for him.

Pushing her hips up toward his hand, she urged him to continue. His fingers scissored inside as his thumb pressed gentle circles on her clit.

"Yes, please," she begged.

"Come on, baby," he encouraged, feeling her inner core tightening on his fingers.

She jolted, rearing back as her orgasm rushed through her, sparks flying outward from her core in all directions.

"That's it," he said, mumbling against her breasts. Sliding his head backward he peered into her face, loving her closed-eyed expression of bliss. "Ride it out, baby," he encouraged.

Lia continued to thrust her pelvis against Aiden's fingers until the last of the tremors subsided and she settled her body heavily on top of his. After a moment of her entire body feeling blissfully weightless, her eyes fluttered open met his, staring straight into hers.

Grinning widely, he slipped his fingers from her wetness and brought them up to his mouth, sucking deeply. She had thought in the early days of her marriage that she and Carl had had a healthy sex life, but she had never witnessed a man take such pleasure in simply giving her pleasure.

The sight of Aiden sucking her juices off his fingers had her mesmerized. He had just given her the best orgasm she had had in her life and had not even gotten off himself. The idea of what he could do when they actually had sex had her anticipation heightening, wondering if it would be possible to die of an orgasmic overload.

Aiden watched the play of emotions cross Lia's face before settling into a smile. His heart warmed and he leaned up, kissing her gently while allowing her to taste her essence on his tongue.

After several minutes he pulled back, lifting his hand to tuck wayward strands of hair behind her ear. "You okay?"

Her smile widened, and she said, "Oh, yeah. I'm not sure I've ever been so okay."

Kissing her lightly once more, he shifted them upward, gently pulling her bra and shirt back into place. Seeing the surprised expression on her face as her eyes dropped to his crotch, widening at the sight, he laughed. "This needed to be all about you."

"But…what about you? You didn't…uh…get off."

"That'll come, sweetheart, when you're ready. When we're both ready. But I want the time to be right for everything we do, and tonight, I just wanted you to feel pleasure. And believe me, it was great for me too."

He watched as she bit her lip, her brows lowered in thought. "Tell me what you're thinking, Lia. I never want to just assume and then make the wrong assumption." He had her settled in his lap, his arms banded about her, holding her close.

"I never meant for this to be all about me," she said, her hand cupping his jaw. She rubbed her thumb along his rough stubble and held his gaze. Though she blushed, she pressed on with what she wanted to say. "It's been a really long time for me. I haven't been with anyone since Carl and, quite frankly, he was overseas a lot of our marriage. So much of my focus over the last few years has been on Emily…I was beginning to wonder if I had become un-sexual, if that's even a word."

He chuckled, staring into her beautiful face. "Babe, you came alive at just the touch of my fingers. You flamed brighter than anything I've ever seen just from our kisses. Believe me, there is nothing un-sexual about you."

Her lips curved slightly. "For a while, Aiden, I was scared. Scared of feeling things for you that would not be reciprocated. Scared of feeling things that I thought you might be incapable of feeling for me. Scared of taking a chance on something, and now that I'm a mom, knowing that I can't just think about myself."

"And now? Are you still scared?"

She stared into his blue eyes, seeing concern, but not fear. She shook her head slowly and her lips curved into a gentle smile. "I learned after Emily was born that we cannot always plan our lives perfectly. And learned after Carl's leaving, and then his death, that I don't want to just sit on the sidelines. I'm ready to take a chance again and I want to take that chance with you."

Her words snaked through him, warming him from the deepest part of his soul. He moved in, his lips touching hers, this time not in lust but as a promise.

"I want you, Lia," he said. "I want both you and Emily. And I'll do everything in my power, if you place your trust in me, to be the kind of man you both deserve."

She pulled him in close, holding his cheek upon her chest, as their arms wrapped tightly around each other.

After a moment, he said, "I can feel your heartbeat against my face."

She did not hesitate to confess, "When I was unsure that Emily was able to hear me tell her that I loved her, I would place her so that her cheek was right next to my heartbeat. I always wanted her to feel it even if she couldn't hear it. She still does that, even now, and I always tell her she can hear my heart...it's the sound of my love."

He remained silent, unsure if she spoke of love for just her daughter or if, perhaps, it might be for him too. But he quickly determined that, at that moment, it did not matter. Just the sound of her heartbeat against his cheek was all he needed.

18

Lia's phone vibrated on the nightstand, jerking her awake. Rolling over quickly, she grabbed it. The screen showed it was just after two a.m. "Hello?" No answer. "Dammit, who is this?"

The call disconnected just before she was going to hang up, frustrating her even more. Replacing the phone back on her nightstand, she flopped on her back in bed, staring at the ceiling. *Who on earth can this be? Prank callers? Teenagers? Someone who's just trying to piss me off?*

Throwing back the covers, she climbed out of bed and padded into the bathroom. Filling up a glass, she took a long drink of water. Sighing heavily, she lifted her eyes to the mirror, her gaze drifting over the slight razor burn down her neck and visible to the V in her silk pajama top. A grin slid over her face as she thought of Aiden's stubble making the slight abrasions.

Putting the irritating phone call out of her mind, she

flipped off the bathroom light and crawled back into bed. With thoughts of Aiden, and the next step she hoped they would take in their relationship, she grinned as she fell back to sleep.

"How's the investigation going?" Scott asked, standing in Lia's office doorway.

She rolled her eyes, but smiled her greeting as she waved him in. He had shed his suit coat, but she liked the way he always maintained his professional appearance, with a white button-up shirt paired with navy slacks and a light blue tie. His hair was neatly trimmed and brushed to the side. It was easy to imagine him being the elder, dapper Mr. Redding's grandson.

"To answer your question, the investigation is simply...going," she laughed. "While I was with a firm in Virginia Beach, I was used to going into larger companies to do an internal investigation into possible fraud. But here in Baytown, it's so different. Everyone knows everyone else. No one really likes to see a forensic accountant coming, because they know that we're looking to see if someone stole money, and if so, who did it. I'm just used to doing that with a certain amount of anonymity."

He chuckled and nodded. "I remember my grandfather used to complain that, while he was completely professional in keeping everyone's taxes and business accountings confidential, people would come up to him in the middle of a restaurant and start asking questions."

"That's what will be very strange here," she said. "Whatever I find out with the fraud investigation, it will be someone that everyone in town knows. And even though it isn't my fault, often it is the bearer of bad news that takes the blame."

Scott appeared to be lost in thought for a moment before looking up and holding her gaze steadily. "And have you found anything definitive yet?"

"Not definitively, but I do feel like I'm heading in the right direction."

"You know, no matter what, the Mayor will want things kept as quiet as possible."

Shrugging, she said, "It's not my say what happens. I simply turn over my findings to the district attorney whenever I'm ready. How the Town Council and Mayor want to handle that is on them."

Standing, he nodded and walked toward the door. "Good luck with everything, partner," he called out.

She stared at the doorway for a moment after he left, not sure what to make of that last comment, before her phone vibrating caused her gaze to jerk back to her desk. She had three calls already where no one answered. Gritting her teeth, she grabbed it up, and said, "Just stop. Just stop calling!"

"Babe?"

"Oh, sorry. Sorry," she babbled.

"What the fuck is going on? What's wrong?" Aiden demanded, his voice laced with concern.

She rubbed her forehead and sighed. "I'm just

getting stupid prank, hang up phone calls that have gotten on my last nerve. I had one in the middle of the night that woke me up and two so far today. I didn't even look to see who was calling when I bit your head off."

"How long has this been going on?"

"For the last week, but I just—"

He shouted, "For the past week? You've been getting hang-up phone calls for a week and haven't said anything to me?"

Each word grew louder until she had to hold the phone slightly away from her ear. "It's just prank calls, Aiden."

"How do you know that?"

"What else could it be? It's not like anybody is making any demands or asking anything of me. Nobody's threatening me. Nobody's breathing deeply into the phone. They're just irritating the hell out of me." By now her voice had risen as well, and she sucked in a deep breath before letting it out slowly in an attempt stay calm.

"Babe, I'm coming over," he stated emphatically.

"Aiden, there's no sense in—"

"I'm coming."

He disconnected and she stared at her phone for a minute, shaking her head. Part of her wanted to be irritated at his high-handedness, but the other part felt it was nice to have someone who cared. Looking back down at her files, she figured she would get a little bit more work done before he came.

Fifteen minutes later, Mrs. Markham appeared at

her door. "Ms. Smith? You have a visitor. It's Police Chief Evans."

"Mitch?"

Mrs. Markham turned to the side, allowing Mitch to step into her office. "Shall I bring coffee?"

Mitch turned and shook his head toward her efficient secretary, and said, "No, thank you. Not on my account."

She stood and offered him a chair, but before she was able to ask why he was there, Aiden came bursting in. Mrs. Markham was behind him, fluttering her hands, but she just nodded that it was all right.

"Good, Mitch. I'm glad you got here," Aiden said, before walking over to her, placing his hand on her waist lightly and bending to kiss her cheek.

Staring up at him, eyes wide, she asked, "Aiden, what on earth have you done?"

"Taking care of you, sweetheart," he said, his voice softer now that his arm was around her.

She blinked, then her eyes darted to Mitch. "I don't know that anything's going on, other than I'm getting prank calls. I'm sorry, Mitch. I don't think this needs to involve the police."

"I'd rather be safe than sorry, Lia," Mitch replied. "Tell me about the calls."

She huffed slightly, then winced, knowing he was only doing his job. "They started over a week ago. No number comes up on my caller ID, it just says *unknown*. There's no heavy breathing," she said with a slight grin, "so I don't think it's a pervert. I can tell the line is open, but no one says anything. The first couple of times it happened, I assumed that someone perhaps had the wrong number. But it's been happening every day, and now has increased to several times a day, including waking me up in the middle of the night."

"Have you ever had anything like this happen before?"

She shook her head, replying, "No. Never."

"I know you do forensic accounting investigations and used to work for a large firm in Virginia Beach. Did you ever have any problems with anyone with that?"

Her forehead crinkled for just a moment, before her eyes shot up toward Aiden and she said, "Uh…"

His brows snapped down and he barked, "Uh? What the fuck do you mean by *uh*?"

She looked back toward Mitch and said, "I have had to testify in the trials of some of the people I investigated. White-collar crime…not like murderers. But, I did have one who was very threatening as he was led from the courtroom in handcuffs. He kept claiming that he did nothing wrong and he was going to get me. The evidence was overwhelming and, unfortunately, with many white-collar criminals, they make many excuses. In his case he felt entitled…he even admitted that lots of rich people are crooks so why shouldn't he be able to get a piece of the pie."

Mitch pulled out a small pad and began taking notes. "Is this man still in jail?"

Jerking slightly, she said, "I have no idea. Quite frankly, after the trial, I forgot all about him until just now."

"Give me his information and I'll check on him."

194

"Tad Marvel." Seeing Aiden's eyes widen in surprise, she offered a slight shrug. "It takes months or even over a year to investigate forensic crimes. Believe me, by the time we have enough evidence for a district attorney to take the case and for it to go to trial, I remember their name very well."

"Is there anything unusual that's happened since you've been here in Baytown?" Mitch asked.

Shaking her head, she said, "No. I've just been doing regular accounting work and now have a forensic case I'm working on for the town, but that's all."

Scott stepped to the doorway, his eyes staring down at a file, and startled as his gaze lifted to see the Police Chief. "Oh, excuse me. I didn't realize you had someone in here."

"No, no. That's okay," she said. "Scott, I know you've met my...uh—"

"Boyfriend," Aiden supplied, his gaze pinned on Scott.

"Yes, nice to see you again."

Shooting Aiden a glare, she continued, "And this is Baytown's Police Chief, Mitch Evans. Mitch, this is my new accounting partner, Scott Redding."

Mitch stood and extended his hand. "Redding?"

Scott grinned and nodded. "Yes, my grandfather, Thomas Redding, was the original owner of this business. I'm glad that Lia is the one who hired me, or everyone would think nepotism was alive and well in Baytown."

Mitch barked out a laugh, and said, "Don't worry about accusations of nepotism. My father was the Police

Chief for many years until his health forced him to retire. And before him, my grandfather was the Police Chief."

Everyone chuckled and she was glad for the release of tension. Feeling the need to explain why Mitch was there, she said, "Scott, I'm talking to Mitch because I've been getting lots of prank, hang-up phone calls. I don't think it's anything other than just probably kids or teenagers, but he's taking notes anyway."

Scott expressed concern before excusing himself from the room, saying, "I've got a few questions on this one account, but we can easily talk later."

Mitch turned his attention back to her, and said, "I'd like to take your phone with me if you can do without it for a couple of hours. We can see what we pull up on it and, with your phone records, do a little digging."

Aiden walked over and placed his hand around her shoulders, pulling her in tightly. Lifting his eyes to Mitch, he asked, "Is there anything else she should be doing?"

Shaking his head, Mitch said, "Unfortunately, no. While it's annoying, no crime has been committed at this time, but we want to be vigilant in case whoever this person is steps up and actually makes a threat. I would just be extremely aware of your surroundings and what's going on."

Unease snaked through her at the thought that the phone calls could be more than just kids. Nodding, she offered a shaky smile toward Mitch as she stood and shook his hand. Handing him her phone, she asked, "Do you know how long you might need it?"

"It shouldn't be too long. I'll get it back to you by tomorrow. Will that be okay?"

She agreed and watched as Aiden walked Mitch out of her office, wondering what they were talking about. As soon as Aiden returned, she opened her mouth, but he jumped in first.

"Don't even start, babe," he said. "I know you think it's nothing, but I'm not willing to take a chance on your or Emily's safety."

At those words, her mouth snapped closed. She had not considered that there might be a threat toward her and certainly not toward her daughter. She nodded slowly, staring up into his face, which mirrored hers in concern. He stalked toward her and pulled her into his body, kissing her forehead.

"I've got you. I've got Emily. And believe me, nothing's going to get to either one of you."

The unease that had moved through her body was now replaced with the warmth of caring. Having handled her life on her own for so long she was surprised to not chafe at the idea of someone else stepping in to help. It did not make her feel weak but, instead, made her feel stronger.

Wrapping her arms around his waist, she held on tight. She felt his heartbeat against her cheek, taking comfort in the sound.

19

Aiden met Mitch outside of Harrison Investigations. Pushing open the door, they walked in together and immediately observed Katelyn coming from one of the back rooms.

"Hey, guys," she greeted. She stared for a few seconds and then tilted her head slightly to the side, asking, "What brings y'all by?"

"Need some help, sis," he said. "Help for Lia."

Gareth walked to the lobby from the back and greeted them as well. Before he could say anything, Katelyn turned to her husband, and said, "Something's going on with Lia."

Immediately Gareth's sharp gaze jumped first to him and then to Mitch. "Come on back," he said, turning and leading them to the conference room. He had been in business as a Private Investigator for a couple of years, hiring Katelyn to be his receptionist. As she became more interested in the business, she earned her PI license as well. Once they were married, they became partners.

The four of them settled quickly around the table and Mitch pulled out Lia's phone.

"She's been getting a lot of calls where no one says anything. She says that she can tell the line is open, but does not hear anyone breathing, nor is anyone making a threat. But it's happening more and more, and it's beginning to unnerve her."

Gareth asked, "Something to do with her business?"

"That's what I wondered, as well," Mitch replied. "She's given us the name of a man she previously testified against when she lived in Virginia Beach and I've got Grant checking to see what the status of his incarceration is."

Gareth reached for her phone, and asked, "This for me to look at?"

"Yeah. I was going to have Bert look at it since he's my best tech officer, but he's not on duty today and I don't want to wait. I also know you've got some fancier toys."

A smile slipped across Gareth's face, and he said, "I'll get right on it. As soon as I have anything, I'll let you know."

Mitch stood and clapped Aiden on the back of the shoulder. "Don't worry, man. I let the rest of my officers know and we'll keep an eye on Lia."

He nodded, then jerked his head up. "We need to let Colt know as well, because she doesn't live in the town of Baytown. She lives just outside the city limits, in North Heron County."

"You got it," Mitch said. "I'll head back right now and call Colt."

Gareth walked Mitch out, leaving Katelyn and him still in the conference room. She did not say anything at first, staring at him for a long time. Finally, moving into him, she wrapped her arms around him and hugged him tightly.

"I can tell you're upset. I know how much she and Emily mean to you."

"It's crazy, sis," he said, holding her tightly as well. "The instant she told me about the calls, I felt cold running through my blood. And then the next thing I knew, I felt boiling rage that anyone might mess with her."

Katelyn lifted her head, her dark hair falling way down her back as she peered up into his eyes, so like hers. "That's when you know it's love, Aiden."

He was silent for a moment and she ventured another question. "Does that scare you?"

He shook his head slowly, and said, "I know you might not believe this, but no, it doesn't." With a final hug, he let her go and walked out of the office, deciding to swing by the Police Station to see what they were finding out about Tad Marvel.

When he reached the station, Ginny greeted him and motioned for him to follow her. They went back to Mitch's office and sat, waiting for him to get off the phone.

"What have you got?" he asked, as soon as Mitch hung up.

"Found out Tad Marvel has served his time and was

released last month. I just got off the phone with his probation officer who says he makes all of his meetings, is employed in a trade, and hasn't given him any reason to think that he would be involved. I let him know what was going on with Lia and he said he would be on the lookout."

Ginny commented, "I don't know, it doesn't sound right to me." His eyes jerked toward her and she continued. "Hang up phone calls don't sound like a man's type of revenge."

"We don't know what kind of man he is," he said. "Maybe he's just the kind of man that likes to dick around with a woman."

Mitch nodded. "Let's see what Gareth comes up with looking at her phone. The probation officer has my information and promised he would call as he checks into Tad, but I don't want us to focus just on this man. She's had other people that she has investigated before and that's not even including what she's doing right now."

"This sucks," he said, slumping down into a chair. "All I want to do is keep her safe, but I don't even know which direction a threat might be coming from."

Ginny and Mitch shared a glance, before she said, "Yeah, welcome to love, buddy."

"Jesus, that's what Katelyn said."

Mitch cautioned, "Keep in mind, it might not be anything. It could be just what she assumed, somebody playing a prank. But stay vigilant and I'll let you know as soon as we find out anything."

With a nod, he stood and headed back outside.

Pulling out his phone, he called the accounting office. When Mrs. Markham connected him to Lia, he requested, "Hey, sweetheart. Until we know what's going on, I'd like to be with you and Emily. I've got an American Legion meeting tonight, but I'll be over just as soon as it's finished."

"Actually, Emily is spending the night with a friend. I'm really excited for her, but kind of nervous."

"Lia, I think that's great," he enthused. "That means she's meeting new friends, which I know you wanted her to do and is really good for her."

"I think so too," she agreed. "How about I come to the Pub after work to meet you when you get there after the meeting?"

"Babe, I can't think of anything I'd like better."

Aiden watched as Grant, the Commander of the American Legion chapter, rapped the gavel on the podium, calling the meeting to order. Ginny closed the doors and she and Brogan walked toward the front, the flagpole in his hand. Once the chaplain had offered the prayer, Grant called for the POW/MIA Empty Chair Ceremony. After having talked with Charles, his mind cast back to the young man that he had sat with as he died. Even though that young Marine was not a prisoner of war nor missing in action, the ceremony still struck him in a different way than it ever had before.

He found himself whispering, "I promise to live life

to the fullest," and for the first time, that meant something different than it ever had before.

After several committees gave their reports, Grant turned the podium over to any of the members who wished to speak. Often, one of the older members would speak about their time in the service. It was a tradition that Mitch had started when he was the Commander, to give the members a chance to get to know each other and often unburden themselves. He was a strong believer that the American Legion was more than just waving a flag. That the meetings should be a time that the members could lean on each other.

No one moved to stand and, much to his surprise, he found himself on his feet. Ignoring the incredulous looks from Brogan and his friends, he moved to the front and turned to face the gathering.

"I recently discovered something about myself. I'd never really connected it to anything from my time in the service but, with the help of one of the counselors at the Mental Health Group, I've been able to put some pieces together. I have listened, in awe, as many of you have talked about your traumatic experiences in the military. But for me, I looked at myself as incredibly lucky. I was not involved in anything that was devastating, I did not lose any close friends, and I came back home to my family. But since then, I've been living for several years always looking to have fun.

"I won't go into all the details, but I did have an experience where I sat with a young Marine, that I did not know, as he was being treated by the medics. We had come across an accident involving his transport vehicle and he was severely injured. So, I sat near his head and we talked about life. Girls we'd like to be with. Music we like to listen to. Things we wanted to do when we got home. It wasn't until the sound of the medivac helicopter about to land that I discovered that he was near death and there was nothing that the medics could do but try to ease his pain.

"He must have known the end was near, because he asked me to promise that when I got home I would live life to the fullest and do all the things we had just talked about. It never dawned on me how my actions when I got home a year later were intrinsically tied to what I had promised. I tried to be a good man, a good son, a good brother. But I was truly living mostly for me, having fun wherever I could.

"But I now know that I was living an empty life. Always chasing something that I thought would make me happy, but in truth, did not. I've now met someone that I care a great deal about and have finally figured out that living life to the fullest isn't about chasing momentary happiness. It's about finding someone that you can connect with and wanting to be the best person you can be for them."

Not sure how to end his speech, he blushed and ducked his head. "Guess that's all."

Grant pulled him into a hug with a back slap before allowing him to head back to his seat. Along the way, most of his friends did the same. Finally, as he moved into the row of chairs occupied by Pops, his dad, and Brogan. Taking them in, he stopped, seeing tears in each of their eyes.

Shaking his head, he gave them one of his typical grins, but accepted their hugs as well. Glad that the meeting was soon going to be over, he could not wait to get to the Pub, knowing Lia was going to be there for him.

Lia threw open the red door to Finn's Pub and walked through, quickly seeing the Friday night crowd. She waved toward some of her friends and made her way to their table. She had heard that many of the legionnaires came to Finn's after a meeting, just like many of the auxiliary members did after their meetings.

It was exciting to know so many people in town already. Katelyn brought over some appetizers while Corrine held little Finn. Nancy and Claire Evans were sitting at the tables also, Nancy with Eddie on her lap. Belle, Jade, Madeline, Jillian, and Tori rounded out the group.

Katelyn slid next to her and said, "Mitch and Aiden came to talk to Gareth. I'm so sorry you're getting those calls."

"I still think it's just a prank," she said. "It's annoying, but I'm not afraid."

"Well, just so you know, Gareth is working on your phone. I haven't done that kind of work before, so he's teaching me as we go. We'll have your phone back to you tomorrow."

"No problem. Since Emily is at a sleepover tonight, Aiden gave me his in case of an emergency or something." Smiling her thanks, she turned her attention to the others as they caught up on each other's lives.

Glancing over to the side, she observed Celia and Sandra at the bar, their heads bent together as they chatted. It was something that normally she would never think about, since both women worked in the Municipal Building together, but after having been there interviewing them, she could not help but take note. Her attention soon went back to the conversations at her table.

Corrine handed little Finn to Katelyn and moved to her side. Leaning over, she whispered, "I hope I don't sound like an over eager mother, but I just want to say that I'm so pleased that you and Aiden are seeing each other."

She smiled widely, her heart warm at the acceptance. "That's really nice of you to say. We're still so new, but… well, that means a lot to me."

Corrine's smile slipped as she stared over her shoulder. "I think you're wanted."

Swinging her head around, she noticed that Sandra was standing nearby, her eyes imploring. Excusing herself, she slid from the booth and walked over to her. She glanced toward the bar and noticed that Celia was no longer sitting there.

Sandra, her eyes nervously darting around, whispered, "I don't know what's happening, but I feel like I should warn you. Please, just be careful."

Eyes narrowing, she tilted her head slightly to the side trying to discern her meaning. "I'm sorry?"

Sucking in her lips, Sandra stepped back slightly. "Honestly, I don't know anything for sure. I just…"

"Did Celia say something? Is this coming from her?"

Shaking her head, Sandra said, "No. Not really. Nothing definitive. There was just an inference."

"Inference?"

Sandra shook her head again, her eyes darting to the side once more. "I just get the feeling that there are some who would rather you not find out anything."

Before she had a chance to respond, Sandra turned and quickly pushed her way through the crowd and out the door. She stood for a moment, lost in thought, wondering what Sandra meant and what Celia may have said to her. Sighing, she knew it was not the first time that she was upsetting people with an investigation. *No one likes having their work checked, even if they are innocent of any wrongdoing, but especially not if they are committing fraud.*

Turning back toward her friends, she heard the sound of a group entering the Pub. Twisting around, she grinned at the sight of Aiden leading the pack. He walked straight to her without hesitation and wrapped his arms around her tightly, publicly claiming her for anyone to see.

She slid her arms around his waist and held on tight, the two of them letting the rest of the noise in the crowd fade away. At that moment, with her daughter happily playing at a friend's house and the man she was falling for in her arms, she could not remember ever being happier.

He smiled as he looked down, her eyes shining and

her smile wide. He ran his nose along hers and whispered in her ear. "What's got that sweet look on your face?"

"Let's get out of here," she said, her voice raspy with need.

His smile matched hers and his blue eyes twinkled. "Oh, baby, I'll take you anywhere you want to go."

With a wave toward their friends, they walked out of the pub together.

2 0

Aiden escorted Lia to her front door, his fingers shaking slightly where they splayed on her lower back. He wondered if it was just him, but as she placed the key into the door, her hands were shaking as well. They entered her house and he was struck with uncertainty, an emotion he rarely felt.

A flash of his previous habits flew through his mind. Entering a woman's hotel room always meant wondering what preliminaries he needed to go through to get her into bed because the act of fucking was the only reason he was with them. Some fun. Some laughs. But essentially…just to get off. And then he was out of there, having no desire to learn more about them or small talk and sure as hell not to stay for breakfast the next day.

But as he and Lia entered her living room and she dropped her purse to the table by the sofa and turned toward him, her own nervousness sent a fierce wave of

MARYANN JORDAN

protectiveness through him. He wanted to comfort her.
Care for her. Hold her. But, suddenly full of self-doubt,
his hands stayed rooted to his sides,

Her warm, wide eyes stared up at him and she said,
"I feel like I have no idea what to do next. Isn't that
crazy? I was married, yet everything before you seems
to have just disappeared. And I'm just standing here
wanting you to want me and not having a clue what I
should do."

Her honesty slammed into him and all the faceless
women before her, their coy smiles, flirtatious manners,
winks and seductive talk, flew from his mind. It was as
though they had never been and all that was left for him
was the beautiful woman staring nervously up at him,
opening her heart.

In two steps he was directly in front of her, his
hands placed lightly on her neck with his thumbs up
toward her chin. "Your beauty fills my eyes, but it's who
you are inside that fills my soul. I've never wanted
anything more than this moment, right here, with you.
Tonight, we only do what you want to do, how you
want to do it, when you want to do it. Just the fact that
you're here with me, is enough."

Her lips curved into a soft smile and her hands slid
around his waist. "I feel like I've been waiting for this
moment for a really long time," she confessed. Lifting
on her toes, she met his lips halfway. Skimming her lips
over his, she pressed her body tightly to him, opening
her mouth to allow him to plunder her soft depths.

The kiss, which started slow, quickly flamed white
hot. With his thumbs still on her chin he angled her

head slightly so that he could explore with easier access. His tongue slid between her lips, the touch light to begin with before becoming more demanding. She answered with a groan that he felt down to his cock as their tongues tangled.

He slid one arm over her shoulder down her back, banding her tightly to him. His erection strained painfully as it pressed against her stomach, but he did not want to move too quickly, preferring to savor the taste and feel of her lips instead.

Lowering her heels to the floor, she separated from their kiss and he stared at her reddened lips for a second before moving up and getting lost in her melted-chocolate eyes. He felt her pull away and the cool between their bodies replaced the heat that had just been there. Immediately, she slid her hand to his, linking their fingers. Stepping away, she pulled him along and they walked up the stairs toward the bedroom.

No pretense. No artifice. Just her letting him know exactly what she wanted.

At the top of the stairs, right outside her door, he halted, their hands jerking slightly between them. She turned and looked up at him, a silent question in her eyes. He tugged her back toward him and with his free hand smoothed the wrinkle in her brow.

"We don't have to do anything you don't want to do," he said. "I want this to be all about you."

He watched the smile slide across her face and she replied, "I just want you. All of you." She sucked in her lips for a moment before lifting her eyes again. "I don't know what this will mean to you but, you should know before we go further, it means everything to me."

Again, her honesty filled him. "The gift you're about to give me is the greatest gift I've ever received. I promise to treat it with care and to cherish it."

With a wordless smile she turned and led him into the bedroom. He cast his eyes about the room, seeing an antique white, queen-sized bed, covered in a light blue bedspread, a matching dresser, and a floral-patterned, comfy chair angled near the blue curtained window. Furniture never held any fascination for him, certainly not what was in a bedroom, but as he took in the space, he realized it was so like her. Understated, but classy.

As she squeezed his fingers, his attention focused back on the woman in the room, her smile wrapping around his heart as her eyes captured his gaze. She stepped closer, her lips melding with his once again. He loved the taste, the feel, the sensations that engulfed him whenever they kissed. He allowed her to take charge and she pulled him tighter. After a moment, his patience unexpectedly snapped and he angled his head for maximum contact, plunging his tongue inside her mouth, the slow kiss flaming hot.

His hand, which had been cupping the back of her head, slid down her arm to the bottom of her shirt. He tangled his fingers in the material and lifted slowly, peeling it upward. When it snagged on the underside of her breasts, she lifted her hands above her head, allowing him to remove it completely before tossing it to the floor.

The pale, soft skin of her breasts spilled over the top

of her satin bra and he sucked in a quick breath before trailing kisses from her mouth down toward the beckoning flesh.

Lia's skin felt alive as each touch of Aiden's lips tingled across her nerves, beading her nipples into tight points. As his face disappeared into her cleavage, she reached behind and unfastened her bra. He lifted his head slightly and, with a quick shimmy, the satin dropped away from her. Instantly, he bent to take one nipple into his mouth, sucking deeply. The jolt sent shockwaves throughout her and she dropped her head back, arching her body into his.

She clutched his waist before grabbing the material of his shirt and sliding it upward. As soon as his abs were exposed, her fingers began to explore the dips and ridges of his hard muscles. She loved that his muscles were honed from a combination of lifting boxes at the pub and the sports he enjoyed, while he maintained a slight softness around his waist, belying he liked to eat and drink as well. *A real man.*

He lifted his head from her breasts and, reaching behind him, grabbed his shirt. Jerking it over his head, he threw it and it landed on the floor next to hers. For a moment the two of them stared at each other, naked from the waist up, their bodies so different and, yet, as they moved together, so perfectly aligned.

The feel of her soft flesh pressing into him had his cock straining even harder, but he wanted to do everything he could to make it perfect for her. He found the side zipper to her skirt and lowered it slowly, sliding the clothing over her ass and down to the floor. She held onto his forearms as she stepped out, kicking the skirt to the side.

As his gaze dropped lower, he stared in awe. Her full breasts, with rosy-tipped nipples, beckoned, but the sight of her satin panties and lace-topped thigh-high stockings dropped him to his knees. He grasped her ass cheeks as he buried his face against the soft skin just below her bellybutton. Kissing his way downward, he breathed in the scent of her arousal. Moving lower, his lips met satin and he could feel her heat. Grasping her panties, he slid them down her legs and she clutched his shoulders to steady her body.

When Aiden's lips latched on to her wet folds Lia gasped, her fingers digging into his shoulders. Too soon, he pulled back and she moaned in disappointment, but he just chuckled and stood, shucking his boots, socks, and jeans, managing the feat without stumbling over. Her eyes moved across his muscular chest but the light trail of hair leading down to his boxers caught and snagged her attention. She wanted to run her tongue over each dip and curve but, from the look in his eye, she knew that would have to wait.

He tossed something onto the bed and she turned to see a strip of condoms now lying on the bedspread. *When did he grab those?* At the sound of clothing being removed, she eagerly looked back just in time to see him jerking down his boxers. Her eyes landed on his jutting cock, long and thick and wide, the veins standing out.

He placed his hands on her shoulders and guided her back until her legs hit the bed. With another nudge, she fell backward, her legs dangling off the side while she balanced her weight on her elbows. He dropped to the floor and disappeared between her thighs. As his lips latched over her heat, she flopped backward on the bed unable to maintain a coherent thought.

Aiden feasted on Lia's wet folds, sliding his tongue deep inside her sex. He loved the scent of her, the taste of her, the feel of her. He felt her hips jerking upward and he grinned. He lifted one hand from her thigh and pressed it flat against her abdomen, holding her in place.

He continued to lick, suckle, nip, and plunge his tongue before moving up, latching onto her clit. She stifled a groan, but he was not having that. Lifting his head, he grinned. "You feel it, you let it all out, babe."

Nodding, he continued and she cried out, her fingers digging into his scalp as her orgasm rushed over her. He lapped her juices as the trembling in her body slowed. Kissing his way from her core, over her belly, to her breasts, he latched his lips around her nipple for a moment. Then, crawling over her body, he leaned his head down, kissing her lips so she could taste herself on his mouth.

With the scent of sex lingering in the air, he lowered his hips between her legs after rolling on a condom. Ready, he stared down at her hooded eyes and hesitated.

Her arms lifted from the mattress and up to his shoulders, where she gave a little tug. "I want you."

Her words washed over him and he marveled that such a perfect woman wanted him. That she trusted her care to him. Her complexion glowed in the moonlight and her long hair spread across the bed.

"Please."

That one-word undid him and he plunged his straining cock deep inside her, fully seating himself in one thrust. Her hips immediately jerked upward to meet his and he moved slowly. Dragging his cock deep inside her sex, he felt connected in a way he had never felt before. With her fingers on his shoulders urging him on, he began to thrust with more force. With each plunge, he felt a wild desire to claim her in every way possible.

The friction quickly built to a crescendo and Lia tried to stare at Aiden's face, but the emotions crashing into her were overwhelming. For only an instant, the face of her husband came to mind. He had been handsome, well-built, and in the early days their sex life had been amazing. She had felt loved and cherished by him, but it was only with time that she came to realize it was because he had an image of the perfect wife and perfect family in his mind. When reality did not meet that image, he was unable to cope. And with that shift in him, he had no longer appealed to her as a man. By not allowing herself to be involved with anyone for years, she had forgotten what this kind of intimacy felt like.

Forcing thoughts of Carl out of her mind, she held Aiden's gaze, understanding the difference. He knew all of her and all of Emily and wanted them both. A smile moved across her lips as she realized how much she had grown to care for this man that was giving himself to her.

As the friction finally engulfed her, all thoughts fled her mind other than the image of Aiden's face above hers, his body rocking into hers, and the emotions swirling between them.

Aiden watched the various emotions play across Lia's face and for an instant he was fearful of where her mind had gone. But, the look in her eyes when her orgasm hit again, told him that she was right there, in this moment, with him. He planted himself deeply and threw his head back, his neck straining as his orgasm rushed from his body, feeling more connected with her than he had ever felt with anyone in his life.

Holding his upper body away from her, propped on his elbows, with his hands on either side of her face, he lowered his head for a kiss. Unsure of the words that were tangled in his head, he poured all of his feelings into the kiss.

She reciprocated, kissing him in return with the same intensity.

After a moment, he leaned away from her and, holding her gaze, said, "I wish I was better with saying what's in my mind, and I hope this doesn't scare you, but I just have to let you know, you mean the world to me."

She replied by holding him close, allowing him to rest his cheek on her chest, with her arms wrapped tightly around him. He shifted his body to the side, taking his weight off her while leaving his head on her chest, reveling in her.

As the air slowly cooled their heated bodies, he listened to her heart beating strongly against his cheek. "God, I love the sound of your heartbeat in my ear."

Well sated, they both began to drift to sleep wrapped in each other's arms and just as sleep claimed him, he heard her whisper, "That's the sound of my love."

21

Sunlight peeked through the slatted blinds, casting the room in a warm glow. Lia blinked open her eyes and for a few seconds wondered how she had slept so late. Then the feel of heat all along her back hit her at the same time she felt the heavy weight of an arm wrapped around her, holding her tight. She smiled and snuggled deeper into the warmth, loving having Aiden wake up with her in her bed.

Having woken up alone for so many years, she noticed everything. The weight of his body on the mattress next to her. His breath, warm against her neck. His muscular arm banded around her. His hand resting at her breast. For a moment, she closed her eyes and all the cares of the world slipped away and she reveled in the feel of this man's body holding her next to him.

With his breath tickling her cheek, he said in a sleepy voice, "I don't really want to move away from here but when is Emily expected home?"

She smiled at his concern for her daughter and said, "Her friend's mom said that she would bring her home about ten o'clock."

He lifted his head to look at the clock on her nightstand then nuzzled her neck. "Then we've got time."

"Time for what?" she asked, hoping she knew the answer. He pressed his hips forward and she felt his morning wood nuzzling against her ass. Grinning that he wanted the same thing she did, she said, "Oh, yeah. We've got time for that."

His heat left her for just a second and she heard the crackle of a condom wrapper. He rolled it on quickly and came back to her, lifting her leg slightly.

She arched her back, angling her ass toward him, and he easily slid his cock through her wetness, deep into her sex. With his hand still at her breast, tweaking her nipples, he thrust his hips over and over again until she thought she would break under the onslaught of feelings.

He slid his other hand over her hipbone and pressed his fingers against her clit. The breathless pants, as though she had been running, leaving her body came to an end as her orgasm washed over her.

Aiden continued thrusting, Lia's tight heat squeezing his cock. As soon as he felt her body slicken even more, he followed her with his own orgasm, groaning with his release.

Lying there, with his cock still deeply embedded in her, their heartbeats slowed. He realized that, for the first time, he had spent the night with a woman and waking up with someone he cared about was the greatest feeling. He was not itching to leave. Did not mind the small talk that would come over coffee. Did not mind the idea of a long morning shower with her.

Leaning up slightly, he whispered, "Now, that's the way to wake up."

She giggled and shifted around in the bed, her hand coming up to rub over his scruffy jaw. Staring into his eyes, she said, "I couldn't agree more."

He sighed, adding, "I hate to leave, but I should be gone by the time Emily comes home. I can take a shower in my own apartment."

She sucked in her lips and he watched as thoughts moved behind her eyes. Not wanting her to worry, he leaned over and kissed her lightly before climbing out of bed.

"Wait," she called out. "There's no reason for you to leave. That is, unless you want to. Which if you want that's fine too. I just don't want you to think that you have to."

He leaned over the bed and stared deeply into her beautiful eyes. "What are you really saying, sweetheart?"

"I'm saying that I don't want you to go."

"And Emily?"

"It's not like she's going to see us here in bed together. I don't think she'll think anything untoward if she sees you here when she gets here. I don't know what you have going on this morning, so I know you might have to leave—"

"Got nothing I'd rather do and nowhere I'd rather be," he interrupted, kissing her lightly again.

Her smile widened until it was beaming. Pulling her gently out of bed, they moved into the shower.

Later, finding themselves downstairs in the kitchen, she plated an easy breakfast of scrambled eggs, bacon, toast, and hot coffee.

Hearing a noise at the front door, she bolted forward and he grinned, knowing she missed Emily. He followed behind and watched as she threw open the door and greeted her daughter with a hug. Emily was chattering away as Lia stood and waved toward the driveway as the other mother backed her van out.

His eyes snagged on a piece of paper taped to her front door and, reaching over Emily's head, he grabbed it. Before he had a chance to look at it, Emily immediately began talking to him as well, telling all about her sleepover.

"It sounds like you had such fun," Lia said excitedly. "Have you had breakfast?"

She nodded, but said, "We just had doughnuts and juice. I smell eggs. Did you make eggs?"

Laughing, Lia smiled, and said, "Yes. Mr. Aiden was just having some as well. Come on back and we'll have breakfast together."

His heart warmed as Emily grinned up at him, took his hand, and the three of them walked into the kitchen. "You had a note stuck to your front door this morning," he said, handing the envelope to her.

She glanced down at it, and said, "Hmm, probably some kind of request for a donation or a sales advertisement. You can just lay it on the counter and I'll look at it in just a bit."

He tossed it down and turned around to face Emily as she continued to tell them about her sleepover. He knew that Lia had been excited for her to spend time with a friend, but also had been a bit concerned. From Emily's excited expression, it appeared that she had had no problem communicating with the other family.

Soon, the three of them were at the table, eating breakfast. If Emily wondered why he was there so early in the morning, she did not question or let on that it seemed odd at all. For him, he cast his eye toward the beautiful woman sitting before him and her daughter, marveling that the only feeling he had was one of a full heart.

Occasionally, Lia would glance his way and offer a shy smile. As they finished breakfast, she sent Emily off to her room to unpack her overnight bag. As he rinsed the dishes and put them in the dishwasher she looked down at the envelope on the counter. Picking it up, she pulled out the piece of paper, her eyes glancing over the words.

A sharp gasp from her drew his attention and he watched as she dropped the paper onto the counter, turning wide eyes to him. Unsure of the reason for her reaction, he glanced down at the paper as well.

Searching will yield only trouble. For you and your daughter.

"Fuck!" he growled, his eyes shooting to her pale face. Moving swiftly toward her, he wrapped one arm around her, pulling her tightly to his side as he jerked his phone from his pocket.

He skipped the police phone line, instead calling

Mitch directly. "Got a problem. A threatening note was taped to Lia's door this morning."

After another few words, he disconnected and, with his lips pressed to the top of her head, he said, "The police are coming, babe. Don't touch the note again cause they're going to want to take it." He felt her body shaking and held her close, wanting to ease her fear while at the same time feeling rage coursing through his blood.

She leaned her head back sharply and asked, "What about Emily? You said the police are coming. I don't want her to get scared."

His mind raced and then he quickly pulled his phone out again. "Mom? Please don't ask any questions right now, but Lia and I could really use you. Can you come to her house and watch Emily for a little bit and keep her upstairs while the police are here talking with us?"

Disconnecting, he looked back down at her and said, "Mom will come. She's great with kids and will keep Emily occupied upstairs while we're down here."

Slumping against him in relief, his arms tightened as he took her weight. "Oh Jesus, Aiden. I don't even know what to think."

"Don't worry about anything right now. Let's deal with Mitch and see what we need to do." He loosened his hold on her just enough to bend slightly so that his face was directly in front of hers. Holding her gaze, he said, "You're not alone. Not anymore. Whatever we face, we face together."

Lia quickly learned that the McFarlanes stick together, each jumping in to offer whatever support was needed. Corrine came over and was now ensconced up in Emily's room playing with her dolls. She had called Katelyn as well, who showed up along with Gareth while Eric stayed at their house to watch little Finn. Ginny had told Brogan when the call came in to Mitch, so the two of them were over also.

To her surprise, when Mitch walked in he was accompanied by Colt. They immediately asked for the note and she showed them where she had left it on the counter.

"While your office is in Baytown, and therefore in my jurisdiction, your house is in North Heron County, and therefore under the Sheriff's Department's jurisdiction," Mitch explained. "But don't worry, Colt and I are used to working together."

Colt handled the note with gloved fingers before slipping it into the evidence bag.

"We looked into Tad Marvel," Mitch continued. "He's out of prison, but he's been in constant contact with his probation officer. In talking with the PO, he reported that Tad's behavior has been model, both in and out of prison."

Nodding, she directed everyone into the living room to discuss the situation. Sure that Emily was unable to hear what was going on downstairs, she and Aiden sat on the sofa while everyone else found seats where they could. She smiled slightly as he wrapped his arm around her shoulders as though it was the most natural thing in the world, taking comfort from the action. Katelyn sat on the other side of her, facing Mitch and Colt sitting in the two chairs in the room. Gareth and Brogan brought in kitchen chairs for the two of them as well as Ginny.

The small room was full, but as she looked around, it did not feel crowded, but instead felt comforting, filled with people that she knew cared.

Leaning forward, Mitch informed her, "The PO also told me that if Tad was involved, he would be very surprised. Now, that doesn't mean that he isn't our suspect, but the note does say *Searching*, which indicates something happening now. I don't want to focus too much on just him."

She nodded again, wordlessly, listening carefully to what he was saying. He glanced to the side toward Gareth, who held her phone out to her.

"I checked out everything I could and discovered that the calls that came to you were made from a burner phone, which means I can't trace it. Mitch and I agree, it's not typical teenage behavior, and that was before the note was found on your door. Whoever's doing this is someone who wants to unnerve you and not leave a trace."

Her front door opened and Hunter stepped through, his eyes moving first to her before sliding to Colt. It was the first time she had seen him in his deputy's uniform and she blinked in surprise.

"I've checked with all the neighbors and no one heard a car or saw anyone approaching Lia's house," he reported.

"Probably came during the middle of the night when

most people were asleep," Colt said. He turned his attention back to her. "What can you tell us about your work right now?"

Still numb from the fact she had actually received a threatening note on her door, she cleared her throat, and said, "At the last audit for Baytown, the state accountants found a deficit of over fifty thousand dollars. The Mayor and the Town Council accepted my proposal for a forensic accounting investigation. All of this is public record but, so far, I have seen nothing in the Baytown Gazette about it, which I'm sure they're pleased about. With Mayor Banks running for re-election, he is keen for me to finish my work and find the discrepancy. He's hoping that it can to be dealt with quickly. Silas is being quite pushy about wanting me to not talk to anyone and to rush the investigation. It's my understanding that he owes much of his position to the fact that Corwin is the Mayor and the two of them get along very well. I haven't been here long enough to become immersed in small-town politics and since I don't live inside the town limits, I won't vote in the next mayoral election anyway. I've read in the paper that there is a new resident, moved in from a larger city, who's also running for mayor. I think Silas is afraid that if news of the investigation gets out, it will look bad for Mayor Banks."

"I can't imagine this staying silent very long," Mitch said. "The Mayor ordered all of the town's departments to not speak about it to the press but, as you say, it's public record."

Colt asked, "Is there anyone that you're investigating

that you would suspect would want you to not do a complete job?"

She snorted, then looked around in embarrassment. "Sorry," she said as she shook her head. "You learn to have thick skin when you're a forensic accounting investigator. You're not exactly welcome when you come into an area to investigate. I have to ask book-keepers and others for all their records which immedi-ately makes people intimidated. I then have to start questioning them about some of their practices, sloppy work, things that don't add up, and things that are just, quite frankly, wrong. That also makes people intimi-dated and then angry. No one likes to have someone check behind their every step, and certainly not ques-tion what they've done."

She shrugged, and continued, "So I'm treated with a great amount of suspicion, sometimes overt rudeness, and most people are glad to see the back of me."

Colt's eyes showed sympathy as he nodded. "Sounds like police work. They're happy when we do our job and it helps them, but otherwise they wish we wouldn't look into their business."

"Exactly!" she said. "I sometimes wonder if I wouldn't be better off just doing what Scott Redding does, which is focus on taxes and business accounting. But," she threw her hands out to the side, "I find investi-gating to be fascinating."

She heard Aiden sigh next to her and twisted her head around. Staring at his face, so full of concern, she whispered, "Are you okay?"

"Right now, I wish you were just a tax accountant," he confessed.

Her shoulders slumped as the full weight of everyone's concern settled on her. The idea that someone might try to harm Emily just to get to her, caused her to drag a ragged breath deep into her lungs at the very thought of it.

Mitch interrupted her panic, asking, "Tell us about the people you are investigating and how your investigation is going so far."

She leaned back against the cushions of the sofa and felt Aiden's arm around her shoulder. Resting her hand on his hard thigh, she drew strength from him.

"The system in Baytown is relatively simple. All of the departments send their invoices, purchase orders, and requests to the town treasurer, Sandra Toski. She's the one who makes the decisions, verifies everything, and has the checks printed. She has the Mayor sign the checks before they are sent out. Mark Weber is her accounting clerk. He is mostly involved in looking over things before Sandra gets them and the input of all the information into the town's financial computer system. If Corwin is unavailable, then the checks are locked in Celia Ring's desk until the Mayor is available. So far, I have not found any discrepancies with the Police, Recreation, Building and Code, or Planning and Zoning departments."

Mitch grinned, and replied, "Well, thank God, the Police Department is clear."

She met his smile with one of her own, appreciating

the moment of levity. Continuing, she said, "I have found small discrepancies with the Library, Harbor, and the Public Works and Utilities. I'm in the process of checking each of those to see if there is an overall problem that appears to be the same, or just some individual mistakes."

"Are you finding things that are small or are you getting the feeling that there is one large discrepancy that could be attributed to one person?"

"From what I can tell from the Library, it appears to be small. What I'm finding is that in the ordering of books and computers, what is approved sometimes gets changed before the order actually goes through. This causes a slight discrepancy between the order and the check that was written. They are very small discrepancies and not what I'm focusing on at all."

"Who has the most to lose from your investigation?"

"My investigation only points to where the discrepancies are, if illegal activities took place or if they were common errors, and who made them. When my findings are turned over to the Town Council, it is up to them to decide if they want to turn them over to the District Attorney for prosecution. He would do so only if an actual crime had been committed and would meet with me to discuss my findings."

"So," Hunter interjected, "it appears that someone thinks you may find evidence of a crime that they committed. If someone's just made some goofs, I can't see that they would threaten you."

She nodded slowly, realizing that he was right. Her investigation was pointing toward someone stealing the town's money, and the threatening note on her door supported that real possibility. Thinking about the previous night, she gasped, drawing everyone's attention to her.

"Last night! I forgot to tell you about last night!"

22

All eyes were on Lia once again, as she said, "I can't believe I forgot about this. Last night, I saw Sandra and Celia at the bar together. I didn't think anything about it at the time, because they work together. For all I knew, they were just two women sharing a drink at the end of the workweek." She twisted around and looked at Aiden, adding, "This was before you came in."

His fingers twitched on her shoulder and she held tightly to his leg. Shifting her gaze back to Mitch and Colt, she continued. "Sandra wanted to speak to me and when I walked over to her, I just happened to notice that Celia had left the bar. Sandra said she wanted to give me a warning."

She felt Aiden's fingers gripping tighter on her shoulder and heard him mutter, "What the hell?"

"What exactly did she say?" Mitch asked.

She scrunched her forehead as she thought, wanting to remember the exact words. "She seemed very hesitant but told me to be careful. I didn't know what she meant so I asked her. She then said she didn't know anything for sure and I asked her if Celia had said something to her. She shook her head and said not really. I still didn't know what she meant, but she said there was an inference. I was getting frustrated because I felt like she was doing nothing but hinting and not really giving me any information. Sandra's eyes sort of darted around, and then she just said that she had the feeling there are some who would rather me not find out anything."

"And that's all she said?" Colt asked.

Nodding, she confirmed, "Yes. Of course, she didn't tell me anything that I didn't already know. As I told you, any investigation will make people nervous and, of course, if someone has perpetrated a crime, then they don't want anyone to know."

Mitch stood. "I'll talk to her and see what I can get out of her. If she now knows that someone has actually made a threat to you, I will encourage her to come clean about who she was talking to."

She stood as well and walked over to take his hand. "Mitch, I can't thank you enough."

He held her gaze and smiled. "You know it's my job, but I want you safe." He looked behind her to Aiden and lifted his brows in silent question.

She twisted her head around just in time to see Aiden nod. Unsure what that meant, her attention was snagged as Colt and Hunter also said their goodbyes. Colt promised that her street would be added to their rotation and that someone would be keeping an eye on her place. Thanking them all, she walked them to the door, shutting it behind them.

Turning back around, she stared at Aiden's family. Katelyn offered, "I'm going to run upstairs and check on Mom and Emily. If they want to come down now, is that okay?"

Nodding, she said, "Yes, thank you."

Ginny stepped over and took her hands. "You know I don't have any jurisdiction in the county, but I'm here for you as a friend for anything that you need." She hugged her and thanked her.

At the same time, Brogan moved to Aiden and clapped him on the shoulder. "We're here for you. You, and Lia, and Emily. Anything you need, anytime."

Aiden pulled his brother in for a hug and acknowledged, "I know that and thanks, bro. That means more than you can imagine."

Just then, she heard Emily bounding down the stairs. Looking in that direction, she spotted her just as she was jumping down the final step, her smile wide. "Mama, Miss Corrine showed me how to cut out paper dolls. She said that's what they used to play with when she was a little girl."

Corrine's eyes darted between the occupants of the room, but finally landed on her. "How can we help, sweetheart?"

Suddenly exhausted, she shook her head and whispered, "I appreciate that so much, but I have no idea. I can't think straight right now."

"Well, I think we should have some lunch. How about I get in the kitchen and rustle up something yummy?" Corrine looked down at Emily and smiled. "Would you like to help me?"

Emily threw her hands in the air and ran toward the kitchen screaming, "Yay!"

Corrine winked at her and with a smile followed Emily into the kitchen.

"Not that I don't want to stay for lunch," Gareth said, walking over. "But I'd rather get back to the office. I want to start doing some digging on a few of the people that you've mentioned today. Anything I find out I'll make sure to get to Mitch and Colt." He shook Aiden's hand, kissed her cheek and, with a promise from Katelyn that she would be along to the office after lunch, he headed out the door.

Ginny and Katelyn walked into the kitchen to assist with lunch. With a chin lift, Brogan followed his wife. Alone for the moment, Aiden pulled Lia in for a hug. Wrapping his strong arms around her, she slumped against him.

"I know you're exhausted and, to be honest, I want nothing more than to take you to bed, encircle my body around yours and sleep. But, I also know you missed some of Emily's excitement and you probably want to spend as much time with her as possible."

She leaned back and looked up into his face, and said, "Will it scare you if I tell you that I'm glad you're here?"

He pressed his lips against her forehead and whispered against her furrowed brow, "No, babe. Not at all. And I can tell you that I'm right where I want to be as well."

After lunch, everyone left, leaving Lia and Emily alone with Aiden. She was not surprised to see Emily was yawning, considering her daughter had most likely stayed up late at her sleepover. This was confirmed when Emily easily acquiesced to her suggestion of a nap.

While Emily was upstairs, she and Aiden sat together in the now quiet living room. Pulling her close, he said, "I've been thinking about this for the last couple of hours and I don't know how you're going to take it, but I don't want you and Emily here by yourself."

She leaned back and looked up at him, and asked, "So what's your solution?"

He held her gaze, his hand drifting up to cup her jaw as his thumb caressed her pulse point on her neck. "My solution is that I stay here with the two of you." She blinked, stunned, but before she had a chance to speak, he jumped in. "I know that when you're in town working you have people around you. But I'm not willing for you and Emily to be out here by yourself at night."

She sucked in her lips, thinking about his suggestion. "I know that you're right, but I don't know how to do this. I don't know how to explain it to Emily."

"I can sleep on the couch. I can get up early and leave before she goes to school. Maybe she wouldn't even notice," he suggested.

She bit her lip, her brow scrunching once more. She felt as though her world was spinning out of control and battled to regain some of it. But no matter what solution she came up with, she kept coming back to the idea that someone might hurt Emily to get at her. Lifting her gaze again, she stared into his blue eyes. "I want you here and can't come up with a good reason why you shouldn't be. I'm a little nervous about what others might say, and downright terrified of giving Emily the wrong idea, but she really likes you and at her age probably won't think anything about it."

He smiled, pulling her in for a light kiss. It was hard to believe that it was just last night that they spent the night making love, the past few hours having put a damper on those feelings. "Brogan is going in and working tonight," he said. "I don't have to work at all until tomorrow. We can have something simple for dinner and explain to Emily that I'm gonna spend some extra time here. How does that sound?"

"Except for the reason we're having to move so fast, it sounds wonderful," she said.

A little bit later, Emily woke from her nap and bounded down the steps, a smile on her face. Seeing Aiden still there, she excitedly climbed up on the sofa and the three of them watched a movie. Halfway through, Lia went to the kitchen and fixed peanut butter and banana sandwiches and put them on a tray with some potato chips, along with some iced tea for the adults and a glass of milk for Emily. She brought it in and set it on the coffee table.

"We get to eat in here?" Emily asked, her eyes wide.

She nodded, smiling at her daughter, and said, "I

thought we'd do something different tonight. Perhaps a picnic in the living room can be our special treat."

In typical six-year-old fashion, her explanation easily satisfied Emily, who dove into her dinner. She looked at Aiden and grinned. "I hope you like peanut butter and banana sandwiches."

Chuckling, he said, "You might not believe this, but they're one of my favorites."

Later that evening, after Emily was bathed and toweled off, she helped her into her pajamas and they moved into Emily's room. She and Aiden had decided not to say anything to Emily yet, just allowing him to leave early the next morning before she woke up.

"Can Aiden read me a story?"

"Um…"

Aiden popped his head around the corner and grinned. "I'd be honored to read the bedtime story." His eyes dropped to her's and he added, "If it's okay with your mom."

She met his smile and nodded. "Absolutely." Turning back to Emily, she said, "You pick out the story and he'll read."

She moved to the other side of the bed and Aiden sat next to Emily as she placed a book in his hands. He began to read and she watched him in awe. His voice was strong and animated at just the right times. Emily beamed, thoroughly enjoying the story.

By the time he got to the end, Emily was yawning heavily. As she slid down in bed, she lifted her hands to him and he bent to give her a hug. Kissing the top of her head, he moved so she could see him and said, "Sweet dreams,

Emily." He stood and walked to the doorway, then looked over his shoulder at her as Lia kissed her good night.

Hugging her tightly, she said, "I love you." After tucking Emily in, she met Aiden at the door and flipped off the light, allowing just the nightlight to illuminate the room.

Several hours later, with extra blankets and pillows, Aiden made his bed on the sofa in the living room. Lia had gone upstairs to get ready for bed and as he heard a noise he turned around to see her standing at the bottom of the stairs. Her hair flowed down her back, her makeup-free face pale in the barely lit room. Her yellow, silky pajama bottoms matched her camisole top, and she had a short robe tied about her waist.

"Are you okay?" he asked, walking over to stand directly in front of her.

She lifted her palms and rested them on his chest, staring up into his face. "I know we've only spent one night together, but I find myself wishing you could be upstairs with me now."

He hesitated, desperately wanting the same thing. The chance to wrap her in his arms during the night. The chance to wake up and make love to her at first light. The pull was strong, but as he stared into her beautiful face, he knew what his answer must be.

"I want you, so badly it hurts. But I want you and Emily safe even more than my physical desires. And right now, I want to make sure that I do this right. So, until we're ready to tell Emily that we're together, I'll sleep on the sofa."

He watched as moisture formed in her eyes and she blinked, allowing a few tears to roll down her cheeks. He slid his hands to either side of her face, capturing her tears with his thumbs.

"I know in the middle of everything that's going on right now, I shouldn't say this. I should guard my heart, but I don't think I can keep this to myself."

His brows lowered as he waited to hear what she was going to say.

"You are such a good man, Aiden McFarlane. And I know it's terribly early in our relationship, and I'm terrified that what I'm going to say will scare you away. But I have to tell you that I'm falling for you."

His arms spasmed and he crushed her to his chest. Words that he had never wanted to hear from a woman before now moved through him, warm and soothing. Not afraid of her emotion, he instead felt connected. Unsure what to say, for fear of not being able to put his heart into words, he kissed the top of her head. Her arms began to loosen from his waist but he did not want to let her go.

He looked down at her face and the doubt he saw in her eyes speared through him. No longer afraid of saying the wrong thing, he rushed, "That means the world to me, Lia. You gotta know, it means the world. I've never been in love before. I've never wanted to be in love before. But what I feel for you and what I feel for Emily, it's stronger than anything I've ever felt in my life."

Her lips curved in a slow smile and she held his gaze

for a moment, then placed her face on his chest, her arms wrapping around his waist once again.

Together they stood in the dark, at the bottom of her stairs, holding tightly to each other, for a few minutes letting their problems fall away.

23

Sitting at her desk, Lia poured over the papers in front of her and carefully dissected the reports and financial information on her computer. She had risen early that morning to see Aiden out and then took Emily to school after breakfast. Corrine had volunteered to pick Emily up from school and watch her for a couple of hours until she got off work. Hoping to get out an hour earlier, she decided to skip lunch and keep investigating.

A knock on her door frame had her looking up, seeing Scott smiling as he walked into her office.

"How's it going?" he asked.

"I'm getting there slowly. Nothing definitive yet, but I know I'll find it."

They chatted for just a few minutes, before he asked, "Have you ever thought about moving the office to a different location? Or maybe expanding this office?"

Curious why he asked, she responded, "I haven't really been here long enough to think about that."

"I know this old office was good enough for my grandfather," he said. "But with both of us here now, we could use the conference room and probably a little bit bigger space."

She observed him as he looked around the room as though sizing it up. He had occasionally called her *partner* but they actually were not. She bought the business from Thomas when he retired. Scott answered her search for another accountant, but until she was sure they would work out she had not offered to take him on as a partner.

"I'll be honest, Scott," she said. "Right now, we don't have the revenue to expand. If you decide to stay, and want to buy in as a partner, then we might be able to check out a larger office space here in town. But as it stands right now, we have to make do with what we have."

A flash of irritation moved through his face, but it was gone so quickly she was not sure it was there.

He smiled as he stood and nodded. "You're right, I know you are. Just to let you know, I do plan on staying. I like Baytown and I like the people that I've met here." Almost as an afterthought, he added, "And I like who I work for."

She heard him leave out the front door after telling Mrs. Markham that he was going to lunch. Just then her stomach growled at the idea of eating and she wondered if Mrs. Markham would mind ordering. She considered the pub but dismissed that idea, not wanting

Aiden to know that she was going to stay in her office during lunch.

She walked out to the reception area and, seeing Jillian walking across the street, changed her mind. "Mrs. Markham, I'm going to run to Jillian's and grab a sandwich to bring back here. Is there anything that I can get for you?"

"No, thank you, Ms. Smith. I brought something from home."

She hurried across the street and entered Jillian's Coffee Shop. Not seeing Jillian around, she ordered a sandwich and sat at a small table in the corner while she waited for it to be delivered. Hearing a familiar voice from the back, she caught a glance of Scott sitting at a table with Celia. Surprised, not ever having seen them together before, she could not help but be curious. Their voices grew softer as they leaned their heads close together, deep in discussion.

She startled as the server brought her bag with her sandwich inside and she quickly paid. Walking back down the street to her office, she could not help but wonder about the possible threat from Celia and why she and Scott were so chummy.

Walking into her office, she plopped down into her seat and pulled her sandwich out of the bag. She rubbed her head, which now had a familiar headache, and grimaced. *I need to get a hold of myself. I'm starting to see gremlins wherever I look.* Taking a big bite of her sandwich, she washed it down with her iced tea, focusing back on the numbers and figures in front of her.

Several hours later, Aiden knocked on her door and

she looked up. "My, my, Mrs. Markham doesn't even announce you anymore," she grinned.

"Well, knowing Mrs. Markham's penchant for professionalism, I take that to mean she must approve of me as someone you don't mind seeing."

She laughed while she pushed her chair back to stand and greeted him with a kiss. "I should confess that I did tell Mrs. Markham we are seeing each other and that you can come to visit me anytime."

He wrapped his arms tighter around her waist and kissed her again. Longer. Deeper. Pulling away regretfully, he glanced at her desk, which was covered in papers filled with numbers, and shook his head. "I don't see how you do it, babe. I'm glad you love your job, because it would drive me crazy."

She glanced over her shoulder at the amount of work scattered around and shrugged. "Numbers make sense to me, I guess. And doing this kind of investigation is like putting puzzle pieces together."

He grew quiet at that, his body slightly rigid. She looked back up at him, tilting her head to the side. "Are you okay?"

He opened his mouth to speak, then hesitated, closing it again. She waited, deciding to let him speak when he felt ready.

Finally, he said, "There's something I want to tell you. Something I'm ashamed of, but if we're going to be together, you're going to find out anyway."

Curious, she remained quiet, hoping that he would feel at ease to tell her anything.

"I'm okay with math," he began, "but numbers can really confuse me."

Unsure what he meant, she tightened her arms around his waist slightly, hoping that he would feel her acceptance no matter what. It must have worked, because he began to explain.

"It's almost like being dyslexic, only with numbers. There's a term for people that don't understand math concepts, but that's not me. I understand the concepts of math just fine, but when I read numbers, I transpose them. If the number is forty-three, then I'll read it is thirty-four. If I really stare at it, and say it out loud, then I get it right. It just takes me longer because I always have to double check the numbers to make sure I haven't transpose them."

"Oh." She blushed and bit her lip, remembering something. "A few weeks ago, when I asked you to double check my work…I'm sorry. I didn't mean to put you on the spot."

He shook his head, saying, "Babe, it's okay. You didn't know. But, yeah. That was…hard."

"Aiden, I'm so glad you trusted me enough to tell me. It's certainly nothing to be ashamed of, but I'm sure it's made you feel weird sometimes."

"Not just weird, but dumb. I always laughed it off but, deep down, it was hard not to feel like the dumb kid."

She held his gaze and nodded slowly. "I worry about that with Emily sometimes. She is so smart, but often people with any type of disability are looked at differently…treated differently."

"You've done a wonderful job with her," he said, his blue eyes holding her captive. "I really mean that."

She smiled. "Thank you. That means a lot to me." Sighing, she added, "I know I can't keep her from being hurt or made fun of, so I just try to make sure she feels good about herself."

"You're an amazing mom…an amazing woman." He slid one hand up to cup the back of her head, tilting her face back so that he could kiss her. Cognizant of being in her office, Aiden kept the kiss light. Just like Lia's declaration of love, he felt her acceptance, warm and soothing as it moved through him.

She sighed with contentment and he felt the loss of her warmth when he had to step back. He knew she had more work to do before going by his parents' house to pick up Emily.

"How much longer do you have here?"

"I plan on leaving at five o'clock exactly and not a second later," she vowed.

"I walked from my apartment to the pub, so how about if I come here at five and we can go pick up Emily together?"

Grinning, she nodded. As he turned to leave, she suddenly thought of something and called out. "When I mentioned that Celia was at the pub having a drink with Sandra, I just wondered if she often comes in?"

"Celia? Celia Ring?" he shook his head, and replied, "Nope. I seem to remember her coming in one time after she first moved to town and started working for the Mayor. She looked like a woman on the prowl and definitely struck me as a woman who was not to be trusted." He blushed slightly, but continued, "I made it clear that I wasn't interested and she's never come back into the pub that I've seen."

With another quick kiss goodbye, Lia watched Aiden leave her office and she sat back down to finish working.

An hour later, Mrs. Markham came back to her office to announce another visitor. "It's Donald Scarsdale," Mrs. Markham said, arching her eyebrows. "It's the man who's running against Mayor Banks."

"What on earth does he want?" she sighed. Standing, she plastered a smile on her face as Mrs. Markham showed him back. Shaking his hand, she offered him a chair, observing the gray-haired man in a gray suit with a light gray shirt. All her fatigued mind could think was that he was very monochromatic and she had to stifle a grin.

"How may I help you, Mr. Scarsdale?"

"I'll come straight to the point, Ms. Smith. I've been reading the public records of the last six months of Town Council meetings and was greatly interested to see the one where you were hired."

He paused, as though expecting her to speak. She simply inclined her head toward him and waited for him to continue.

"I know that there is money that's suspected of being missing and wanted to find out where you are in your investigation."

"Mr. Scarsdale, the investigation, at this point, is still private and confidential. I have come to no conclusions

MARYANN JORDAN

and to speak at this time would be a breach of ethics and considerably premature."

He glowered, saying, "The situation is public knowledge."

Nodding, she agreed, "Yes, Town Council minutes are public record. But my investigation, until I have given them a report, is not up for discussion."

He leaned forward, his sharp eyes pinning her, and said, "Ms. Smith, it is my intention to become the new mayor of Baytown. In my opinion, Corwin Banks has held that position far too long. If the public knew that he was responsible for misappropriating funds, then the townspeople would be able to make the obvious choice for a new mayor."

Irritation flew through her veins, but she forced her breathing to remain steady as she maintained a professional demeanor. "I understand exactly what you're saying, Mr. Scarsdale. My investigation has absolutely nothing to do with the Mayoral election and I assure you that I will not, under any circumstances, give in to any coercion. When my financial investigation is complete and I make my recommendations to the Town Council, then it will be public knowledge."

His face grew redder and he argued, "And if Mayor Banks is at fault? If he's won the next election, and it turns out that he's the one at fault, are you willing to take on that responsibility as well?"

Standing, she lifted her arm toward the door, and said, "Mr. Scarsdale, our meeting has come to an end. You will know the results of my investigation when it is ready to be made public record. We have nothing further to say to each other."

He stormed out of her office and a few seconds later Mrs. Markham scurried to her doorway. "Are you all right?"

Nodding wearily, she said, "Yes. He's just another political blowhard."

Rolling her eyes, Mrs. Markham shook her head. "Lord save us from another one of those!"

As Mrs. Markum walked back to the lobby, she nodded to herself. Sitting down, she began working once more, this time praying for no more interruptions. Her luck did not hold out. Thirty minutes later, she overheard a ruckus in the lobby.

"You cannot just go back there!" she heard Mrs. Markham say. "I need to see if she is available and announce you. And if she's not available, then you need to make an appointment."

"As town manager, I have imperative business with Ms. Smith that cannot wait. "

She looked up just in time to see Silas stalking into her office with Mrs. Markham fast on his heels. At the end of her rope, she stood and, with her hands fisted on top of her desk, growled, "How dare you come storming into my office. How dare you push your way past my receptionist."

Silas, his face appearing sharper than ever, glared back as his lips twitched. "I don't have time for niceties," he argued. "Our entire town's future rests solely on your shoulders—a thought that keeps me awake at night I can assure you!"

She opened her mouth to retort, then snapped it closed again as she noticed Mrs. Markham was still standing in her doorway, shooting daggers at Silas with her eyes. "Thank you, Mrs. Markham. I'd like you to stay as a witness to this statement." Pinning Silas with her glare, she warned, "If you ever push your way into this office again, I'll call the police." Offering a polite nod to Mrs. Markham, she said, "I'll take it from here."

Mrs. Markham retreated, now with a smile on her face.

Turning back to Silas, she took in his stunned expression. "Now, why don't you tell me what it is you want to say and get it over with."

"I just got a phone call from Marcella, over at the Baytown Gazette. She wants an interview with me concerning the missing funds!"

Refusing to say anything, she simply stared.

He continued, "She told me that if I don't talk to her she's going to come straight to you."

Throwing her hands up into the air, she plopped down into her seat. "I'll tell you the same thing that I told Mr. Scarsdale, and that—"

He gasped and backed up a step, as though struck. "Scarsdale? Scarsdale was here? Oh my God! What did you tell him?"

She leveled a hard stare his way, and said, "I am a professional. I am running a professional investigation. My findings will be public knowledge as soon as they are given to the Town Council and not a moment before. I showed him the way to the door, just as I'm getting ready to do with you."

"So, you're not going to talk to the newspaper?" he asked, his voice high and strident.

Walking around the edge of her desk she lifted her hand to the door. "It seems this is my day to show people out. I will no longer talk about the investigation to you unless," a slight smile curved her lips, "I am interviewing you about the missing money."

He opened and closed his mouth several times, but no words came out. It was the first time she had seen him speechless and she was glad for it. Calling out for Mrs. Markham, who appeared at her doorway in an instant, she told him it was time to leave. After a moment's hesitation, she and a still angry Mrs. Markham watched him storm away. Turning back to her desk, she shook her head, feeling tired to her bones.

When five o'clock finally came, she gratefully shoved all of her papers into files and placed them into her briefcase. Shoving her laptop in there as well, she grabbed her purse and waited as Mrs. Markham locked the front door.

Aiden peered up into the stands, his eyes easily landing on Lia. It was also easy for him to discern her unease as she nibbled on her fingernails. He had been excited for Emily to play in her first game, but now looked down in concern as well. The game was with their younger group of children and he knew that Emily was on par with most of them so he had nothing to worry about. Still, he wanted this to be a great experience for her. Blowing out a breath, he willed his nerves to steady.

As she stood at bat, he placed himself close by so that she would easily be able to see him. The volunteers who were umpires knew why he was there. Bending down in front of her, he said, "Just like we practiced. You've got this."

She grinned up at him and nodded. He stepped back and glanced toward Jason at first base, making eye contact to assure himself that he was ready for her. She swung a couple of times, striking on the first two, and fouling on the third.

He was not disappointed, knowing that it would take her a while to become more comfortable with hitting the ball. On the next pitch, her bat made contact and the ball rolled between second and third base.

He signaled for her to run to first base and she did, her little legs taking her as fast as they could go. His eyes jumped to Jason, who was signaling for her to stop on first base. He grinned widely as she jumped up and down with joy, giving Jason a high-five. Turning as he heard the cheering from the stands, he watched as Lia screamed as loud as anyone.

He was not only glad to see all of their friends there, but his mom, dad, and Pops had come to cheer Emily on as well.

When the next child hit the ball, Jason signaled for Emily to run to second base where Zac was waiting for her, signaling for her to stop. He could not have been prouder of his friends for their ability to adapt to her needs so that she could play the game. And as he watched her jump up and high-five Zac, he could not have been more impressed with her either.

The next couple of children struck out and the inning was over, so Emily did not get to run to home base. But the joyful look on her face was shining and he knew at that moment she was as happy as she could possibly be. On her way running back to the dugout she ran straight to him, jumping into his arms for a hug.

He swung her around and his gaze shot back up to the stands, seeing Lia accepting congratulations from those around her just before she blew a kiss toward him.

After the game was over and the sports equipment put away, most of the crowd had dispersed. The coaches and their significant others were all heading to Finn's, as usual.

Walking up to Lia, he threw his arm around her shoulders and she twisted her head up to plant a kiss on his lips, the simple act sending warmth through his whole body.

"Thank you," she whispered, as Emily was talking with some of her teammates, teaching them a few signs as well.

"You don't gotta thank me, baby," he said.

She gave a subtle head jerk toward Emily, and said, "You see that smile? That right there, is what you did for her."

He bent, taking her lips again, keeping it light. Grinning at the spark of lust he saw in her eyes, he gave her waist a squeeze.

"You guys coming to Finn's?" Brogan asked.

He looked at Lia and she nodded. "I've only taken Emily a couple of times, but she's loved it. Especially their fish and chips!"

"What's this I hear about someone liking fish and chips?"

He turned around to see Pops walking up to them, a big grin on his weathered face. "It seems that Emily's a fan of our food at the pub," he answered.

Pops turned toward Emily and he felt Lia stiffen next to him. Bending over, he spoke directly to Emily so that she could see his face. "How about you and me lead the group over to the pub for some fish and chips?"

Lia relaxed, seeing that Pops had no trouble communicating with Emily. Emily glanced up at her mom, shifted her eyes over to him, and then back to her mom, her face hopeful.

"Yes. We can go. If you would like to walk with Mr. McFarlane, Aiden and I will be right behind you."

Pops held out his hand, taking Emily's much smaller one in his grip. Looking directly at her again, he said, "You can call me Pops."

Emily laughed and Aiden felt Lia relax further into his side. The group heading to the pub was huge, including all of their friends, his parents, Mitch's parents, Jillian's parents, and a few others that he figured she had met at the Auxiliary meeting.

Once inside, he headed behind the bar with Brogan and their dad to get drinks for the large crowd. Lia walked to the back, seeing Emily ensconced between Pops and Corinne, who was holding little Finn. Emily was entranced with the little baby, tickling his tummy and laughing as much as he was.

Looking across the bar, Aiden saw Lia standing still, her gaze resting on the gathering, and wondered what she was thinking.

"This it for you?" Brogan asked, drawing his attention over to his brother.

Nodding, he smiled. "Abso-fucking-lutely."

"Well, all right," his dad said, coming up behind them. "Nothing more your mom and I want to see than all three of our children happy."

A few minutes later he walked over to the crowd and his mom stood to allow him a chance to kiss his nephew before sliding in next to Lia. He watched as his dad leaned down to kiss little Finn also before kissing Corrine. A glance to the side showed Ginny, her arms wrapped tightly around Brogan, leaning up to receive a kiss from him as well. Swinging his head back around, he watched as Pops and Emily dug into their fish and chips.

"Hey," Lia's soft voice sounded next to him, drawing his attention back to her. "Are you okay?"

Nodding slowly, he stared into her eyes, his lips curving. "I've got my whole family surrounding me, including you and Emily, to fill my heart. I couldn't be more okay."

As he leaned over to give her a kiss, her wide smile settled in his heart.

Aiden, once more sleeping on Lia's sofa after having had a fun night with she and Emily, woke as his phone vibrated. He sat up quickly and reached for his jeans, remembering his phone was stuffed in the front pocket. Pulling it out, he was surprised to see Mitch's number, but knew that a call in the middle of the night could only mean bad news.

Connecting, he said, "Mitch? Talk to me."

"You at Lia's?"

"Yeah, but I'm downstairs. She's upstairs. What's up?"

"I need you to get her and bring her downtown. I know it's gonna take a few minutes because you've got to get somebody to watch Emily. Grant is on night shift and has been driving around town. He just passed her office and saw that her front office door has been broken into and was hanging on the hinges. He called for backup and they went in. No one is there, but her office has been trashed."

"Goddammit!" he cursed.

"I decided to call you instead of driving straight out there. Ginny is not on duty, if you need to call her and Brogan to stay with Emily."

Rubbing his hand over his face, trying to think of the best thing to do, he said, "You're right. I was going to call my mom, but I don't really want her out here by herself. Of course, I know my dad would come too, but maybe if Ginny and Brogan came together that would be the safest Emily could be."

"Okay, make the arrangements so you can get Lia here. We're going in to dust for fingerprints now but won't touch anything until she gets here to see what may have been taken."

Disconnecting, he felt rage coursing through his blood once again. He immediately dialed Brogan and as soon as his brother answered, he explained the situation. He could hear Ginny in the background and Brogan put his phone on speaker. They both expressed anger over what had happened to Lia, promising to be there just as soon as they could get dressed.

Disconnecting, he pulled on his jeans and the clean shirt he had brought with him. Still in his bare feet, he padded softly up the stairs, bypassing Emily's room. He stepped into Lia's bedroom, closed the door, and walked to the bed. He stared at her for just a moment, the moonlight casting a soft glow over her. She was so beautiful, so peaceful.

Inwardly cursing that he was going to have to wake her, he gently shook her shoulder, while whispering, "Lia, babe. I need you to wake up, sweetheart."

She jerked awake, sitting up so quickly she bumped her head lightly on his chin. "What? What is it? Is it Emily?"

"Shhh, quiet, babe," he whispered, flipping on the light next to her bed. Seeing her blink up at him, her sleep-tousled hair falling about her shoulders, he dreaded what he was going to have to say. "Honey, I hate this, but you're going to have to get up and get dressed. Mitch called and said that your office has been broken into—"

Her eyes widened and she gasped, "You're kidding!"

He shook his head and said, "You know I'd never kid about something like that. I've already called Brogan and Ginny and they're coming over in just a few minutes. They'll stay in the house to make sure Emily's safe 'cause Mitch needs us to come downtown. They're dusting for fingerprints right now, but you're going to have to go through to see what might have been taken."

He watched as his words finally sunk in and she threw back the covers, bolting from the bed. She rushed into her en-suite bathroom, jerking her camisole off as she went. A moment later she came back, wearing only panties, having splashed water on her face and run a

MARYANN JORDAN

brush through her hair. He ignored the sight of her almost naked body and whispered, "I'll be downstairs."

A few minutes later, she ran downstairs carrying her shoes in her hand. She greeted Ginny and Brogan, who had just entered the house and were talking to him. "Thank you all so much for coming. Emily's asleep and should stay asleep for a couple of hours. If, for whatever reason, she wakes up before I'm back, just tell her that I had to go to work to check on something and you guys are babysitting. Honestly, she'll believe you."

They assured her that everything would be fine and she nodded. Sliding her feet into her shoes, she grabbed her purse and looked up. "I'm ready, but I've got to tell you, the more I think about this the madder I get."

He put his arm around her and kissed the top of her head, squeezing her waist. "I know, baby. I fucking feel the same."

Aiden turned onto the street of Lia's office, seeing several police vehicles as well as Colt's Sheriff SUV. Parking as close as he could, he heard Lia gasp and jerked his head around so that he could see out her window. The front door of her business was now hanging awkwardly.

"Oh, my God," she breathed, her voice filled with incredulity.

Before he had a chance to stop her, she threw open the door and jumped down from his truck. Cutting off the engine, he leaped out and followed her. Reaching her where she stood outside her office and putting his hands on her shoulders, he leaned down and whispered, "Babe, it'll be all right. I promise."

Mitch met them at the door, his eyes moving from Lia's stunned face up to Aiden's angry one. "Lia, I need you to come in and look around. You're the only one who would know if anything is missing and, if not, what they might've been looking for."

She nodded silently and followed Mitch into the reception area with Aiden close behind. The first thing they were shown was that Mrs. Markham's desk looked untouched, except for the filing drawer, which had been pried open.

"Mrs. Markham would have to be the one to tell you if anything is missing, but I can assure you that nothing confidential is kept here at all. This is really just her file drawer."

Mitch nodded and stepped into the hall that led to the two offices and small staff room. Peering first into Scott's office, they could see that the filing credenza behind his desk had been opened as well, with some files emptied onto the floor.

Shaking her head, she said, "I'm really uncertain what anyone would have been looking for."

They then followed Mitch into her office and she gasped loudly at the sight.

Her office was much more trashed than the rest of the business. The filing credenza behind her desk had all the files out of it and spread around. Her desk drawers had been broken into and the contents were strewn around, as well.

She sucked in a shuddering breath and he wrapped his arms around her from behind. Leaning down, he whispered in her ear again, "Breathe, babe. It'll be all right. Mitch'll find out what's happening."

Hearing someone else enter the room, they twisted their heads at the same time to see Colt standing there.

He nodded toward Mitch, and explained, "Mitch and I are still going to work together on this, because whoever's targeting you is obviously targeting you both at home and at your business."

She nodded numbly but he was glad that she was going to have the benefit of all of the local law enforcement.

"Lia, what can you tell us is missing?" Mitch asked.

Looking around the room, she said, "I would have to go through this mess to see if I can identify what somebody was looking for. I find it strange that my office was targeted more than Mrs. Markham's or Scott's. But, then, that just leads me to believe that whatever this person was looking for they knew it must've been with me."

Watching her closely, he noticed as an inkling of suspicion began to settle in her mind, anger forcing its way past the shock. Her fists landed on her hips as she whirled around, staring at the each person in the room in turn. With her voice shaking with rage, she said, "It has to do with the investigation of the town finances. Since I came to Baytown, the only work I've done is tax accounting for several of the businesses here. Nothing weird. Nothing strange. Nothing unusual. I haven't had a disagreement with one single client. But when the Mayor and the Town Council accepted my bid to do the forensic accounting work for them, the threats started."

Mitch said, "I know this is hard for you to do, with this mess in here, but we need you to go through everything to see what might be missing."

Before she had a chance to reply, a noise came from

the front lobby, sounding as if Grant was in the process of detaining someone.

"This is an official crime scene. You can't come in here."

"I work here!"

Lia's gaze jumped toward the door as a man pushed his way through. He was wearing jeans and tennis shoes, with a slightly wrinkled polo. She blinked. She had never seen him in anything other than a button up shirt, tie, and dress pants. Blinking again, she wondered why she was noticing something as ridiculous as his clothing when they had much more important things to be concerned about. "Scott. That's my other accountant, Scott Redding. I called him before I got here."

Mitch stepped out of the doorway and spoke with Scott and Grant. After a moment, he stepped back into her office, Scott following. His eyes grew wide as he looked at the mess scattered about the floor, and he breathed, "Holy shit", before his gaze jumped to hers. "Are you okay?"

She started to nod automatically, then realized that was a ridiculous reply. "Quite frankly, no. I'm furious as hell and was trying to figure out what might be missing. Did you look at your office?"

"I took a glance in, but it's not nearly like this." He rubbed his chin, and said, "Although I've only been working for a short time here, so my file cabinet was not as full."

Grant was standing at the doorway, looking unhappy at having been bulldozed over, and Mitch said, "Scott, please go with Officer Wilder and take a look in your office. We finished dusting for fingerprints in there, so you can go ahead and look through what might be missing."

Scott sent her a sympathetic grimace before turning and following Grant back into his office. After they left, Colt confirmed, "I assume your partner, Scott Redding, is Thomas Redding's grandson?"

"Yes," she replied, suddenly feeling very tired. Giving her head a little shake, she added, "Not that it matters, but he's not actually a partner. Technically, he's my employee." Colt raised an eyebrow in question and she explained, "I bought the business from Thomas Redding when he was retiring and ready to sell. He mentioned that he had a grandson that was an accountant but was just out of school. I had only been here a few months when Scott contacted me and said that he would be interested in working here. Even though he was Thomas' grandson, I didn't want to take on a full partner until I knew that we would work well together." She shrugged, and added, "He's been doing great work and prefers doing the taxes, which is not my personal favorite. We haven't talked about him becoming a full-fledged partner, yet, but I don't see why that might not happen as long as things keep going well."

Mitch rubbed his chin, his expression thoughtful for a moment, before walking over to close her office door. "Is there any benefit to him for you to not succeed?"

Rearing back in surprise, she tilted her head, and asked, "Not succeed? I don't know what you mean."

Aiden stepped closer again, standing right behind her, with his hands on her shoulders. "I think Mitch is asking if there is any reason why Scott would want you to leave Baytown or back away from the investigation."

She twisted her head around to look up at him before glancing back to Mitch. Shaking her head, she said, "No. That wouldn't make any sense. I'm being paid for the investigation, or rather, my accounting business is being paid for the investigation. For my firm to be financially stable, I need to have customers that pay. Scott's on my payroll, just like Mrs. Markham. For him to want me to leave would be about as silly as Mrs. Markham wanting me to leave."

Mitch nodded, and said, "Don't worry about my questions, Lia. I just have to consider all possible avenues of inquiry."

A knock sounded on the door and Colt turned around to open it. Grant was standing on the other side with Scott behind him. Grant said, "Mr. Redding has been through his office and reports that he doesn't see anything that's missing."

Her shoulders slumped underneath Aiden's fingers and he pulled her back tighter to his front. Looking at Mitch, he asked, "Do you want her to go through her files now?"

"The sooner, the better, but I know you probably want to get home to Emily."

She sighed heavily, her mind racing with what she needed to do. "I'm sure Emily will sleep for another couple of hours. I could go through things now, and then go home to be there when she gets up. Then I can take her to school and come straight back. I just want to be here before Mrs. Markham gets in, because I'm sure this is going to upset her."

Scott's eyes landed on her, and he offered, "If you want to get home to Emily, I can come back early and be here when Mrs. Markham first gets here. We'll also need to get someone in to repair the door. I don't mind handling that as well."

She nodded in appreciation and said, "That'd be great Scott. I'll look at things quickly right now, but will leave to get home to Emily soon."

Mitch looked at Scott, and added, "I will ask that you not move any of Lia's files. I need her to make sure she knows what is here and what might've been taken."

She looked up, and said, "I can let you know right now that, if they were looking for anything to do with my investigation into the town's finances, they wouldn't have found it here." That statement had Mitch, Colt, Grant, and Scott pinning their gazes on her. She explained, "I planned on working on that at home, so those files were in my locked briefcase along with my laptop. So, if someone was in here looking for that, it was a waste of their time."

Later that day, after Emily was safe at school, Lia went back to her office. She had been able to warn Mrs. Markham of the events that transpired before she got in so when she arrived she, once she got over her shock, immediately jumped in to begin straightening up. Scott had procured someone to come replace the door and

MARYANN JORDAN

she was grateful that he was able to do so quickly, not wanting to draw untoward attention to what had happened on the inside.

She went through all of her files, finding everything that should have been there was, and Mrs. Markham came in to help her reorganize them before placing them back into the file credenza. It was lunchtime before she knew it, and her office was descended upon by Jillian, Katelyn, Belle, and Tori. Not surprised her friends had heard, she gratefully accepted the food they brought by.

"I couldn't believe it," Jillian said, opening the containers of sandwiches, "when Grant told me this morning what had happened. What the hell was someone looking for?"

She did not answer at first, too busy chewing her bite of sandwich and then gulping from her cup of sweet tea. Blushing, she replied, "Sorry. I didn't realize how hungry I was!" The others chuckled and gave her a moment. Finally, she said, "The only thing I can figure is that someone really wants to hamper the town investigation. But who would have broken in here? I have no idea."

Tori's eyes narrowed, and she said, "But that wouldn't stop the investigation. It would just mean that you'd have to start over, which would be a pain in the ass, but it wouldn't stop it."

Nodding, she agreed. "I've had two interesting visits recently. One from Mr. Scarsdale—"

Katelyn gasped. "The man running for mayor

272

against Corwin?" She nodded again and Katelyn continued. "What the hell is he after?"

"My guess is that he's trying to find some information that he could leak to the public before my investigation is finished. Something that would implicate the Mayor in some kind of wrongdoing. But I told him that I am unable to release any information about my investigation until it is complete and goes to the Town Council. At that point, it will be public information, but not before."

Shaking her head, Belle said, "I had no idea small-town politics could be so vicious. I guess that's just very naïve of me."

She looked at her and offered a small smile. "It's not just you, Belle. This has been a real shock to me, too."

"Who was your other visitor?" Tori asked.

Wiping her hands on a napkin, she replied, "Our favorite town manager, Silas Mills." At that, all four women groaned and she chuckled. "Yep. He, on the other hand, doesn't want me to find anything that might harm Corwin's chances for reelection."

"So, what are you gonna do?" Jillian asked, folding up the remnants of the lunches and putting them back in the plastic bag.

"I'm going to keep doing my job," she said. "I've got the police here in town and the Sheriff's Department where I live keeping an eye on things. I've got Aiden staying overnight, so we're safe." She was quiet for a moment and the others let her gather her thoughts. Finally, she looked up and said, "It's not the way I

MARYANN JORDAN

expected my relationship with Aiden to progress, and I guess it seems a little fast."

"Not as far as I'm concerned," Katelyn quipped. "You and Emily are perfect for my brother and he appears to be right for you as well. If ever there was a good man who just needed a good woman, it's him."

She smiled, staring at Katelyn, and the others jumped in. "I've known Aiden my whole life," Jillian said. "Katelyn said it perfectly. You two are meant for each other."

"He's so good with Emily," she admitted. "It was hard to trust again after Carl, but Aiden has turned out to be the man for us."

As her friends hugged her goodbye and left, she went back to work, finally with a smile on her face.

26

Aiden stood in Lia's kitchen, heating the casserole that his mother sent over. He had picked Emily up from school and the two of them practiced batting in the backyard before coming inside so that he could get dinner ready.

Perched on one of the stools at the counter and asking lots of questions, she barely gave him a chance to answer before asking another one. "What was it like to grow up near the beach?"

"It was a lot of fun. Me and my friends would spend the summer on the beach or, when we wanted to get away from the girls, we had a boys-only hideout."

"Why would you want to get away from the girls?"

Chuckling, he said, "Because sometimes the girls would get on our nerves. And we wanted to do guy things."

"What kind of guy things?"

His chuckles turned into laughter as he tried to

think of an answer. "Well, to be honest, I can't really think of any right now. But when I was ten years old that seemed important." Shrugging, he added, "But my sister, Katelyn, would climb trees and almost always find us."

"What was it like having a brother and a sister?" she asked, her eyes wide as she stared at him.

"Most of the time it was really great, because I always had someone to play with. But, sometimes it was a pain to have an older brother always telling me what to do and a younger sister always wanting the attention."

She grew quiet after that, her face contemplative. Scrunching her nose, she looked up at him again, and said, "Sometimes I get bored and wish that I had a little brother or sister, but my daddy died and Mama said that it takes a mama and daddy together to have a baby." She was quiet for another moment, before startling him when she asked, "Do you think you and Mama will give me a little brother or sister?"

Stammering, he said, "Uh...well, um...I...you'll have to ask your mom."

"But you've kissed her. I've seen you kiss her. Don't you want to make a baby with Mama?"

The room felt small as he tried to think of what Lia would want him to say. The idea of being settled, much less being married and becoming a father, had been a far-flung idea until he met Lia and Emily. Now, no longer afraid of those new roles, he actually looked forward to that possibility. But considering that he and

Lia had not spoken of that yet, he was terrified of saying the wrong thing to Emily.

Much to his relief, he heard the front door open and close. Looking toward Emily, he said, "Your mom is home."

In typical little girl fashion, she jumped off the stool and ran toward the front door, her arms waving in the air to greet her mother. Leaning against the counter, Aiden blew out his breath, grateful for the reprieve. A moment later, Lia walked into the kitchen with Emily and moved straight to him. She reached up to give him a kiss but, taking in his expression, stopped short, cocking her head to the side in question.

Leaning down, he kissed her lightly, aware that Emily was staring at them with a wide smile on her face. Whispering so only Lia would hear, he said, "Little ones have big questions. We'll talk later."

Her eyes widened and she glanced down at her daughter before looking back up at him. Grinning, she nodded before turning her attention to the casserole sitting on the counter. "That smells amazing," she said, diverting Emily's attention. "Since Aiden fixed our dinner, why don't we set the table?"

Later that night, as Lia tucked Emily into bed, Emily asked, "Are you and Aiden going to get married?"

"Uh…," she stammered. "Why do you ask?"

"Because I want a new baby brother or sister. One of my friends at school, her mom just got married and is gonna have a baby. So, since you and Aiden kiss, I thought you would get married, too."

"Emily, sweetheart, I do like Aiden a lot and I'm glad

that you like him also. But we just started seeing each other not too long ago. For people to consider marriage, they should get to know each other really well."

Emily's nose wrinkled as she pondered that. "Are you going to keep getting to know him really well?"

She could not keep the grin from her face. "Yes, I think so. And, hopefully, he wants to keep getting to know us as well."

Emily seemed satisfied with that answer and slid down in bed. She tucked her in tightly, bending over to kiss her forehead. "Sweet dreams, baby."

Just as she walked to the door and flipped off the light, Emily said, "Mama? I'm glad you like Aiden. If you want to marry him, it's okay with me. I'd like him to be my daddy."

The air rushed from her lungs and tears stung the back of her eyes. Other than talking about her dad having gone to heaven, Emily had not said much about not having a father. Carl was a memory to Emily, a face she most likely only remembered because of the photographs placed in frames on her dresser. Blowing her a kiss, she walked out, shutting the door behind her.

She only made it about halfway down the stairs before her legs gave out from under her. Plopping down, she dropped her head to her knees.

Aiden heard Lia begin her descent, but after a few minutes she still had not made it to the living room. Walking to the bottom of the stairs, he observed her sitting halfway up. "Babe? Are you okay?" He hurried up and sat next to her, wrapping his arm around her. "What's wrong?"

She lifted her gaze to him, staring deeply into his eyes. "I guess I need to know what you and Emily were talking about when I got home."

"Oh, that sounds serious." He stood, assisting her upward, and they walked downstairs. Once settled on the sofa, he tucked her into his side. His fingers drifted along her arm and she began to relax.

"It started with her just being inquisitive. You know, she wanted to know what it was like growing up near the beach, what I did with my friends when I was little, and...what it was like to have a brother and a sister. "

Twisting her head around to look at him, she nodded for him to continue.

"Then she asked if you and I were going to give her a baby brother or sister."

She shook her head and chuckled. "Yeah, she pretty much asked me the same thing just now."

"What did you tell her?"

"I wondered what prompted her question and when I asked her she told me that a friend's mom just got married and they're gonna have a baby."

"So...what did you tell her?" he repeated.

She leaned forward and twisted around on the sofa so that she could face him. As she drew nearer, he placed his hands on her hips and shifted her so that she was straddling him. Face to face, she said, "I always try to be honest with her. I told her that I really liked you and that we were getting to know each other. I also let her know that her friend's mom had probably been dating that man for a long time."

"And?"

Huffing, she asked, "Do you really want to know everything she asked?"

He reached up and cupped her face with both of his hands, smoothing his thumbs over her satiny cheeks. "Yeah, babe. I really do."

She sucked in her lips for just a minute, and then said, "I told her that I wanted you and I to keep getting to know each other really well." She held his gaze, and added, "I suppose I should be as honest with you as I am with her. She then told me that she really likes you too and if we wanted to get married, it was okay with her."

As soon as the words were out of her mouth, she blushed deep red. "Please don't take that the wrong way. I'm not saying that we—"

He pressed his fingers against her lips, stilling her words, then, smiled as he leaned in, kissing her forehead before sliding his lips down to kiss her nose. He continued his path of kisses, landing on her lips. "That's one of the nicest things that anyone has ever said to me, babe. Please don't feel embarrassed about what she said."

"I told the girls at lunch today that this seemed to be going so fast, but Katelyn disagreed. She said that when something is right, you just know it."

"That sounds like Katelyn." He chuckled, then added, "And I find her usually right."

They began to kiss and it quickly flamed into making out on the living room sofa like two teenagers. As his hand slid up her shirt and cupped her breast, she grabbed his wrist.

"Sorry, babe," he said, shifting on the couch to ease his erection pressing against his jeans.

"No, no. I don't want us to stop. I just want us to take this upstairs."

He leaned back and eyed her carefully. "Are you sure? We don't have to do this."

She moved forward the inch that their lips were separated and latched onto him, putting all of her emotions into the kiss. She placed her palms against his chest and pushed gently, until she could slide out from under him. Standing, she reached her hands out and said, "I want this. I want you. I know we need to be careful and I know we need to be quiet. We'll lock my door, so there's no chance that Emily could walk in on us. I have no reason to think that she would get up during the night, but if she does, we can be dressed."

He held his breath, yearning to hold her while they lay in bed and, yet, wanting her to be certain. She smiled and took his hand, leading him to the stairs. He followed eagerly and once in her bedroom, she clicked the door lock, assuring privacy.

He pulled his phone from his jeans pocket and set the alarm. "This will ensure that I wake up and can be downstairs before Emily wakes."

Lia smiled and he smirked, asking, "What's that look for?"

"Nothing. Just realized that falling for you is no longer a possibility, because I've already fallen." His heart nearly exploded at her confession and his mouth fell open, wanting to say something but not sure how to put it into words. "Give me just a minute," she called over her shoulder, as she headed into the bathroom.

He sat on the edge of the bed and quickly divested himself of his boots, socks, and shirt. He had just started to unfasten his jeans when she walked back into the room, clad in a silky, pale blue robe. With the bathroom lights behind her, her hair appeared even more shiny, a halo about her head. He itched to bury his fingers in her tresses.

She sashayed straight toward him, her hands loosening the tied belt. Keeping her eyes on him, she stopped only when her breasts brushed against his chest.

He watched, enraptured, as she continued to loosen the robe's belt, the lapels hanging open showing her cleavage and the tops of her plump breasts.

His hands lifted to the edges of her robe, pushing it over her shoulders, unwrapping a delectable present. With very little effort, the silky material landed in a pile at her feet. Dragging his eyes downward, he lovingly gazed over her body from her breasts to her tapered waist that flared out at her full hips. Her legs were long and toned and he could not wait to have them wrapped around his waist.

Bending quickly, he lifted her into his arms and lay her gently onto the bed. His cock, already pressing against the zipper of his jeans, was straining to be relieved.

She leaned up on her elbows, dropped her gaze to his crotch, and said, "That looks painful."

"It is," he smirked. "Do you think you have a remedy for my...uh...pressing situation?"

Lia giggled then clapped her hand over her mouth to stay quiet. Whispering, she said, "Yes. I think I have exactly what you need." Giving in to the urge to be more daring than she had been, she slowly opened her legs, exposing herself to his lust filled gaze.

"Damn, babe. You could make any man drop to his knees just to worship at your body."

"And you're the only man that I want," she said, her eyes shining. As Aiden kicked off his jeans, she lowered her gaze to travel over his body. His dark hair was a little shaggy and she could not wait to run her fingers through it. She continued her perusal from his muscular chest to his defined abs and as he dropped his boxers, she feasted her eyes upon his erection. "You are so gorgeous," she said, staring at his muscles flexing as he leaned over her.

"Oh, Lia, I was just going to say the same thing about you," he fisted his cock up and down its length, "but before I give in to the urge to plunge inside your warmth, I have to taste you first." With that, he knelt on the floor, pulling her legs toward him.

As he kissed her inner thighs, she flopped back on the bed, heady sensations rolling through her. He licked her folds attentively, as though memorizing the taste of her. She jerked and he grinned as her hips lifted from the bed. Sliding his fingers inside her channel, he used his mouth as he nipped, licked, sucked and worked her into a frenzy.

Just when she thought she could take no more, he

sucked on her clit while sliding a finger deep inside. Moving his finger in just the right way, it hit the spot that he had been aiming for and she moaned as quietly as possible as her orgasm rushed over her. After a moment, she relaxed, boneless as she lay sated on the mattress.

Barely able to raise her head to watch as he crawled over her body, she whispered, "This may kill me, trying to stay quiet while you're making me feel things I've never felt before."

He stared at her quizzically. "Never?"

Realizing her comment had inadvertently brought Carl up, she shook her head. "I'm sorry. I didn't mean to bring up…well, what I mean is…" She sighed. Holding his gaze, she explained, "No. I thought what Carl and I had was good, but I've never felt like I do when I'm with you."

A slow smile curved his lips and he leaned down to kiss a path across her breasts. Lifting his head, he held her gaze, and said, "You're the only woman who makes me feel this way. I've never had a connection with anyone the way I feel with you. And Lia, you have to know, I only want you." He placed a kiss over her heart, before sliding his lips up to hers.

Just like earlier, their kiss turned wild and flamed hot. The soft mounds of her breasts pressed against his chest and he slid back down her body to feast upon her nipples. She lifted her legs and wrapped her ankles around his waist, pulling him toward her.

"Babe, are you on the pill?"

Her gaze held his, searching. "Yes, I am."

His expression was pained, as he said, "I completely understand if you don't want to, but I'm clean. We have to be tested as volunteers for the fire department, and my last test was about three weeks ago, and have the results on my phone. I can get tested again whenever you say. But I promise, I have never gone ungloved. Ever."

"I believe you," Lia breathed against his lips, stealing Aiden's breath.

He held his weight off her chest, balancing on his forearms, and sealed his lips over hers. He plunged his tongue into her mouth, intoxicated with her very essence. Moving his straining cock to her sex, he looked down at her face, her eyes holding nothing but trust.

"Tell me what you want," he begged, holding his cock just at her entrance. He battled the urge to plunge deep inside her but forced himself to go slow. Inhaling, he kept his eyes on her, carefully watching her face as she held his gaze.

"Aiden, all I want is you."

Hearing the words she was giving him, he smiled as he entered her slowly, stretching her, his cock hitting every nerve along the way. Building the friction quickly, he kissed down her neck, sucking on the tender area where her pulse throbbed.

She reached her hands around his shoulders, feeling the muscles bunch and cord underneath her fingertips. Her legs entwined around his waist, opening her up as much as she could, willing to give him all of her body. He groaned and she lifted her hips, matching his rhythm.

As the friction continued to build, she felt jolts of electricity firing through all of her nerves. The world fell away, taking with it all of the cares that she had been holding onto. Only feeling the rocking of her body as he powered into her, the tremors that began in her core soon exploded outward.

Aiden watched as Lia pressed her kiss-swollen lips together in an effort to keep from crying out. He would have preferred hearing her unbridled passion, but it was worth it to stay quiet just to experience the gift that she was giving him.

Wanting to prolong their pleasure, he rolled quickly, flipping her on top of his body. "I want to see you," he begged. Moving to her knees, she leaned over and placed her hands on his chest, her long hair hanging down in a curtain around them. Lifting herself before plunging back down, she quickly got her rhythm and began riding him.

Unable to believe that she was going to come again, Lia threw her head back, her smile wide on her face.

"Please, babe," he begged. "I want to see your face when you come."

She dropped her chin and focused her dark eyes on his, her smile beaming down at him. She felt her inner muscles clenching and he reached between them, pressing on her clit. Pinching her lips together once more, she rode out her orgasm, muffling the sounds of her pleasure.

She watched in fascination as his orgasm rocketed through him. His head pressed back into the pillow as he continued to thrust upward until the last drop had been wrung from his body.

She fell forward onto his chest, and a loud grunt emitted from his lips. She giggled and he rolled them so that they were lying side by side. For several minutes they held each other's gazes...neither speaking, nor needing to. Words were no longer necessary as love flowed between them.

Aiden knew what he felt, and he knew it was different than any other time in his life. Sex had always been an action, but never an emotion. But Lia had changed him, and he had no desire to ever go back. Knowing he had to say what was on his heart, he could only pray that she was ready to hear the words. "I love you, Lia. I can't hold that back anymore. I have to let you know. I love you and I love Emily. And I want us to be together."

She held his gaze and his heart quickened as he a tear slid down her cheek. He wiped it with his thumb, uncertain what to say.

"I love you, too, Aiden."

"Then why are you crying?"

She swallowed deeply as another tear slid down her cheek and he captured it as well. "Because I'm happy, and I never thought I would be happy like this again."

He kissed her once more, this time with all the emotion that was swirling around them. As their sweat-soaked bodies cooled, he reluctantly climbed from the bed. He bent down to pull on his boxers and looked over his shoulder at her. "Sweetheart, as much as I would love to lie all night with you, skin to skin, I don't want to risk Emily trying to find you during the night and us not being ready."

Kneeling on the bed, Lia felt even more love for Aiden, knowing that he cared so much for her daughter. Walking to her dresser, she pulled out her pajama pants and a camisole before moving into the bathroom. A moment later she came back into the room and crawled into bed with him.

He wrapped his arms around her, and rubbed his hands up and down her sides. "I will never again feel silk and not think of you."

Smiling wide, she could not remember the last time she felt such peace. Right now, it was as though all the cares of the world could not touch them.

As her body drifted into slumber, his arms wrapped tighter around her, cocooning her in protection and love.

27

Aiden was in the kitchen early the next morning, stirring oatmeal and flipping bacon, when Emily came down the stairs. She was dressed in her school clothes, but looked up at him sleepily.

"Where's Mama?"

"She's upstairs getting dressed for work. Would you like some breakfast?"

"Uh huh."

He grinned as he dished up breakfast and set it in front of her on the counter. She was staring up at him, her nose scrunched, and he could see her mind working behind her eyes.

"You were here last night, when I went to bed."

"Uh...yeah."

"And you're here this morning, when I got up."

A sweat broke out on his forehead and once again he wondered where she was going with her inquisitive mind. "I want to make sure that you and your mom are taken care of."

"Then why don't you just stay here all the time? You could move in and be with us."

He stared at her, now looking up at him with such hope, and his heart pounded in his chest. Just then, he saw Lia step into the kitchen, her eyes wide, and he knew she had heard what Emily asked. Dropping his gaze back to the little girl staring so trustingly into his face, he replied, "I'd like that, Emily. When the time is right, I'd like nothing more than that."

The wide smile on Emily's face combined with the curve of Lia's lips caused his heart to nearly burst.

Lia stepped further into the kitchen so that Emily could see her, and said, "Aiden and I will figure out the right time to make that kind of decision, sweetheart. But, until then, we have him with us lots of the time."

Emily, obviously satisfied with that answer, dug into her breakfast. Lia walked over and wrapped her arms around him, rising up on her tiptoes to kiss him lightly. As he stood watching his two women eat and get ready for their day, calm slid through him.

This is it. They are mine. He now knew what his parents had...what Ginny and Brogan had...what Katelyn and Gareth had. And he knew his days of playing Peter Pan were over.

Lia walked into the Municipal Building and made her way past the first receptionist, walking straight to

Celia's desk. Celia looked up, a grimace marring her fake smile, and said, "Oh, yes. I forgot that you made an appointment, didn't you?"

"Yes, I did. I assume you have a place where we can talk?"

Celia nodded, but made her wait as she straightened her desk, which was already neat. Finally, after delaying another minute, she stood, smoothed her hands down her tight skirt, and clicked her stiletto heels toward the conference room. She followed Celia in and closed the door behind her.

Celia blinked when she heard the door shut and gave a nervous laugh. "Oh, my, this must be very official."

Lia took a seat and opened her briefcase, pulling out several files before opening her laptop. Celia slid into a seat across from her, her fingers twitching for a moment before she clasped her hands together.

"I want to question you further about the security of the unsigned checks in your desk. Specifically, how long are they there while waiting for Mayor Banks' signature?"

"I…uh…"

"While the final results of my investigation will go straight to the Town Council, I will let you know that one of my recommendations will be that this step be eliminated. There is no reason why the Treasurer cannot maintain control of those checks until she watches the Mayor sign them himself. To have an interval of time where they are out of her hands, or his, is not good practice."

"I…uh…just do as I'm told," Celia stammered.

Celia's demeanor changed to one of uncertainty and Lia continued to push. "How often would you say that the folder with checks is given to you instead of directly to the Mayor?"

"Uh…about twice a month, maybe," Celia replied, her brow furrowing in thought.

"Are they ever left unattended? For example, when you go to lunch or, perhaps, even overnight?"

Her head bobbing, Celia answered, "Yes. I mean, certainly when I go to lunch." She licked her lips, and then added, "A few times…uh…overnight as well. If Corwin…um…Mayor Banks does not come back from a meeting or doesn't want to be bothered at the time, then he will sign them the next day."

"Is there anyone who knows that they are in your desk?"

This time, instead of answering, Celia huffed. "I don't know what you're getting at. I don't know why I'm here being treated like a criminal. I've done nothing wrong. I'm just doing exactly what I've been told to do by Mayor Banks!"

"Ms. Ring, I'm not making an accusation," she said calmly. "My job is to investigate. And in order to do so, I have to have an understanding of how procedures work, where they are failing, and what may have happened in order for someone to have taken money."

With lips pinched, Celia continued to answer her questions as succinctly as she could get away with. When they were finished, she thanked her and Celia pushed her chair back sharply, stood quickly, and marched out of the room almost slamming the door behind her.

Since the conference room was quiet, and she knew that she might want to question others, she stayed, continuing to work. Thirty minutes later, she walked to the door, wanting to question Mark Weber again. With her hand on the doorknob, she halted as she heard voices just outside.

"What did she want?"

Knowing she should not eavesdrop, she nonetheless leaned her ear closer to the door, recognizing Silas' nasally voice.

"She just wanted to know more about the folder of checks that stays locked in my desk at times. I tell you, it's downright insulting to have my work questioned like I'm some criminal."

"Well, what did you tell her?" he asked.

"I told her what I do. They are locked in my desk until Corwin wants them. I don't even know why he bothers. He doesn't even look at the checks that he signs! Obviously, I didn't tell her that, but she was taking notes on everything I said. Who knows what her damn investigation file folder has in it."

There was a moment of silence before Silas spoke again.

"Are you available tonight?"

Lia winced, knowing how unprofessional it was to have her ear to a door in the first place, but doubly so because of what she'd just heard. Before she could lean back, Celia answered.

"For what? Dinner? Or just a fuck?"

Silas whined, "Don't be like that."

"Those days of *easy access* are over. I told you that the last time you broke things off to be with your fiancée. Now *ex*-fiancée. Anyway, I have a date tonight."

"With who? That new accountant? He's only in town to see if he can wrangle his grandfather's business away from that newcomer."

"Jealous? That particular emotion doesn't become you, Silas."

The voices faded away and she heard the tapping of Celia's heels as she walked down the hall. Blowing out her breath, she wondered about the comment made concerning Scott. *He's after the business?* Giving a mental shake, she pushed that thought to the side.

Stepping outside the conference room, she had the opportunity to stare closely at Celia's desk. Unlike the metal, utilitarian desks of the receptionist in the front, Celia's desk was large, polished wood, with drawers on one side and a filing drawer on the other. *It would be so easy for someone to have made a spare key to her desk. Or, she might have given a spare key to someone. But who?*

Walking around Celia's desk, she made her way to the hall where Sandra and Mark's offices were. Just as she got to the door, she heard their voices inside.

"She was with Celia for a long time. What do you think she knows?"

She recognized Mark's voice and lifted her hand to knock, refusing to eavesdrop again, but before she could make a sound, she heard Sandra's reply.

"I can't imagine what's going to happen if she keeps sticking her nose in everything."

With her hand still in a raised position, her fist halted on its way to the door, cold dread seeping through her. It was an unfamiliar feeling, considering she had never been threatened during an investigation before, at least not before it went to trial. Frozen in place, she continued to listen.

"I only do what I've been instructed to do," Sandra continued. "But what Celia does beyond that? Well, I have no idea, but I don't trust her."

"Yeah, but Corwin does. He acts like he can't do his job without her right there."

"Humph. I'd say he was getting some on the side, if I didn't know Corwin's wife. That woman knows everything and she'd string him up by his balls if he ever cheated on her."

"I'll be glad when the whole thing is over and I don't have to worry about Amelia Smith anymore. Her investigation just feels like someone snooping into what we've done."

Sandra finished with, "Well, just remember that there's only so much she can find out from looking at the reports, so keep your wits about you when she talks to you. She's so thorough, she probably sleeps with that folder of notes and reports she keeps on all of us."

Carefully tiptoeing down the hall, Lia then turned and walked firmly back toward the office. No longer hearing any voices, she knocked on the door before turning the knob. Swinging the door open, she saw Mark and Sandra sitting on opposite sides of the room.

Plastering a smile on her face, she said, "Mark, I've got a few more questions to ask you. You can meet me in the conference room in about five minutes." She shut the door without giving him a chance to protest and walked back to the conference room. Closing her eyes and gathering her wits for a moment, she steeled herself for another long afternoon of interviews, hoping she would not overhear any more threats.

Aiden stood in the open doorway of the Baytown Fire Station with Brogan and Zac, discussing an upcoming meeting with all of the volunteer firefighters. Zac was the former Fire Chief and was now the Captain of the Rescue Services. As they chatted, his attention was drawn by the sight of Scott and Celia talking across the street of the Municipal Building.

"Hey, you listenin' to us?" Brogan asked.

Jerking his head to the side, he asked, "Either of you ever notice Lia's new accountant, Scott Redding, hanging out with Celia?"

Both men shook their heads, but Zac laughed. "Hell, Celia's tried to bang just about every eligible man that's come through town. Not surprised that she's set her sights on him."

Brogan, studying him carefully, asked, "What's got you interested?"

He shook his head, his fist planted on his hips. "I don't know. With the threats coming into Lia, I'm spooked about everything. Obviously, Celia is one of the people having to be investigated with the whole town finance mess, and it just seems like Scott and she got chummy awful quick. Probably nothing…like I said, I'm just suspicious."

"Everything okay between you and Lia?" Zac asked, his gaze assessing.

A grin slipped across his face, easing the concern creases next to his eyes. "Yeah. You want to know the damnedest thing?" Seeing that he had both Zac and Brogan's attention, he continued, "Emily told me last night that she wanted me to stay there. She wants me to keep dating Lia. Said she'd like us to be a family."

"Damn, Aiden. That is serious."

"He's got this," Brogan said, a slow smile curving his lips.

"And that doesn't scare me one fuckin' bit," he pronounced, offering a chin lift to his brother for his support. "Well, I should amend that. I think becoming anyone's father is scary. But with Lia and Emily, I'm all in."

Lia shoved all of her papers and her laptop back into her briefcase, securing it firmly. Slinging it over her shoulder along with her purse, she walked to the door of the conference room. On the wall right next to her was the door that led straight into the Mayor's office. Just as she was ready to enter the hall, she heard Corwin's blustering voice.

For the third time that day, she halted, listening to

what was being said. Inwardly, she tried to convince herself that if she had not been threatened she would not have succumbed to such an unprofessional habit.

"I know she's been here all day. I've heard nothing but complaints from some of the department heads. My wife is on a rampage about the fact that I've got a possible thief amongst our workers and my secretary is threatening to quit!"

"We need to make sure that her findings are not reported before the next election."

She recognized Silas' voice again and dropped her chin to her chest. She was beginning to think that the town offices were filled with vipers.

"I know that, but I'm ahead of Scarsdale in the latest Gazette polls."

"Voters can change on a dime," Silas bit back. "It's bad enough that the Town Council is having her look into everything, but you've got to keep convincing the public that everything is under control here. At least until after the election!"

"Well, if you can think of a way to keep her from reporting sooner, that's fine. Drag your heels, put her off. Whatever. For me, I've got to look like everything is hunky-dory with the town's finances."

The two men must have moved further away from the door, because she was unable to hear anything more. Sighing heavily, the depressing weight on her shoulders was growing. Longing for nothing more than to see Emily and Aiden, she threw open the conference room door and stepped out into the hall. With barely a nod to the others standing around, she moved quickly out of the building.

———

"Mrs. Markham? Do you know if Lia is going to be coming back today?" Scott asked, popping his head into the lobby.

She smiled at him and shook her head. "No, I believe she's going straight from the Municipal Building, home."

Nodding his thanks, he moved back to his office and looked down at his desk. He rarely took work home for the weekend, but remembered Lia commenting that she kept her current work with her in her briefcase, along with her laptop. With his hand on the doorknob, he pondered for a minute before shutting the door. Walking back through the lobby on his way out, he called goodbye to Mrs. Markham. "Have a nice weekend. See you on Monday."

Deciding to have a drink before he went home, he headed to Finn's. Sitting at the bar, alone, he overheard Aiden and Brogan chatting about the weekend.

"I know that Ginny's off-duty this weekend," Aiden said. "Why don't you take tomorrow off and hang with your wife. I've got it covered here."

"You sure?" Brogan asked.

"Fuck yeah, bro. Don't you think I can handle it?" Aiden said, a wide smile on his face.

Brogan popped the dishtowel out toward him and he jumped back quickly, laughing as it missed him.

"Stop cussing in front of the customers," Brogan growled.

He watched the playful banter between the two brothers as he nursed his beer. Finishing a few minutes later, he threw some money on the bar and slipped out.

28

Aiden manned the grill on the back deck after Lia confessed she rarely cooked on it. While she was inside chopping vegetables, Emily clambered up on a chair so that she could watch what he was doing. Afraid that she was too close to the flame, he swooped her into his arms and dragged the chair back several feet, before plopping her down in it again. Finding her as inquisitive as ever, he laughed at her many questions and constant chatter.

She watched as the meat dripped grease onto the coals, turning her good ear toward the sound. She scrunched her nose and, recognizing that look, he knew a question was coming.

"How long does it take for the hamburgers to cook?"

He shrugged and winked. "I guess it takes them just as long as it needs to. They'll get done when they get done."

"Mama never cooks out here. How did you learn to cook on a grill?"

"My dad taught me. He taught me a lot of things." He described the camping trips on the beach that his family used to take when he was a little boy, building campfires, roasting marshmallows, and his dad teaching him how to fish.

Fascinated with the idea of camping, she asked, "What was it like to sleep in a tent?"

"Well, usually, my brother and I would drag our sleeping bags out so that we could sleep under the stars."

Eyes wide, she exclaimed, "But what about crabs?"

"When I was a kid, I guess I never really thought about them. At least, we never got pinched by one."

Wistfully, she said, "I wish I could go camping sometime." Looking up into his face, she added, "I never had a daddy to teach me things like that."

Lia picked that moment to step outside to check on the burgers and heard what Emily said. His gaze jumped to hers and he saw pain slash across her face. He had never met Carl, of course, but at that moment felt torn between hating the man for abandoning Lia and Emily, regret that Carl had died in the course of his duty, and gratitude that he had them in his life now.

Before Lia had a chance to speak, Emily's face brightened and she said, "But you're here now with us. You can take us camping and you can teach me things, just like you were my dad."

He smiled at Emily and, catching Lia about to step forward and intervene, he shook his head slightly at her.

Squatting down so that he could be right in front of Emily, he said, "That's right. I am here now, and this is exactly where I want to be, with you and your mom."

She threw her arms around his neck and he hugged her tight. Looking past her shoulder, his gaze moved to Lia. The smile on her beautiful face told him that she felt the same. Setting Emily down, he said, "Looks like your mom's getting anxious for the hamburgers so we better get to work."

Emily turned around and looked at Lia before plopping her hands on her waist. "Mama, they'll be done when they get done."

Laughing, Lia headed back into the kitchen.

As the evening continued, he enjoyed every moment. Eating dinner with his girls and cleaning up afterward. Piling up in the living room and watching TV, Lia snuggled up close to him, and Emily coloring on the floor. Checking the house to make sure it was secure while Lia got Emily ready for bed.

When it was time to tuck Emily in, Lia called for him. At the top of the stairs, he looked into her face questioningly and she smiled.

"Emily wants you to say good night."

Grinning, he went to her bedside and hugged her tightly. He felt as though his heart had slid into place as he kissed her good night.

Hours later, as he lay in bed after making love to Lia, he held her close, tucking a strand of hair behind her ear. "I want you to know that I've never said this to anybody else. I love you. I want us to be together."

"I love you too. I used to wonder if I could love

again…trust again." She held his gaze, her hand drifting over his jaw, her thumb gliding over his lips. Her breath warmed his face, as she said, "With you, I know I have found love again."

Clutching her to him, he rolled so that his hips were nestled in her warmth, proving his love with his body.

Not used to sleeping in on the weekends, Lia enjoyed a leisurely Saturday morning. Aiden had already left for the pub. He had told her that they had some deliveries being made early and he wanted to make sure he went over them, giving Brogan a rare day off to be with Ginny all by themselves.

Still lying in bed, she stretched, her muscles slightly achy from the night's activities. A smile spread across her face as she remembered their vows of love.

Life was strange, she thought, with its many twists and turns. When she had first met Carl, she saw him as mature and steady. It was easy to fall in love with the idea that they would have the perfect marriage. For better or worse, in sickness and health. Then, Carl had proven to not be the kind of man who could hang in for the long haul when things did not go the way he wanted them to. Funny, how he was able to lead men in battle, but unable to deal with the unexpected challenges with his own daughter.

Aiden, on the other hand, a man that she did not think would relish responsibilities, had proven to be just the man she and her daughter needed. And loved.

Hearing a noise across the hall, she realized that Emily was awake. Jumping from bed, she pulled the covers up in a jerky fashion before throwing open the door to greet her daughter.

"Good morning," she said, accepting a hug from Emily. "I'll go down and fix some breakfast for us."

"Isn't Aiden here to fix my breakfast?"

"No. Remember, he had to go into work today." Seeing her face fall, she said, "Hey, that's okay. You can still hang with your mom, just like we used to."

Emily giggled and agreed. "We can have a girls' day, right?"

Kissing the top of her head, she said, "Absolutely! After we eat, I'm going to do a little housework and then we'll have a fun girls' day."

After breakfast, Emily headed back upstairs to get dressed, promising she would pick up her toys in her room. Smiling at her daughter as she disappeared up the stairs, she pulled out the vacuum cleaner.

Lia finished vacuuming the living room and connected the stair attachment before bending over to vacuum each stair, carrying the canister vacuum with her. At the top, she popped her head into Emily's room and waved, seeing her busy placing her dolls on her bed. Continuing to vacuum down the hall, she entered her bedroom and did a thorough cleaning, including vacuuming the baseboards.

The scent of wood burning captured her attention

and she wondered if any of her neighbors were burning the piles of leaves that they had raked. Always worried about leaf fires getting out of hand, she walked over to her window and peered out, curious if she would be able to see anything.

Smoke was billowing up but, to her surprise, it was right next to the back of the house. It took a few seconds for her to realize that her back deck was on fire. Screaming for Emily, she turned and ran out of her room, down the short hall, and burst into her daughter's room.

Signing and speaking, she exclaimed, "Fire! We have to get out!"

Emily's eyes widened in understanding and she jumped up, running to her. Grabbing her hand, she ran into the hall and started down the stairs. *My phone!* Remembering it was in her purse by the front door, she stumbled to a stop at the bottom of the stairs, seeing flames licking the front door.

Turning quickly, she looked down at Emily and yelled, "Stay!" She rushed forward and grabbed her purse and briefcase, feeling the heat from the fire on the other side of the door on her face. Fumbling inside the large bag, her fingers clasped the phone and she quickly dialed 9-1-1.

Forcing her voice to remain as calm as possible, she said, "Fire! There's a fire in my house and I can't get out. Me and my daughter. The back door is on fire and so is the front. Fifteen Magnolia Street." As the words left her mouth she was struck with the thought that this was not an accident. It couldn't be, not with fire on both sides of the house. Her stomach clenched as she realized someone was carrying through with their threat.

29

Aiden's phone dinged a message and, picking it up, the text was an alert to volunteer firefighters to check in with the station for an emergency. Just as he was telling the staff at the pub to continue taking care of business, his phone rang. Seeing it was Zac, he immediately connected, assuming he was getting special instructions.

"Aiden, hold on to your shit, but get to Lia's house as fast as you can. That's where the call came from. Fire at her house."

"Fuck!" he shouted, his knees buckling as he started to rush out. Tripping, he righted himself and burst through the door of the pub, out into the sunlight. Pulling his keys from his pocket, he raced around the corner to his truck, calling Brogan on speed dial.

"Hey," Brogan greeted. "I thought you were going to handle everything—"

"Fire at Lia's house! Just got the call—"

"Hang on, bro. Ginny and I'll be right there."

Throwing open his truck door he climbed into the driver's seat, slapping his phone into the holder. He pulled out onto the street, praying he made it in time. The idea of not having Lia and Emily in his life... *Fuck that!*

As the operator told Lia to remain calm and that the fire truck was on the way, she jerked her eyes to the window in the dining room, seeing there were no flames on that side. She took a step in that direction but then stopped, remembering it was stuck with old paint.

Grabbing Emily's hand, she rushed back up the stairs, her phone still in her hand. "I can't get the down-stairs windows open," she called out to the dispatcher. "But the window in my daughter's room is near a tree and I know it will open."

"Ma'am, stay on the line," the operator said, her voice calm.

Barely listening, she said, "I can't hold the phone and get my daughter to safety. Tell them we're at the second-floor window on the east side of the house. There's an oak tree next to the house."

Reaching Emily's room, she shoved the phone in her pocket with one hand and pulled Emily along with the other. Turning, she squatted, forcing her words to be steady as her heart pounded erratically. "I'm going to open your window and see if we can reach a branch to climb down."

Emily nodded, but Lia could tell she was terrified. She flipped the latch and let out a relieved gasp when the window slid open easily. She cursed as she fiddled with the screen before it popped out and fell to the ground below.

She could hear sirens in the distance and she placed her palms on the window sill, leaning out to see how close the thick branches were to the window. *Shit!* There was one substantial branch that she could probably grab onto, but then she would have no way of getting Emily onto it as well.

Looking to the street, she saw two fire trucks racing into her driveway, followed by a number of SUVs, cars, and trucks. For an instant, she was stunned at the number of vehicles, then remembered Aiden had told her about the mostly-volunteer crew. *Maybe he'll be here, too!*

Running back to Emily's bedroom door, she slammed it shut. Grabbing a blanket off the bed, she shoved it against the bottom of the door. In case the smoke came up the stairway, they would still be partially protected.

Dashing to the open window, she leaned out again. "Over here!" she began screaming, waving her arms. Within a minute, she saw firemen rushing from the trucks and vehicles, swarming to her house.

Aiden, his heart in his throat, squealed his truck to a stop behind the fire trucks, Zac pulling the ambulance in next to him. Firefighters poured out from every-where, running to the fire trucks, assisting the ones who were already in full gear.

His feet pounded the ground as he raced toward the front door, unheeding the calls for him to stop. Brogan, who had arrived just before him, ran from the side and almost tackled him, bringing him to a stop.

Grabbing his arms, Brogan shouted, "Aiden! You gotta be smart."

He turned toward his brother, his face ravaged in panic, and shouted, "My girls! My girls are in that house!"

As the firemen battled the flames in the front and the back with their hoses, the Fire Chief ran to him. "The side! They're upstairs on the side."

Rounding the corner, he looked up, hearing Lia shouting from Emily's open window. He shouted back, trying to gain her attention. "Lia! Lia!"

She looked down, making eye contact, and yelled, "I can get to the tree, but I can't get Emily there."

"Get engine eleven over here!" the Chief ordered.

Engine eleven had a turntable ladder, which would easily reach to her second floor. "Baby!" Her attention stayed riveted on him, and he yelled, "I'm coming for you!"

Lia nodded, pulling Emily close to her at the window in case the smoke came into her bedroom. Hoping to keep Emily diverted, she looked down and said, "Watch the fire truck. It's going to come over here, and they'll send up a ladder."

Emily turned her face from her and peered out the

window, just as the fire truck drove through their yard, around the corner of the house and parked as close to the tree and house as they could.

She kept a running dialogue as she knelt next to her daughter, pointing out the stabilizing legs of the fire truck and the way the firemen maneuvered the ladder around and then upward toward them.

She did not recognize Aiden at first, who had slipped into his firemen's uniform, complete with hood and hat. By the time he had climbed part way up the ladder, and the firemen had maneuvered the top to her window, she realized who was there and her heart leaped.

He smiled at her, his lips tight, and asked, "Can you help Emily get to the windowsill? If not, I'll come in and get her."

"I've got her," she said. "What do you need her to do?"

By that time, he was at the top of the ladder, with his body right at her window. He smiled widely at Emily, and said, "Hey, Sweetie. Looks like you're having an adventure. You're going to come with me and we're going to get down the ladder together. Okay?"

Emily looked up at her, uncertainty on her face. She held her close, and said, "You'll be fine. Aiden will make sure of that."

Hugging her tightly, Lia lifted her daughter to the windowsill and held her securely while Aiden quickly fastened a safety belt and line around her. As his sure and steady arms locked around her, he held Lia's gaze for a few seconds.

"I love you," she said.

"And I love both of you," he replied. With a forced smile, he added, "I'll be right back, babe." With that, he hustled down the ladder with Emily secure, her little arms wrapped around his neck. Continuing to talk, he was not sure she could hear him, but in case she could, he wanted her to hear his voice. He felt her body shiver as he quickly met Brogan on the bottom of the ladder.

"Hey, Emily," Brogan said. "You're going to come to me now, sweetheart, so that Aiden can go up and get your mom."

She nodded and, with little trouble, made the transfer, wrapping her arms around Brogan's neck.

Aiden kissed her forehead and, bending low, said, "Don't worry, I'll get your mom." He watched for a second as Brogan made it easily to the ground with Emily in his arms, Zac ready to whisk her over to the ambulance.

Climbing back up the ladder quickly, he reached the windowsill. Lia was ready for him, with one leg already slung over to the outside. Just as efficiently, he secured the safety belt and line around her and maneuvered her body tightly to his and onto the ladder. "Hang on, babe. They're going to bring us down."

The ladder began to descend, and Lia focused her eyes solely on Aiden's face, clinging to him, knowing he was taking her to safety.

At the bottom, other firefighters reached out their arms to assist him with her, but he shook his head, throwing his hat to the ground. "She's mine. I've got her." As he unhooked her from the safety belt, she jerked her head from side to side trying to find Emily. "It's okay. She's with Zac at the ambulance." Tossing the safety line down, he grabbed her hand and together they ran over to the ambulance.

Lia's face broke into a wide smile as she rushed to Emily, scooping her into her arms and holding her in a crushing hug. Aiden wrapped his arms around both of them, and together they stood for a moment reveling in the fact that what could have been a greater disaster had ended in all lives saved.

Looking down at Emily, she said, "We're safe, sweetheart. We're okay." Emily leaned forward again, her cheek pressed against her chest and her little arms wrapping around her waist. Looking back up, Emily said, "Mama, I hear your heart."

A sob ripped from her lips and tears pricked Aiden's eyes.

Aiden sat with Emily in his lap and one arm tucked around Lia in the Baytown Police Department conference room. Mitch, Grant, Ginny, and Lance were in the room, as well as Colt and Hunter from the North Heron Sheriff's Department.

Mitch and Colt were starting to question her, but she found it hard to focus with Emily there. She really should not be hearing all this. Just then, Corrine showed up and popped her head into the room. Her gaze quickly skimmed the occupants, landing on Emily. She smiled widely, and said, "Hi, Emily. Can you come to keep me company out here for a few minutes? I brought some cookies and milk."

Emily's gaze darted from Corrine to her and, when she nodded it was okay, she slid from Aiden's lap. Tucking her hand in Corrine's, she walked toward the reception area.

"Brogan called her. Thought you'd appreciate it, not having to worry about Emily overhearing this," Aiden explained.

Nodding in relief, she slumped closer to Aiden and began answering the questions. "I didn't see anything and because I had the vacuum cleaner going, I didn't hear anything either." She sucked in a shuddering breath, her fingers flexing on Aiden's thigh. Shaking her head slowly, she said, "I know that Zac said that the fires were started using an accelerant, so obviously one or more people set them. I just can't imagine why someone would want to do that to me, especially knowing my child was inside."

The reality of what could have happened hit her and a sob burst forth from her chest. Without a second thought, she turned to bury her face in Aiden's neck and his arms wrapped tightly around her. The gathering stayed quiet, giving her a chance to cry. After a moment, she lifted her face and accepted the tissues being pressed into her hand. Wiping her eyes and blowing her nose, she sucked in another deep breath and let it out slowly.

"Even if this is about the report for the town, I still can't imagine that it's happening."

Mitch leaned forward, his eyes warm as he asked,

"Lia, how close are you in your investigation to knowing who may have been stealing the money?"

"I'm close. I think I know what has been happening and have eliminated some of the people in my inquiries. I need a little bit more time to know definitively, and then I'll be able to present my findings to the Town Council and see if they want to turn the investigation over to the District Attorney."

Corrine popped her head into the room again, this time her eyes wide. "Uh, I think you all need to hear what Emily has to say."

She jumped up, thinking Emily was ill, and said, "What's wrong?" She was already stepping over Aiden's feet to get to the door, when Corrine shook her head.

"No, no. Nothing's wrong, but…" Turning her head, Corinne smiled, and said, "Emily, honey, will you tell the nice policeman and your mommy what you just said to me?"

Emily, with her hand in Corrine's, walked back into the room and looked at her. "I looked out the window when I was cleaning my room," she said, "and saw the Mayor-man walking around our house."

3 0

The room, silent as a tomb for a few seconds, suddenly came to life as numerous people spoke at the same time.

"Quiet!" Lia called out, immediately cutting through the cacophony. Moving quickly to Emily, she squatted and wrapped her arms around her daughter, holding her close. Pulling back slightly, so that her face was directly in front of hers, she asked, "Did you see someone at our house?"

Emily nodded and she felt her breath rush from her lungs. "Have you ever seen him before?"

Emily nodded again, and she asked, "Where did you see him? Why did you call him the Mayor-man?"

"He was at the park the night I got lost. You know, Mama, the music in the park."

Brow scrunched, she was aware that all eyes were centered on her and Emily. "And you saw him at the park that night?"

"He was the Mayor-man. The one up on stage when the band wasn't playing."

She remembered Mayor Banks greeting the crowd, but that had been when Emily was with her friend. Lifting her eyes to Aiden and seeing his angry expression, she shot her gaze over to Mitch.

"We need a search warrant," Grant said, at the same time the others began to plan out loud, several talking all at the same time.

"There," Emily's small voice called out.

Hearing her daughter's voice, her gaze shot back to her. She was staring up at the wall, arm stretched out, pointing with her finger. Looking over her shoulder in the direction Emily was indicating, she saw a photograph of the Mayor surrounded by the members of the Town Council.

Everyone quieted, staring at the picture, except for Aiden, who jumped from his seat. He stalked over and lifted Emily in his arms. "Emily, sweetheart," he said, his smile warm. He walked toward the picture and held her in front of it. "Do you see the man who was at your house this morning?"

Emily nodded, and he said, "Can you show me who he is? Can you point to him?"

Lia moved next to them, her hand resting on Emily's back encouragingly. She tensed a little, feeling the others in the room step closer as well. Emily's reached out and touched the picture with her finger. Staring at the man's face, she sucked in a quick breath.

It was not Mayor Banks, it was the man standing next to him…Silas Mills.

Silas protested loudly as Mitch placed him under arrest, but his protestations turned to whining when they produced a search warrant for his car. As suspected, a gas canister was found in his trunk. When the reality struck that he was going to be charged with multiple counts, ranging from grand larceny to attempted murder, he quickly decided he was not going to go down alone. Confessing to the theft of town money, he turned on Sandra as his accomplice.

Two days later, Lia stood before the Town Council, along with Mayor Banks, and presented her findings. She explained that sloppy procedures made it easier for Silas and Sandra to be able to steal over fifty thousand dollars from the town.

"Their system was crude, but effective," she explained. "Sandra realized that when the Mayor was unable to sign the checks she brought him immediately they were left vulnerable, unsecure in Celia's desk. Silas, who at one time dated Celia, had the opportunity to lift her key and made a copy. Silas would get into Celia's desk, after hours, and Sandra would manually alter a few of the checks after they had been printed. Overpaying some of the vendors would result in a refund check. I noticed that Mayor Banks' signature did not always look exactly the same. This is not necessarily an indication that someone else is signing, but it was enough that I became alerted. When I started receiving personal threats, I knew that I was on the right track.

"My full report is in front of you, detailing the past

thirteen months and the discrepancies I found. I am now working with the District Attorney, going over Silas' and Sandra's personal bank accounts.

"My report also includes my recommendations on how to close the gap in the sloppy procedures so that this cannot happen again."

Casting a glance to the side, she noticed Mayor Banks shifting in his seat. She knew that this information could reflect negatively on him for the upcoming election, but pushed that out of her mind.

The Chair of the Town Council looked up and thanked her profusely. She nodded and rose from her seat. Saying her goodbyes, she walked out of the conference room and back through the Municipal Building hall. Several people standing around in huddles, whispering, quieted as soon as she walked out. Celia, whose face was often set in a hardy smirk, was pale and wide-eyed.

Mark walked over and shook her hand. "I want to thank you, Lia. Sandra has been around for a long time and I'm the new kid on the block, but there were just some things that did not add up to me and some of the procedures she insisted were normal around here were just not what I had learned in school."

She accepted his handshake and smiled. "That's often how things are found, Mark. Someone gets the feeling that things just aren't right."

"At least temporarily, I've been moved up to Sandra's position. I'd like to work with you to make sure any recommendations you have will be put in place."

Agreeing to meet with him at a later time, she

walked out, heading to her car. Back at her office, she reported the meeting to Mrs. Markham, who clucked over the news of Silas' arrest, and Scott, who nodded his head while congratulating her on her investigation.

As Scott and Lia walked back to their offices, she paused and lifted her gaze to him. "Um…Scott? It's none of my business, but you and Celia?"

He blushed and looked away, squeezing the back of his neck before meeting, and holding, her gaze again. "I thought I was interested, but it didn't take long to figure out she's a man-eater. I used to think she was beautiful but now when I look at her all I see is a preying mantis."

A laugh bubbled out and she pressed her fingers over her lips in an attempt to stifle the sound.

He chuckled as well, shaking his head. "It's hard, being new in town. And…well, dating is hard in general. At least, for me…"

She cocked her head and reached her hand out, resting it on his arm. "Oh, Scott, don't worry. You'll find someone special, I'm sure." She hesitated for only a few seconds before adding, "I've been meaning to talk to you about becoming a partner." Encouraged by the spark in his eyes, she said, "Let's set up a time next week to discuss the particulars."

With a huge grin, he nodded. "Absolutely. I've decided to make Baytown my home, so this'll be perfect."

Saturday morning dawned bright and sunny, and Aiden

took Emily to the ball game early. Arriving after the game had started, Lia slipped through the crowd and walked toward the bleachers behind the dugout. Standing next to the fence before climbing up to sit with her friends, her eyes searched the field, landing on Emily at third base. Thrilled that her daughter had made it that far, she leaned against the fence and watched.

Her gaze swept over the rest of the field, recognizing Brogan, Jason, Zac, Grant, Mitch, Lance, and, of course, Aiden. She saw Katelyn and Ginny near the dugout, but in the outfield she saw someone that she did not recognize. It was a man, muscular, in an American Legion T-shirt and cargo shorts. What held her attention was that he had a prosthetic right leg. She wondered if he were new, since she had not seen him before.

Her attention was diverted as the crowd cheered. A batter had hit the ball toward the outfield and was running full out. She jerked her gaze around as the third base coach told Emily to run. Jumping up and down, screaming and waving, she watched as Emily ran to home plate, scoring a run. Aiden was there and he swung her up in his arms, celebrating. Behind them, the crowd was on their feet, many of them with their hands in the air, waving in the American Sign Language sign for applause.

Tears pricked her eyes as she watched Emily grin, throwing her hands in the air in thanks. At the end of the game, her attention was once more snagged as the man from the outfield jogged closer. Her mouth hung open in surprise as she recognized Scott. He caught her eye and grinned, jogging over to where she now sat with her friends.

"Scott, I had no idea." As soon as the words left her mouth, she felt foolish, but he quickly jumped in.

"Well, I tend to not wear shorts to work," he laughed. He glanced down at his prosthetic leg and shrugged, saying, "My souvenir from Afghanistan."

Jason walked up and clapped Scott on the back. "Glad you decided to coach. We're all heading to the pub, will you join us?" With a grin and a nod, Scott agreed, and they walked off together.

Barely having time to process that new information, Emily came running to her. Throwing her arms around her daughter, she congratulated her. As the crowd dispersed, they walked down the street toward the pub with their friends. Emily ran ahead and chatted with some of the others, leaving her to walk alone with Aiden.

He looked at the smile on her face, and asked, "Happy?"

She linked fingers with his, and said, "I don't think it's possible for me to be happier."

He grinned. "Well, let's see if I can find a way to make you even happier. Grab Emily and we'll skip the pub. I've got something to show you."

Gaining Emily's attention, she motioned for her to come back. Promising them a surprise, Aiden herded them to his truck. A few minutes later, they were driving down the road and as they pulled onto her street her house came into view. She and Emily had moved into Tori's Sea Glass Inn while she worked with the insurance company about repairing her house. The only real fire damage had been the back deck, including the back door and part of the kitchen wall, and the front porch, along with the front door and entryway. There was also water damage in the living room and the kitchen. The rest of the house was fine, but she did not know how long it would take before they could move back in.

As he pulled up to the front of her house, her mouth dropped open in awe.

"Wh…what's going on?"

"Look, Mama. Our house is getting fixed!"

Looking nervous, Aiden turned to her. "I know I was taking a big chance, but your insurance adjuster is part of the American Legion and so is the owner of North Heron Construction. I wanted them to hurry and start the reparations, so I put up the initial money until the insurance money comes in."

She turned and looked at him, realizing he was doing everything he could to give her and Emily a home again. Tears pricked her eyes as she said, "Aiden, you're amazing. Thank you so much."

The three of them climbed down from his truck and walked a little closer to the construction.

Emily, piping up again, said, "But Mama, our house is getting bigger!"

Paying closer attention to the work being done, she noticed the construction workers were busy not only repairing the front but, from what she could see, were also adding on to the side and back of the house.

"What's happening?" she asked, facing Aiden.

"This is what's happening."

He dropped down on one knee and took a ring box out of his pocket. Opening it, inside was nestled a diamond solitaire. Her mouth fell open and she glanced to Emily to see her reaction. She was looking between the two of them, her gaze shooting back and forth, and grinning widely.

"Amelia," Aiden said, gaining her attention again. "I hoped one day I would meet someone that I would want to spend the rest of my life with. Amelia, you're that person. I want to build a life with you and Emily and thought a great place to start would be with your beautiful home. Will you marry me?"

With tears sliding down her face, she nodded. "Yes, yes I'll marry you." She stared at her hand as he slid the ring onto to her left ring finger, waiting for him to rise, but he stayed on his knee. So, she bent over, clutching his face, kissing him. As she stood, she was surprised that he continued to stay on bent knee.

He then pulled out another ring box and flipped it open as he faced Emily. Inside was a tiny diamond solitaire on a necklace chain. Emily's eyes widened and her mouth dropped open.

"Just as I love your mother, I love you too," he said. "Will you let me be your daddy?"

Her tears continued to flow as she watched Emily jump into his arms, holding him tight. Dropping to her knees, their arms tangled together as they held each other close. With Emily squished in between of the two of them, she looked up, and grinned. "Now I can hear both of your hearts."

Baytown Boys (small town, military romantic suspense)
Coming Home
Just One More Chance
Clues of the Heart
Finding Peace
Picking Up the Pieces
Sunset Flames
Waiting for Sunrise
Hear My Heart

Lighthouse Security Investigations
Mace
Rank

Heroes at Heart (Military Romance)
Zander
Rafe
Cael
Jaxon
Jayden (coming March 2019)
Asher (Coming 2019)
Zeke (coming 2019)

Saint's Protection & Investigations (Military Romantic
Suspense)
Serial Love
Healing Love
Revealing Love
Seeing Love

Honor Love
Sacrifice Love
Protecting Love
Remember Love
Discover Love
Surviving Love
Celebrating Love
Searching Love

Alvarez Security (military romantic suspense)
Gabe
Tony
Vinny
Jobe

Sleeper SEAL
Thin Ice

Letters From Home (military romance)
Class of Love
Freedom of Love
Bond of Love
The Love's Series (detectives)
Love's Taming
Love's Tempting
Love's Trusting
The Fairfield Series (small town detectives)
Emma's Home
Laurie's Time
Carol's Image
Fireworks Over Fairfield

Please take the time to leave a review of this book. Feel free to contact me, especially if you enjoyed my book. I love to hear from readers!

Facebook

Email

Website

Made in the USA
Middletown, DE
26 December 2018